HIDDEN JUSTICE

HIDDEN JUSTICE

Hidden Justice Book One

NOLON KING

DAVID W. WRIGHT

STERLING & STONE

To YOU, the reader.
Thank you for your support.
Thank you for the wonderful emails.
Thank you for the thoughtful reviews.
Thank you for reading and loving our stories.

Chapter One

Frank

BREAKING into a person's home was the easy part.

Suffering was born from the stolen nostalgia.

Frank Grimm never took anything that didn't belong to him, tried to keep his presence invisible — like he'd never even been there at all — and tamped down the vicarious thrill he occasionally felt stalking lives like he did. Because the breaking and entering was never about excitement. Frank sneaked into his neighbors' homes and turned them inside out while they were away for one reason: to find the person who murdered his daughter, Jenny.

One day, he would find and kill the man responsible.

Then the world would be a slightly better place. And Frank might finally be able to sleep through the night.

Right now, he was in one of the newer rebuilds in the cul-de-sac. The Jhasti family moved in four years ago, less than a week after the Bensons loaded everything into a big Mayflower truck and a much smaller U-Haul. Frank wasn't sure where the Mayflower had been bound, and back then, he didn't care enough to ask, but both of the Benson children were all grown up. So Joseph and Leslie had decided to buy a tiny house, an acre of land, and all the peace of mind that accompanied solitude and a severe lack of attachment.

Now Frank thought about that all the time. Getting the hell out of Creek County. Finding a quiet place to live out the rest of his miserable life, knowing he could never, ever be happy again.

Not without Jenny.

Not without Sarah.

And not without answers or quenching the vengeance that lived inside him like a thirst.

Frank moved from Peter's room to Tabitha's, trading posters of the Justice League and McLarens for One Direction and My Little Pony.

Tabitha was probably too old for those toys now, even though she had a battalion of them arranged on her nightstand. Jenny got her first Pony on her fifth birthday from one of the girls in her kindergarten class, and for the next six years, she was *obsessed*. She was already starting to grow out of it and hadn't really been playing with them much anymore when the unthinkable happened. Looking down at the Ponies now was a painful reminder, same as always was.

Every time he'd ever been inside this room.

It wasn't that Frank had lost count of how many times that had been so far; it was that he didn't want to think about it. Or acknowledge his obsession.

Tabitha was fifteen, the same age Jenny would have been if …

He swallowed and tried to rinse the thought from his

mind. It was already nested there whether he liked it or not, growing scabrous inside him. He was here for answers, not to reminisce.

He picked up one of the ponies and felt a stab of pain with the realization that he knew its name. *Pinky Pie*, Jenny's favorite.

He palmed the pony, then went to sit on the edge of Tabitha's bed, thinking.

He shouldn't be this comfortable in another person's home and was breaking one of his own rules by getting lost in his thoughts like he was. But this house was different and always had been. Tabitha and Jenny were the same age, so being in her room kept him haunted by the same recurring thought.

It could have been Tabitha instead.

Tabitha was just as innocent. She had just as much potential.

Would the life that had been squeezed out of Jenny have destroyed Bill Jhasti just like it ruined Frank?

The girls had just begun getting close. It took more than a year after the new family moved into the cul-de-sac before they started playing — or *hanging out*, as Jenny insisted — together.

But they never got to have a sleepover.

They never got to paint each other's toenails and probably never got to talk about boys from school and who they each might have a crush on.

Or girls. Frank would never get to know that part of his daughter — who she might have liked if some sick bastard hadn't—

He stood from the bed and returned General Pinky Pie to the front of her battalion.

He should really be going.

There were no answers here.

But Frank looked around the room again anyway. He saw a battered flute case over by Tabitha's desk. She had apparently signed up for band because the instrument hadn't been there the last time Frank had broken into the house, just over a week ago.

Bill Jhasti was innocent. He knew that, same as he knew that this particular home wouldn't have any answers. But it fed something inside him to be there; a loaf of bread for a man starving to both remember and forget. Going through Tabitha's things would never help him catch the killer, but it was a compulsion he couldn't do much about.

Or maybe he could.

If Frank were willing.

And since he wasn't, maybe he was as broken as the man he would one day murder.

Two sides of a shattered mirror.

Staying here in Tabitha's room and drowning in pilfered nostalgia kept Frank away from the truth. Jenny's case had never produced any DNA evidence, so his only hope of catching the killer was to find a trophy, photos of his daughter that someone shouldn't have, anything that might tie a suspect to her.

Frank's longest-running theory was that someone in their neighborhood had been obsessed with Jenny and finally acted on their wicked fixation. Specifically, someone in his cul-de-sac, where she could have been seen playing on the front lawn like she once loved to do — *ring-around-the-orange-tree* — before her life was stolen away.

A few months before she'd died, she told her mother that the neighbor had been creeping her out. When Frank had asked which neighbor, Jenny had refused to answer, saying it was nothing, not wanting to cause a scene. Had she seen into the eyes of the man who would kill her? Frank couldn't help but wonder.

Only one home on Heirloom Cove was exempt from suspicion, and only because the family had moved in six months ago, half a year too late. The two-story Victorian with a family of three that had so far kept to themselves. The daughter looked about Jenny's age. Another friend she would never get to have.

Breaking and entering wasn't just a way to cope; it was Frank's only way to gather the kind of evidence he couldn't legally obtain as a cop. The only way he could subsist or survive after Sarah—

No.

He couldn't think about her either. Or that.

None of his to-dos could be done here at the Jhastis', so Frank needed to go.

He stood with a sigh and was smoothing his indent from Tabitha's perfectly made bed when he startled at the sound of a car pulling into the driveway.

Three long steps, and Frank was looking out the window.

He clenched his fists, angry at both his indulgence and his incompetence.

Bill was never home at this time of day. Frank had never seen him stay home sick — or pretending to — even once in the entire time he'd been paying close attention. He left for work with his prissy tie knotted too tightly like always.

Bill slammed the door to his Audi, either speaking to someone on Bluetooth or muttering to himself like a madman. He looked upset. His movements seemed erratic and frantic.

Frank had a minute at most.

He spent six seconds making sure the bed looked like a glass tabletop, then took flash inventory of his situation. His options were either slogging through wet concrete or waiting for it to dry at his ankles.

He couldn't afford to panic.

Frank closed his eyes for a moment to calm his nerves.

He'd always been prepared for this inevitability. He was breaking into homes while his neighbors were away. He had run the scenarios to sharpen himself, knowing he might need to cut his way out of an unexpected situation. Without killing.

His target couldn't be found at the Jhastis', and yet here he was having to decide between getting caught by Bill or jumping out a second-story window. A subpar option; not only would the coast need to be clear of any neighbors walking their dogs or out for a late morning stroll — that loudmouth Iggy liked to treat the cul-de-sac like his private trail — but landing would make a loud noise for sure.

Bill would almost for sure hear Frank's escape, in addition to any curious neighbors opening their own windows to investigate the disturbance. And, perhaps most obvious, was that Frank was too damned old to be jumping from second stories. He could very well break a leg or two.

The front door opened downstairs.

Bill's furious voice filled the house. "—whatever he did! Let me ask you something, Wally: am I a man you know to unnecessarily swear?" A beat for Wally to answer. "Exactly, Wally. So you should be extra concerned when I remind you that this is FUCKING RIDICULOUS!"

Bill Jhasti might be the nicest guy on the street. Frank felt genuinely curious to know what Wally had done to upset him, but he needed to make a move more than anything else.

Bill was already stomping up the stairs.

At least he was mad enough, and talking loudly enough, that Bill wouldn't be able to hear Frank moving quietly around. He looked around the room again — a futile gesture to buy him a breath or two. Tabitha's closet was the only place he could possibly go.

He slipped inside and closed the door like a whisper behind him.

"I'm going to make this as clear as I can make it. No — you don't get to respond right now! This isn't just a fire-able offense. I feel like using my life savings to hire an ex-Mossad agent to kill you. Not Orson, not Greenburg, and not Farrow. *You*, Wally."

Bill marched right by Tabitha's room, then loudly yanked open the door to his home office and went inside, giving Wally a moment to defend himself.

This was bad.

Frank couldn't get caught.

Even if he managed to escape undetected, the Jhastis couldn't suspect that someone had been inside their house. If the sheriff's office traced the break-in to him, his life would become unbearable again. The media spotlight was too bright for Frank. Its heat too much for him to take.

Innocence didn't matter. The attention was damage enough.

And, of course, they would bring up Jenny.

And Sarah.

Again.

Bill was still yelling up a storm. Like Wally, Frank didn't know Bill Jhasti as a man to swear without intent, but he'd also just heard him scream, "I HOPE YOU DIE SHITTING!"

Tabitha would be home in an hour and a half.

So Frank should get out in the next minute or so.

Bill's voice got louder as he emerged from his office and passed Tabitha's room while walking back toward the stairs.

"I understand *sorry*. I can relate to *sorry*. I might even be able to see how *sorry* could relate to this situation — IF YOU HADN'T COST THE COMPANY THE CARLSON ACCOUNT!"

Bill sounded like he was halfway to the ground floor.

"You know what else you cost me?" No chance to answer. "*My job*, Wally. This is probably going to cost me my fucking job."

Frank sure hoped not, for Peter and Tabitha's sake. And Nicole's.

The Jhastis were good people.

And he shouldn't be here.

It sounded like Bill was now yelling at Wally from the kitchen or thereabouts.

Frank took a series of exceedingly cautious steps, out of the closet, then down the stairs, and into the living room. He looked both ways, feeling like he was attempting to cross a highway at midnight, then dared another eight heart-stopping steps toward the front door.

Bill was still barking at Wally like a rabid dog, but Frank was positive he'd see him opening the front door or hear him closing it and running over to investigate.

But Frank made it to the other side with a pounding heart.

This was too risky going out the front instead of the back like he usually did, but it wasn't like he could wave at Bill on his way out the kitchen door.

He looked up and down the street to make sure he was alone.

Then he exhaled with relief as he cut a sharp right onto the sidewalk and aimed himself toward home.

Frank made it ten steps before he looked up and saw the girl at 47 Heirloom — much too skinny and always dressed in black — staring down at him from her second-story window.

She'd seen him escape.

Chapter Two

Mal

FRANK FUCKING GRIMM.

Mallory Black took a sip of the coffee she shouldn't be drinking, looked down at the file she shouldn't be reading, and pushed herself away from the desk she shouldn't still be sitting behind.

"You should probably put that away," Mike said.

She looked over at her partner. He was doing two things he really enjoyed, the second more than the first: sifting through forensics reports and telling her shit she didn't need to hear.

Mal said, "You should probably start bitching about how *Dexter* treats the fine science of blood splatter. It's getting late, and you haven't even told me that no one in the world can expertly analyze the arrangement of blood at a crime scene so quickly and accurately—"

"You know it's ridiculous."

"Sure." She shrugged. "But I don't *care*. You seem to have a vendetta against Showtime."

"There is some science in liquid pattern analysis, but the variables involved in any—"

"Does Gina like it when you talk nerdy like this? Is that what does it for her?"

"Screw you, Mal." But Mike was laughing.

Her phone rang with the opening notes of Maroon 5's "Kiwi."

"Your husband awaits."

"Hey, hon." Mal threw him a look: *I don't want to hear shit about this song choice again.*

"Hey," he said.

But then nothing else. Ray always did this shit; it was like when he just texted *Hi.*

"Yep, we covered that." Mal looked down at the file again. It might as well have been photos of child actors who'd grown up to look hideous the way she kept scraping her eyes across the thing. "What's up?"

"I was hoping you could grab a few things on your way home for dinner?" He didn't wait for Mal to answer. "I'm making moo shu, and Ashley's in charge of the pancakes. She also wants real popcorn for movie night instead of the 'greasy microwave stuff,' so maybe you could pick up—"

"Sorry, hon. But I've gotta work late tonight. You'll have to save me some moo shu and maybe skip the pancakes."

"Mal."

The one word was enough.

Ray got what he wanted; the guilt was now chewing through her.

"I need to work late, not super late. I'm sorry."

"No, I can tell when you're sorry, and you're not sorry. If you were, you'd stop doing this. You promised …" He sighed. "You promised that you were going to stop doing this."

"I'm not *doing* anything." But she was, and she knew it. "I'm not clocking crazy hours right now. You *know* this occasionally comes with the gig. Sometimes there's a hot lead, and it's my job to follow it. I'm sorry that—"

"Just come home as soon as you can, okay? We'll go ahead and eat dinner without you, but we'll wait to start the movie."

"You don't have to—"

But Ray was already gone.

"—wait for me. I don't mind missing the first few minutes," Mal finished, so she wouldn't have to hear Mike give her any shit. "Okay. Love you, too."

"Hot lead, huh?"

Mal ignored him and dropped a folder on top of the one she'd been looking (obsessing) over.

Mike laughed. "That wasn't even remotely subtle."

"I don't know what you're talking about." But really, why bother? Mike had already caught her, and now he wasn't going to let it go until he finally got his partner to fess up.

"Hot lead on a cold case?"

"Maybe I thought of something."

"Oh yeah, what?" Mike asked.

"I'm still working it out."

"Sure you are." He shook his head. "Go home, Mal."

"I'll go home when I'm finished here. What's it to you?"

"You're my partner and, for some damned reason, my friend. I'm sick of seeing you throw your family life away for an obsession."

"I'm not 'throwing my family life away.'"

"Okay."

"Don't 'okay' me, Mike. I hate when you 'okay' me."

"*Okay*." He laughed. "You guys just went through this. I feel sorry for your husband."

"I took last Saturday off to play miniature fucking golf. We ate frozen yogurt, and I paid way too much for some supremely subpar toppings. I didn't lose my shit when the twin toddlers two tables away started screaming at the top of their lungs. And I explained, for the umpteenth time in my nicest voice, why we can't just adopt a puppy when no one is home to take care of it all day long."

"That all sounds like what I like to call 'parenting,' and even the worst of it's better than poring over this old case. It's closed, Mal. Frank didn't do it. You need to—"

"He *did* do it." Mal was getting mad fast — few things made her angrier than Creek County's handling of the Grimm case, and Mike shining all his doubt onto her desk made her want to strangle him.

"And again, even after all this time, the only thing you have to go on is your gut."

"You've always trusted my gut before," Mal argued like always. "Literally, *every other time*."

"That's because your gut has always been right before."

"So why can't you give me the benefit of the doubt now if it's always been right?"

"Because that's not how guilt and innocence work." He shook his head. "You know that."

"You just don't want to admit that someone you know could do something like that. But you've been at this job long enough to have learned that the exact opposite is true. *Anyone* is capable of anything."

"How about *you*, Mal? You capable of that?"

"You know what I mean."

"Not sure I do."

"It's *always* the father."

"It's been at least a day since I heard your strongest argument," Mike said. "Got anything new?"

"I told you, I'm still working it out."

"It was the homeless—"

"It wasn't the homeless guy."

"—that everyone saw before and no one saw after."

"Everyone and no one?" Mal raised her eyebrows. "Those are some scientific numbers. You gonna use those on the stand when they catch this mysterious hobo?"

"You're not supposed to say hobo. That's offensive now."

"Bullshit." Mal shook her head. "Bum is offensive. Tramp is offensive. Hobo is a goddamned compliment."

"How so?" Mike asked.

"Tramps only work when someone makes them; bums don't work at all, though they might pretend for a drink or two. Hobos are traveling workers."

"You're making that up." A beat, then, "And you're changing the subject."

"I'm tired of the subject," Mal said.

"If you were really tired of the subject, then you'd let it go. He didn't do that sick shit to his daughter."

"He did the pick."

"Again with the pick." Mike laughed, shaking his head in defeat. "The man had lint on his shirt."

"He also had his knees pointed to the door. And he crossed his arms when Signal Eight was questioning him.

Mike laughed louder and harder. "You know, half the time, I think you're actually just fucking with me."

"You were standing right next to me, Mike. Watching the same thing I was. If it hadn't been Grimm in there, then we wouldn't be seeing two different things."

"So you've been telling me for a year now."

14

"He lied, Mike. About something he didn't even have to lie about!"

He had. That was indisputable, and it was infuriating that Mike kept refusing to acknowledge it. Signal Eight had asked Frank where he'd been earlier that morning, the day his daughter was murdered. He said that he'd been at Provisions because it was his turn to do the grocery shopping. Sarah always wanted him to go when they were barbecuing because he was fussy about his meat. If it had been up to her, she would've eaten chicken marsala every night.

But that was bullshit.

Mal had seen Frank at HomeWork at the exact time the former detective said he was shopping at Provisions. She didn't see what he bought because she couldn't have cared less. Ray had been giving her shit about not doing enough around the house, so she went to buy a new faucet to replace the one that had been gushing like a water show in the kitchen. The DIY project proved she was doing her part while also giving her a reason to get the hell out of her house for an hour on a Sunday when Ashley wouldn't stop asking her questions. Last thing Mal had wanted to do was strike up a conversation with Frank.

She made an about-face the second she saw him, then took her faucet to the farthest register.

"For the last time, it doesn't matter why he lied about where he was three hours before she went missing," Mike said. "Frank has an alibi. He was with his wife and then visiting a source."

"Both who are now dead."

"Don't even go there," Mike said. "Reginald got killed in a drunk driving accident and, well, Sarah … losing a kid so horribly could make any parent kill themselves."

"Especially if she covered for her husband that did it."

"Stop, Mal."

"Little lies lead to bigger ones. *You know that.*"

"He was never charged." Mike pulled another tired and irrelevant point out of his bag. "With *anything.*"

"His body language was all wrong."

"If the State Attorney's Office doesn't think he did it, why would you?"

"Because he's guilty." Mal refrained from crossing her arms to avoid looking as pouty as she felt.

"He's one of ours, Mal. Why can't you—"

"Pretend he's innocent? Jesus Christ."

"Of course, I don't want you to *pretend he's innocent.* Don't insult me. I just want you to give the guy the benefit of the doubt."

"Is that what you usually do, Mike?"

"Yeah, actually. Isn't that what we're all supposed to do? Innocent until proven guilty, isn't that how it works in this—"

"You and I both know there are a lot of guilty fuckers running around out there—"

"And innocent men and women in jail." Then he added, "Mostly men."

"That's sexist."

"You know it's not," Mike said.

"Cops shouldn't get special treatment when it comes to breaking the law."

"How many laws do you break on a regular basis?"

"Tiny ones." Mal pinched her fingers together and showed him the approximate size of her illegality. "Not murder and—"

"I'm not arguing that Frank should have gotten any special treatment."

"Well, he did."

Mike shook his head. "You and I are just going to have to disagree on that. Again."

"He's part of the Old Boys Club, and you know it. So no, Mike. He's not one of mine."

"Come on, that's not—"

"He was supposed to be one of the good guys, making sure justice was served, instead of perverting it."

"You're talking like it's a fact that he's guilty."

"Maybe he is," she said.

"That's dangerous thinking. *Deciding* that someone's guilty."

"I'm not *deciding* anything. Except that Jenny Grimm's killer deserves justice."

"Mob justice, or the regular kind?" Mike stood, still holding his smile. "Come on. Let's leave all of this until tomorrow and go home to our families."

"Fine. I give up." Back on her feet and grabbing her jacket from the back of her chair. "For now."

Mal waited for Mike to turn around, grabbed Grimm's folder from under the pile, dropped it into her bag, and followed him out the door.

"I'm right behind you."

Chapter Three

Frank

FRANK WANTED to pretend that the girl at 47 Heirloom hadn't seen him slipping out of the Jhastis' home and that she wasn't still staring at him as he tried to look casual, just another early retiree out for a late morning walk. He wanted to tell himself that even if she *had* seen something, his new neighbor wasn't about to call the police on him.

But Frank didn't suffer lies, including those he told himself.

And the girl was still staring at him from what had to be her bedroom window.

Still, she couldn't *know* he'd been sneaking out. Maybe he and Bill were buddies, and Frank went over there when he wasn't home all the time.

The police might be on their way right now.

Maybe it had been a mistake, leaving 47 Heirloom off of his investigation list. He knew so little about the people inside. It was a rental property, a couple and their teenage daughter. Dad was always in a polo shirt. Mom looked like life had been batting her around for a while. And the kid dressed like a goth teenager.

They looked like just another average American family, unhappy for the most part but going through the motions all the same. But the father couldn't have had anything to do with Jenny, and his home held no happy nostalgia for Frank.

He crossed the street. Stole a glance and saw that the girl was still staring.

If she hadn't moved from the window, then maybe she hadn't called the cops.

He tried to collate everything he knew into an orderly list in his mind. But there wasn't much. Frank had only run into the family once while out walking. The mom and her daughter avoided eye contact, but the dad had shot him an unmistakable and territorial look: *What are you looking at?*

He'd taken note but didn't need to get into a pissing match with some alpha male jerk-off. Frank was well acquainted with the type from his time with the sheriff's office. No reason to squander his temper; measured control was the best weapon he had.

He'd seen the goth girl walking to the bus stop a few streets down in the mornings but never had reason to pay any attention before now. Even after six months living on a friendly cul-de-sac, she was always alone. An outcast. Maybe she wouldn't have been if Jenny were still alive.

Kids like that broke his heart. He'd seen that during his time on the force, too. The toughest, weirdest, most problematic kids were often the weakest and subject to abuse from bullies and their enablers. Nowadays, humiliation and torment could arrive with an invisible yet unrelenting force. With online bullying, and kids killing themselves or bringing guns to school so they could take others on their way out, Frank was grateful that he'd managed to keep Jenny safe as long as he had.

Two-thirds of the way to his house, and the girl was still looking.

Still *staring*.

His neighbor, Mrs. Goldberg, was just up ahead.

He would give every dollar in his wallet to avoid her, but that wasn't an option. He needed to stop and talk like he always did. Anything less would be suspicious. Mrs. Goldberg was a kind, lonely old woman who only wanted to be heard. She'd had a classroom full of fifth-graders for nearly forty-five years before retiring from the district. Just two years out of teaching, it looked like she'd aged a decade already. She used a walker after recovering from hip surgery and could now barely keep up with her unrelentingly energetic chihuahua, Dolly.

But even with a pair of decades on him, Mrs. Goldberg could still exhaust him into conversational submission. His best strategy was to rope-a-dope the exchange, listen to everything she'd been dying to get out, then say something, like "uh-huh" or "hmm, interesting," to show he'd heard every word.

"Frank!" Mrs. Goldberg called out with a friendly wave and a wide smile.

"Mrs. Goldberg." He returned her smile and added a nod.

Maybe he could tip his head, tell her to have a great morning, then keep on walking.

Of course, she'd try to engage him, but he could say he was sick and that he really had to use the restroom. Right now, he needed to escape a long and exhausting exchange. Not because he didn't have the patience for Mrs. Goldberg — he understood the cost of his extracurricular activities — but because he wanted to get back in his house and away from the creepy girl's penetrating gaze. Frank felt like he was standing in the crosshairs while a sniper stared from their perch across the street.

Frank sped his pace and offered Mrs. Goldberg another nod, but as he moved to pass her, she reached out and touched his arm. "It really is a perfect day for a walk, isn't it?"

He stopped, still feeling that gaze at the back of his skull.

I'm so sorry, Mrs. Goldberg, but I really need to use the restroom.

"It sure is." But really, it was hot and humid. Same as most Florida days, and maybe more than usual. "I'm so sorry, but I—"

"Too bad I can't enjoy it like I want to, with this hip still giving me issues and Dolly always tugging at me like she does."

Mrs. Goldberg cast her walker an accusatory glance, then turned her gaze on the chihuahua. Dolly yanked on her leash and started yapping. She wanted to escape this conversation, same as Frank.

"It's been miserable since the surgery. I can only afford to have Leona come in twice a week now, and Jessa just had a baby, so it's not like she can ever really help with anything or would even want to if she could. So there's that. I've also been thinking a lot about what the mayor said last week; can you believe the garbage coming out of his mouth? Doesn't anyone have any decency anymore? And you know what I realized this morning? 'Brown Eyed Girl' is almost fifty years old! Did you have any idea?"

She didn't want an answer.

Frank let her keep going.

Dolly tugged harder and yapped louder.

"I *loved* that song. It was the summer of love, you

know." Mrs. Goldberg laughed to let him know that she used to be young. "And I was doing quite a lot of loving. But you know who wasn't? Van Morrison. And you know why?"

Frank didn't, but she wasn't offering him the opportunity either way.

"Because it was a pop song, and Van Morrison didn't want to be a pop artist. He was supposedly horrified when the album came out, and he saw that psychedelic-looking cover, which I also *loved*, by the way. Did you ever have that album?"

"I did not," Frank answered before Mrs. Goldberg could say anything else. He needed a way out of this now, and he wanted to see if the girl was still watching.

The police could be here any second.

He said, "But I am sorry to hear that Leona can't come over as much anymore. Once Jessa's baby is a little older, she'll appreciate you more. That's just how motherhood works." He shook his head in solidarity. "The mayor doesn't always think before he speaks, and even though I never had the album, "Brown Eyed Girl" is one of the best rock songs — or *any* songs, really — ever recorded. Now," he extended his hand in offering, "why don't you let me finish taking Dolly on a walk for you, then you can rest your hip?"

"Oh my." Mrs. Goldberg seemed both pleased and flattered by the offer. "You're much too busy to be walking my dog for me. But yes, that would be wonderful."

"I'm not busy at all. And I'm out here walking anyway. I'm happy to help." He shook his empty hand, prompting her to fill it with the leash. "I'll have her back in a few minutes, tired enough to give you some rest."

Mrs. Goldberg handed him the leash. Just as he'd been hoping, his offer robbed her of words.

"Would you mind bringing in the mail for me on your way in? That way, I don't have to walk all the way to the mailbox."

The mailbox that was on her way to the door.

"Sure thing, Mrs. Goldberg."

"Rachel." Apparently, they were friends now.

"Rachel," Frank repeated, then he tightened his grip on the leash and walked away.

His back was still to 47 Heirloom. He didn't know if he could feel the teen's still-burning gaze or whether his sixth sense was paranoia. His skin crawled as he listened for sirens. His eyes and body were on full alert, expecting to see a sheriff's cruiser pulling onto the cul-de-sac any second.

Picking up the mail wasn't his idea, but he was glad that she'd had it.

Because now he had an excuse.

If the cops showed up and said a neighbor caught him sneaking out of the Jhastis' house, Frank could tell them that he was just dropping off a piece of mail that got delivered to him by mistake on his way to help out Mrs. Goldberg. A former brother in blue, playing the good neighbor card.

He rounded Heirloom and saw that the girl was still in the window, still looking at him.

Frank allowed himself a second to believe that she hadn't moved a muscle and thus could not have called the cops. But that sounded too much like it might be a lie.

He kept pretending not to notice her while letting Dolly sniff every blade of grass on the street. Ten long minutes and still no sirens. Not a single police car turning onto the street. He spent those ten long minutes stealing glances to see if the girl was still staring at him.

She always was.

So after dropping the chihuahua off to Mrs. Goldberg — *Rachel* — along with a fat stack of junk mail, Frank turned around and finally met the girl's eyes as he started walking back toward his home.

Then he did the strangest thing, feeling a flash of surprise both before and after he did.

Frank gave the girl the slightest nod.

And then she gave him one back.

A minute later, he was back inside his house, gulping water and trying not to hyperventilate, wondering if this was the end of everything.

FRANK WENT TO THE WINDOW, parted the curtains, then glanced out at Heirloom.

He needed to stop. He'd been looking out the window compulsively all day, and it wasn't doing him any favors. So he left his nest, went into the dining room, and sat to eat.

He looked down at his plate and wondered the same thing he did every night.

Is this my life now, or is this my life forever?

Chicken marsala with aged Romano. Sarah's favorite dinner.

He'd gone from eating it on Fridays like they had for years to making it a few nights each week because why not? It was easier to cook in batches, anyway. But Frank had been eating the same thing every day for a while now. The only thing that changed was how much wine went with his meal. A half glass graduated to a full bottle, and then Frank seriously considered letting a second one breathe before washing his dishes. The second bottle could be his starter for the following day.

He took a bite.

Delicious and terrible.

The flavor was earthy, but the memories bitter.

"I almost got caught today," Frank said across the table to a Sarah who would never be there again.

He always set out a plate for her, though he wasn't wasteful or foolish enough to fill it with food. He needed someone to hear him at the end of the day, even if it was only her empty seat.

"It was stupid. I was over at the Jhasti place, but I never should have been. We both know Bill didn't have anything to do with what happened to Jenny."

He smiled at Sarah's spot because, really, the only thing she ever knew about any of this for sure was that she didn't want anything to do with his "miserable little hobby."

"Bill came home while I was up in Tabitha's room." He slowly chewed a bit of marsala. "Only reason I even made it out of the house was because Bill was yelling at someone."

Another bite.

"Then when I got out, that new goth girl across the street was staring at me." Big gulp of wine. "And it wasn't my imagination, Sarah. Like I said, she was *staring*."

No comment, one way or the other.

More chewing, more wine, then finally more sorrow. "I miss you so much."

Followed by regret.

"I'm sorry for everything. I know it wasn't just Jenny … and I understand why you had to go. But I wasn't trying to … I never thought that … It's my fault. I get that now. I'll get it again when I read your letter tomorrow. I just …"

There wasn't any good end to that one, so he ate and drank and collected himself, then he changed the subject. "I'll find out who did it to her, Sarah. To *us*."

Might as well polish off the glass.

Refill it and take another long swallow.

The sooner Frank was drunk, the sooner he would be asleep.

He couldn't wait until tomorrow for yet another chance. Tonight he could do only three things: drink, wallow in his miseries, and loathe himself deeply for both.

"I messed up all over the place. Not just with how I handled things after Jenny, but even today. It's like I can't get anything right. I wasn't looking for her killer. I was just trying to have a moment of normalcy, even though I knew I couldn't *really* have one."

Another swallow, this one to stop the tears.

"You too. I'm not trying to make this all about me. It's always been about us. I wish I could go back to that day …"

Sarah finding his second gun had led to the worst argument of their marriage. The battles only escalated after that night. She knew, and there was no way Frank could argue his way out of it. He already owned a gun for the P.I. firm he insisted on starting in lieu of his early retirement but had yet to get off the ground. A second untraceable gun could only mean one thing.

She knew her husband was bent on revenge, and that was the last thing Sarah had wanted. She begged him until she was hoarse, trying to convince him that it was a mistake to hunt the killer. A quest for revenge would only warp him into the same kind of monster.

"Being a vigilante is only cool in comic books," she'd said.

But Frank didn't agree.

Maybe he couldn't.

The argument never changed.

Frank would always insist that he was the only one left in the world who could ever get justice for their Jenny; his only option was a fierce pursuit of the truth and the vengeance to follow.

Sarah stood firm, demanding through her tears that Frank stop being obstinate and just listen to reason or her. Revenge was *never* the only option. She always ended these exchanges with some pithy little quote, usually about how an eye for an eye would leave the whole world blind.

But they never resolved the argument.

And eventually, Sarah gave up trying.

His plate and bottle were both empty. But Frank didn't want anything more to drink.

He stood from the table and returned to the window for yet another glance outside.

He'd stopped expecting to see cop cars a few hours ago. Now looking out the window felt more like the ticking of a box. Something Frank felt compelled to do on his way to finishing some invisible checklist.

But this time, he saw something that stopped his heart for a beat or two until his brain filled in a few of the blanks, and he could finally understand what he was seeing.

Experience told him it was an unmarked cop car in their cul-de-sac. But after a blink, Frank realized that it almost for sure had nothing to do with his breaking into the Jhasti house.

That sort of crime didn't require a stakeout. If the girl had called the cops on him, then officers on the scene would know precisely where to go and what to ask Mr. Grimm at 93 Heirloom. But more to the point, Frank was fairly sure that the cop who appeared to be stuffing her face with a giant burrito from inside the cabin of a late model Ford Explorer was Mallory Black.

And if so, Frank knew exactly what this was about.

Mallory had been the lead detective on Jenny's case.

She thought he was guilty from day one, had never entertained any other suspects, and ended up harassing him for long after the investigation into Jenny's death went cold.

He did understand, but it was difficult not to take it personally. Mallory had been a colleague, a fellow officer of the law. And it was hard to swallow her seeing him as the kind of monster who could rape and murder his own daughter. Thinking about it made Frank want to clench his fists, break glass, maybe hurl something through a window.

Mallory was the kind of detective that followed her gut. Frank could relate, but it was a looking-glass nightmare to see how much a warped perspective could ruin a cop. Her instinct couldn't be connected to any legitimate evidence because none existed. He was never especially friendly to her because that wasn't his manner with anyone, but he had gone to bat for her a few times in the past. Not that Mallory had any idea. She must have thought poorly of him due to his longstanding friendship with Sheriff Claude Barry, a man she'd often been at odds with, before his replacement with Gloria Bell.

He knew from his first interrogation: Frank Grimm was Mallory's man, and that's just how it was going to be. He was never worried. Sure, plenty of innocent men had gone to prison for crimes they didn't commit, even with little or no evidence. But in those cases, a DA, a department, or a collection of many someones were convinced of the defendant's guilt. Unless Frank's old friends were all lying to him, Mallory was the only one who didn't believe in his innocence, the only one who didn't see him as a good man who unjustly suffered when a horrible thing befell him.

At least inside the sheriff's department.

Outside was a whole different story.

Frank was sure that Mallory wouldn't have been nearly as combative with him if not for Ty Kirby.

An ambitious reporter at Channel 4, Kirby built a career on his sensationalist coverage of Jenny's murder. Not even thirty years old yet, the kid was delusional, seeing himself as a hard-hitting journalist, willing to stop at nothing on his quest for the truth. But his ruthless exploitation of his subjects' emotional states and willingness to tell whatever story might earn his segments the most clicks on social media made the man loathed by law enforcement and many of his subjects.

Except for Mallory, when his reporting helped to support her bias.

Ty interviewed Sarah when Frank was away, following a lead that went nowhere. He'd tricked her into thinking the network could help find their daughter's killer. But it was merely a witch hunt, a trap to make the sheriff's office look bad because the network had it in for the sheriff. Kirby asked a lot of manipulative questions and buried a seed of doubt in her head. It took an hour of pounding, relentlessly working to make Sarah say that no, nobody could truly know everything in their spouse's heart.

She refused Ty's every attempt to contact her after that, but the damage was done. Both to Sarah's sanity and their marriage. Kirby's seed of doubt had grown into a weed and uprooted their lives. A sudden gulf between them made it harder for her to communicate with Frank about everything.

He was stupid enough to believe that Ty might back off after he threatened the reporter's life, telling him that no one would ever find his body if he ever bothered Sarah again.

An idiot's mistake, and Frank knew it before he was even back in his car.

Of course, Ty would make the threat public. Of course, it would make Frank look violent and unhinged. Of course, that would only increase Mallory's interest in him as a suspect. Of course, Frank should have seen it all coming.

Even young as he was, Ty had been carrying a grudge for years. Ever since Frank once shoved the reporter against a wall for harassing an accused (but innocent) rapist out on bail. The poor guy was a scapegoat who never made it to trial, hanging himself two days before he was due to appear.

Ty knew that the sheriff's office didn't think he was guilty, but that never stopped Ty from mentioning that the real killer hadn't been found and that Frank was surely a suspect for a reason.

Frank could never allow himself to hit the news cycle because Ty would be ready the second he did. And all the old garbage would be back: Ty alleging that sources within the sheriff's office believed someone in the department was burying Frank's involvement in the crime; Ty exposing an old affair between Frank and a fellow officer, which had nothing whatsoever to do with the case, but did help to further destroy his marriage; Ty revealing that Officer Grimm had been suspected of taking kickbacks from some Russian mobsters — that last one didn't even have a molecule of truth, and was surely character assassination from someone with an ax to grind with Sheriff Barry and his administration. Probably Gloria Bell or her proxies.

Frank stepped away from the window.

It took a healthy measure of self-control to stop himself from hating Mallory. To remind himself that she was only human and doing her job. Everyone had their blind spots, including him. Wondering if his own blind spots had led to Jenny's death kept him whimpering in his sleep.

On those times when Frank couldn't keep himself from getting angry, he focused his fury where it belonged. Not on the insults to his character, but on the truth that Jenny's killer had gotten away with his crime. The monster was still out there somewhere. He escaped justice.

And justice, when Frank allowed himself to consider it — which happened more often than not these days — would come with the killer's death by his hands.

If Mallory had just listened, then maybe they could have caught Jenny's killer together.

Instead, she seemed intent on ruining his life.

He was tempted to go outside and have a little chat with her. Maybe offer Mallory some of his leftover marsala. Not that she'd be hungry after that giant burrito.

Part of him wanted Mallory to know he was on to her. But all of him knew it was stupid to let her know anything.

Why encourage her to do a better job hiding? One little slip and his life could be over. If Frank got caught breaking and entering, old complications would bubble up to the surface.

Ty Kirby would work to defame him. And Mallory would work tirelessly to see him in prison.

Chapter Four

Mal

MAL CURSED herself the entire way from the Heirloom cul-de-sac to her home.

It was almost five in the morning. Ray was going to murder her. Not that he needed to; Mal's back had the job half-finished already.

She fell asleep in the Explorer a few minutes after deciding it was finally time to go home. Now she would have to rush through her shower and grab a bite before heading back into work.

Of course, it wouldn't be that easy. Ray would want to "talk." And that little tête-à-tête would get louder and louder until one of them eventually said something ugly to spoil their morning and sour their day.

She had only herself to blame.

And sadly, Mal didn't understand how to hold herself accountable.

She was acutely aware of her levels of self-sabotage but

didn't understand why she was doing it or what needed to happen before she could finally stop.

Yes, Mal would be grateful to have a better strategy. But no, she didn't believe it would come from a shrink, and she was sick of Ray's incessant suggestion. A therapist's number one job was to keep their clients coming back week after week, which meant picking at old scabs that time should have healed. Their income literally depended on it.

And besides, Mal didn't need to see a shrink because she already knew what they would say.

That her bad habits were feeding something inside her. Offering a kind of comfort that she wasn't getting anywhere else. But the pop psychology insisted that Mal didn't know what she was doing, that it was all happening at a subconscious level. But she knew just fine. Mal was perfectly aware of the dopamine hitting her brain whenever she did something she wasn't supposed to.

Her working theory didn't require spilling her guts or spending money she didn't and wouldn't ever have. She needed candy. It really was as simple as that. Mal was forced to eat her vegetables for nearly every meal of every day, seeing guys like Grimm escaping justice and walking free. Sometimes she needed the sugar rush she could only get after working to expose them.

She had been parked for more than five minutes but still hadn't opened her door. She wanted a shower and something to eat. Plus, last night's burrito wasn't sitting well in her stomach this morning. She just didn't want to face Ray.

She swallowed and quit procrastinating. Got out of the SUV and quietly entered her house.

Sure enough, Ray was waiting in the living room. And *furious*.

It didn't show in his face or in the sound of his voice, but Mal could clearly see it in the set of his eyes, smoldering with anger he was doing his very best to bottle.

"You promised me, Mal."

"I know. I'm sorry. There was a lead I had to follow and—"

"There's *always* a lead to follow. But you know what? There's always a family at home, too."

"I know. I'm sorry," she tried again, hoping he'd hear her better the second time.

"It's not right what you keep doing to us."

"You act like I'm having an affair."

"You *are* having an affair, Mal."

"I am not!"

"You are. With your work. With your old case files. Like Grimm."

That stopped her.

She hadn't expected him to be so pointed.

Had Mike said something to him? Maybe Ray called him last night after she hadn't shown up at home? No, Mike would have texted her if that had happened, and she checked her messages when she woke up in the car with drool all over her chin. She didn't have any texts from anyone.

"I'm not having an affair with my work, Ray." Now she was defensive. "I'm doing my job. Trying to get guys like Grimm off the street so that girls like Ashley are safe."

"Girls like Ashley just want their mommy around."

She sighed. "I know. I'm sorry."

Third time's a charm.

"You should have seen her face, Mal. I don't know if I've ever seen her more disappointed. And I'm not trying to snipe at you, but I've seen her disappointed an awful lot lately. She was sad that we weren't going to make moo shu, so I told her we could order a pizza. She asked if I thought Mommy would be home before it got there. Of course, I didn't, but I said we could hope so. She didn't want to eat it without you, so I had to microwave her slices by the time she finally agreed to eat them. That was an hour into the movie and about five minutes before she fell asleep."

Ray stopped and looked at her but didn't really give her a chance to respond. "I know. You're *sorry*." He sighed. "But I don't need you to be sorry. I need you to be better."

"I—"

"You promised. Over and over and over. You made me believe that things were finally getting—"

"They *are* getting better," Mal insisted. "You know they are."

"I know they *were*."

"I promise to make it up to you both. Tonight. I'll knock off early, and we can all see the Puppy Detective movie together. Ashley's been talking about it for months, and—"

"I'm sure you'll just complain about how unrealistic their crime lab is or something."

"That's not fair. I'm trying, Ray."

"I understand that's what this looks like to you."

"You're talking to me like I'm a child."

"I'm sorry you feel that way."

But then he looked at Mal. She couldn't even tell if what she saw on his face was disappointment or disgust.

"I promise to do better."

He nodded. "I've heard that promise before."

"People mess up, Ray. I said I'm sorry, and I meant it. Things are a lot better than they used to be, but you know what? *I'm human.*"

He looked exhausted more than argumentative but

35

made the point out loud anyway. "I waited up for you all night; I'm too tired to fight."

"Why didn't you just text me?"

"It's not my job to text you, Mal."

"*Hey, honey, when are you coming home?* Or maybe, *It's late. I'm worried about you.*"

Ray stared at Mal for a long second before answering. "Are you really going to act like you would have responded? Because that would have been the first time you ever answered a text on one of your long work nights. You usually ignore them and wait for us to have the battle live."

"I don't want to fight either. Can we please just … Can you please just believe that I'm trying?"

"I will continue to believe what I see," Ray answered without sounding unkind. "Why don't you take a shower while I make breakfast?"

"Okay." She gave him a timid smile, then felt a grateful thrill when he offered one back. "Thank you."

"You're welcome, and good morning."

Ray stood and walked toward the kitchen.

Mal tromped upstairs to their bathroom.

She started the water, then went to her medicine cabinet and grabbed a bottle of NoDoz.

She shook a few into her palm without counting.

It was going to be a long day, and there was no such thing as too much caffeine.

Chapter Five

Frank

FRANK LOOKED at their spread with a devious smile.

Stan shook his head and broke into a laugh. "I don't know why you do this."

"Because you like to eat."

Stan nodded. "Sure. But I don't like being obnoxious."

Frank disagreed. "You've always liked being obnoxious."

"Not about how much food I order."

"You didn't order it. I did. Just pretend you're eating Sloppy's."

"It would be awesome if you ate with me instead of watching. It's weird, you know. Almost feels like a fetish."

"I can assure you, my fetish is certainly not watching my cousin eat."

"Then what is it, bitch?" Stan grinned at him.

"I buy you all this food, and you still insist on calling me a bitch?"

"I told you, bitch, I don't want you to order all this food."

"And yet you eat most of it and take the rest home." Frank kept the argument going because that was half of the fun. "Every time."

"You're retired. You should be watching how much you spend."

"Are you kidding? You think I want all the money I have?"

"Then why don't you give it all away?" Stan asked.

"Because I'm not an idiot." Frank plucked a thick strip of apple-smoked bacon from the table and stuffed half of it into his mouth. "Man, that bacon is good."

"Damn right, bitch." Stan grabbed two pieces. "So, why'd you want to have breakfast? You finally gonna start your P.I. business and need a partner who's smarter than you?"

"Because it's been a few weeks since I've seen my cousin stuffing his face. I thought it might be nice to—"

"Bullshit. You want something."

"You didn't let me finish. I was going to say that I thought it might be nice to talk, and maybe I might have a question or two you could answer over breakfast."

"Ha. Okay." Stan started digging into his omelet. "Don't be a bitch and start beating around the whatever. Ask me before my waffle gets cold."

"What's with your addiction to that word?"

Stan looked genuinely confused. "*Waffle*?"

"No. The other word … the b-word."

Stan shoved a piece of waffle into his mouth while laughing. "*Bitch?* You seriously can't even say the word?"

"I can. I *choose* not to."

Stan shook his head. "I never got that; what kind of cop doesn't swear?"

"The kind without a limited vocabulary."

"Bullshit. I know some *very* loquacious folks who like to swear. Including yours truly, using the word *loquacious* like a boss just now."

"Too bad you misused it," Frank said.

"I used it just fine."

"Loquacious means talkative; it doesn't mean that you actually know what you're saying or that you're an eloquent orator."

"Sure." Stan shrugged, his fork now on its way to a pancake. "But you need a lot of words to be talkative, or loquacious as it were, so checkmate, bitch. Now, what did you want to ask me?"

"Profanity is the effort of a feeble brain to express itself forcibly."

"I'm one-hundred percent positive that you didn't just make that up." Stan scrunched his face. "Quote of the day calendar? You seem too old-school for an app." Stabbing at the omelet. "Now, what did you want to ask me?"

"I was wondering if you knew about any reports of break-ins in my neighborhood."

Stan answered through a mouthful of food. "Sure. Of course. I keep all crime reports related to your neighborhood at the edge of my mind and the tip of my tongue. I read them right before bed, then catch up in the morning when I wake up, just in case I've missed something. That way, I'm always ready if you ask."

"You don't have to be a smartass."

"Better than being a dumbass. And a serious question: *Is ass not a curse word*?"

"It's… *historically* acceptable."

Another laugh from Stan to go with what looked like an entire third of his waffle. "You really are a bitch. Why are you asking? Say what you wanna say."

Frank opened his mouth, but he didn't get a chance to say anything.

"Wait! I got it. This has something to do with Black, right? She's like one of those Japanese soldiers who never knew that World War II was over."

Frank laughed because it was better than breaking a plate. "She was staking my place last night. She probably got indigestion and a throbbing back."

Stan shrugged. "What do you care?"

"Am I not allowed to want my privacy?"

"Sure. But maybe you can see this another way."

"And what way would that be?" Frank could only hold out for so long. He stabbed a piece of waffle, dipped it into the butter, and then the syrup before putting it in his mouth.

"Black has it out for you, but she's the one wasting all her time. She has nothing and never will, so why sweat it when you can laugh at her. Hell, you should box up some of your marsala and go out and feed it to the bitch."

"You don't have to call her that."

"Why not, man? She's fucking with your life."

"There are other ways to express yourself."

"Oh yeah." Stan rolled his eyes. "I already forgot. You do know that studies have shown that swearing can display a *greater* rather than a *lesser* use of intelligence, right?"

"Is this study funded by Dullards For The Erosion of Society?"

Stan, still talking with a full mouth: "Swearing is linked to the experience and expression of feelings and emotions. I can see why you'd have a hard time with it."

"What's that supposed to mean?"

Stan whispered like it was a secret, "You've been a little robotic since Sarah."

Frank pulled the waffle plate toward him, then started eating instead of insisting that he wasn't being robotic.

"You need therapy, man."

"Not this again. Can we please just not—"

"Make you a deal …" Stan cut him off. "I'll stop mentioning therapy if you acknowledge the elegant beauty of the word *bitch*. Or better yet, you start using it yourself."

"It's an ugly, sexist word that's been used to keep women down throughout history.

"*History,*" Stan repeated. "Always consider intent. The problem is never in a word; it's always in the nuance. I bet your therapist will agree when you meet her."

"I'm not going to a therapist. And if I did, what makes you think it would be a woman?"

"So you've told me—many times. But guess what, cuz? There's no shame in needing help, man or woman. That was some hard shit you went through."

"Who knows, maybe Mallory's not even after me anymore." Frank changed the subject. "Maybe something else is happening in my neighborhood. Can you do me a favor and just let me know if you hear anything?"

"In your neighborhood?" Stan stopped eating to look at him across the table. "You mean that tiny little cul-de-sac? What is it you *think* is happening?"

"Nothing specific." Frank shook his head. He might have already stepped in it, yet another sign that he might be losing his edge. "Just a hunch."

"Ah," Stan nodded, obviously not believing him. "*A hunch.* Got it."

Then he winked and went back to eating. Nearly half of the spread was already gone.

No more interruptions from Frank. He wanted Stan to finish the meal, so he could get back home and figure a few more things out. He'd gone to bed a quarter past midnight;

a few minutes after seeing that Mallory had fallen asleep, then he woke up in enough time to see the girl from 47 Heirloom walking down the block toward her bus stop. Frank was glad to see she was gone, even if he couldn't follow that early. He could break in and learn a little about his new neighbors after breakfast with Stan.

Frank looked down to realize that he'd been eating for a while now.

"Finally." Stan looked satisfied by more than the food. "Now *that's* how you clear a table." Then, because Frank didn't respond, his cousin added, "*Biiiiitch.*"

* * *

Frank stared out the window, through the thinnest sliver of the blinds, waiting for the girl from 47 Heirloom to round the corner on her way home.

He could never see the school bus as it pulled up or away, but he could hear both and imagined the sound of its door hissing open and closed.

Frank had been waiting for this ever since coming home from breakfast. He'd had every intention of going over and seeing what he could find out from inside her house, but his instinct wouldn't quit itching. Maybe it was paranoia at having been seen or even his close call with Bill coming home early, but Frank just couldn't get himself to shed the thought that he'd get caught if he made the mistake of going over there. He kept picturing the worst-case scenario: getting seen, having to squirm through an awkward explanation, then having his entire life upended again.

He went outside on three separate occasions but only rounded the cul-de-sac twice, feeling more and more like a coward. He was out more than usual and drawing unnecessary attention to himself.

Something had withered his judgment. So no, Frank

didn't trust himself enough to be breaking in anywhere today. Instead, he waited by the window like the lonely old man he was.

Muriel, Tabitha, Peter, and Capri.

After the last of the first four kids that lived in the cul-de-sac all rounded the corner, Frank started counting backward from ten. He was on three when he saw the girl from 47 Heirloom.

Dressed in all black, like usual, but for the first time, Frank noticed something he hadn't before. In the past, he saw her attire as a costume, a uniform, to prove how apart she was from the norm, just like all the other goths.

Now, even from his window, Frank could see the truth of her sadness.

But maybe not. Maybe it was a put-on. The girl was looking right at him. She *wanted* him to see her.

He flinched back from the window.

Frank didn't think she actually saw him, or even really believe that she could, but it was clear she expected him to be watching.

She fixed her eyes right on his house and didn't break her gaze until she was standing directly across from it. Then she stopped, stared for several paralytic seconds until she finally gritted her teeth and dragged her eyes from his house to hers.

Then she turned back, gave Frank a decisive nod — whether she knew he could see it or not — and walked the rest of the way to her house without looking over before disappearing inside.

Frank kept looking, waiting to see if she'd appear in her upstairs window.

Less than a minute passed. He didn't see her in the second story, but Polo Dad did swing his old Buick into the driveway. He killed the engine and was out of the car in a flash as if running late and allergic to the idea of his daughter being alone in the house.

Did he always come home just moments after the bus?

More proof that Frank had been asleep at the wheel.

Dad was halfway to his front door when he turned and looked behind him — a direct glance back at what Frank definitely felt was his house. As if the man could sense him staring and wanted him to know it.

He let go of the blind he was holding up, closed the curtain, and stepped away from the window, then did what he should have done months ago and went to look up his neighbors.

He'd been a fool to trust Erin Duvall. She said the family had moved to Creek County from Hanover, but after a quick search he could and should have made when they moved in, Frank discovered that the dad, Patrick Dahl, had worked in the county during Jenny's murder, before he moved with his wife, Irene, and daughter, Freya, into the modest Victorian.

So now Frank knew two things:

Patrick Dahl was a suspect in Jenny's murder.

And Freya might be in trouble.

Chapter Six

Mal

MAL FORCED herself to look again at the corpse in the woods behind the shopping plaza as she added to the initial crime scene sketch in her notepad.

The girl, a Caucasian female with long brown hair, looked to be around fourteen or so. She was nude, hands bound in rope in front of her crotch, throat slit, eyes fixed in a dead gaze to the afternoon sun. It was a similar scene to the one that had hosted Jenny Grimm.

She looked to make sure the tarps they set up around the scene to block anyone's view of the girl hadn't fallen over in the cold wind now picking up. Everything was secure. The wide perimeter had kept looky-loos confined to the northeast corner of the parking lot, along the side of a Winn-Dixie.

"Lividity along her backside," Mike said into his camera's microphone as he turned the girl slightly to reveal purple splotches from blood pooling. "Body is still stiff, rigor mortis not yet reversed. So she's been here less than a day." He'd already detailed the time and temperature to help establish a time of death.

Bile rose in her throat as Mal finished her sketch and walked deeper into the woods to collect herself.

She looked at the people hanging around the parking lot like they were at a taping for CSI, wondering if the killer was among the viewing audience. She'd already had one of the officers discreetly take video of everyone there. She'd also requested the shopping center's security footage facing the woods and for security to pull copies of all recordings from every available camera in case the killer or victim had been in the parking lot or store.

But she didn't think the killer was still here.

Mal would have spotted her suspect in a second.

The first cops on the scene already interviewed the worker, an older man who'd spotted the body on a smoke break. They didn't like him as a suspect, given his age and general state of frailty.

Mike finished recording video and photos and walked over to update her on his findings — no weapon, flashlight had no prints, but they'd bagged it anyway. He had the photo of the girl run against the missing persons' database. There were no missing teens matching the girl's description in Creek County, but it could be too early for a parent to have noticed her missing. Or she could be from elsewhere in the state or even out of state. Somehow, an inordinate number of the nation's runaways wound up dead in Florida.

As he spoke, she could feel the conflict brewing in the cooling autumn air. Not that she wanted an argument, but there was no way to say what she was thinking without him pushing back. Even after a year, he still didn't — maybe couldn't — get it.

Mike, staring at her, asked, "Whatcha thinking?"

"I don't think you want to know."

He eyed her suspiciously. "What?"

"Think it's a little similar to Jenny Grimm."

He nodded. "Yeah, with the rope. But Jenny was stabbed, and her face covered with her shirt."

"Yeah, because the killer knew her. Like, say, her father."

"Please don't start again. You gonna tell me that Frank did this one too? Since he didn't know her, he didn't feel a need to cover her up? That he also decided on slitting her throat instead of stabbing the body nineteen times?"

"It's worth talking to him, don't you think?"

"Let's just finish working the scene, maybe see where this girl's even from before we go grab Frank Grimm, eh? Isn't the dad always the first suspect? This girl probably has a dad we should talk to first, don't *you* think?"

She shook her head and let out a sigh. "Why not talk to him while we're waiting to get info on this girl? That girl is the same age as Grimm's daughter. Killed almost the same way. You really think it's a coincidence? You don't think he's a suspect?"

"Why are you asking me questions you already know the answer to?" Mike seemed genuinely annoyed. "He never should have been a suspect in the first place. So what, you want to add insult to injury? *Hey Frank, sorry about what happened to your daughter. It really wasn't fair, everything that you had to deal with. I can't imagine what the last year's been like for you. But hey, while we have you, why not tell us about your whereabouts last night? We have a body Jenny's age, and we figured—*"

"Fuck you, Mike."

"Okay." He shrugged.

"I'm tired of you acting like it's *impossible* that Grimm could be guilty."

Another shrug. "Well, I'm tired of you grasping at straws."

"I'm not—"

"You want to put this on Frank because you have a vendetta against the guy. You're so sure he got away with it that you'll attach him to anything remotely similar. Even if these cases are connected, and I'll grant you, it's possible, that doesn't make Frank our suspect. In fact, I'd argue that it makes it *less* likely he killed Jenny."

"How's that?"

Mike shook his head. "If I need to tell you, then maybe that proves my point, Mal. Think about what you're suggesting. For a second, just imagine that this was anybody other than Frank. If you'd be questioning them."

"I *am* thinking about it. You're the one who's not willing to see what might be right in front of us. I'm not saying Grimm did this. I'm saying it's ridiculous to exclude him as a possible suspect."

"Mal." His tone made her stop. "I'm not excluding anybody yet. We just caught this case. Shit! You need to let go of your obsession with Frank. It's distorting your professional judgment."

She didn't know how to respond.

Mal could feel the truth in what he was saying, but he wasn't doing the same for her. "Can't you just acknowledge that it's *possible* that Grimm is guilty?"

"Of course, it's possible. But that *possibility* shouldn't drive everything. It's time to let it go."

"How?" Mal asked, feeling close to tears but not even sure why she was getting emotional. "How do you not imagine your own kids falling victim to some monster like this? And how is it okay to know that some guy is out there free, still killing kids? That *we* didn't catch him? Or worse, we had him, and we let him get away?"

Mike's face finally softened. He reached out and touched her on the shoulder. "It's—"

"Fucking dammit," Mal cut him off.

"What?"

But then he saw.

Ty Kirby, getting out of his news van, quickly approaching a deputy with a cameraperson right behind him. The first of the reporters to show up, and Creek County's Public Information Officer still wasn't on the scene. The deputy he was talking to was a rookie, and Mal wanted to make sure the officer didn't give this shit-bag any information.

Kirby was a bottom feeder in endless pursuit of the most sensational possible headline. He sold fear but packaged it as concern, as if he or the channel he worked for gave a damn about anything but the maxim, *if it bleeds, it leads*. He was the kind of guy who deserved a pounding from karma and yet still somehow always managed to get more than his share out of life.

"Do I need to tell you to behave yourself?" Mike asked as she approached the perimeter of the scene.

"No, but I'm sure you will anyway."

Kirby looked past the deputy he was talking to, caught Mal glaring at him, and gave her a friendly but surely sarcastic wave.

He would have made her Shit List based on his smarmy, artificial, parasitic personality alone. But Mal mostly hated Ty Kirby because he was one of the biggest reasons that Grimm had wiggled his way out of justice.

The reporter started early by claiming that the sheriff's office was protecting one of their own. But that wasn't even close to the truth. There was a big difference between giving a colleague the benefit of the doubt and burying the truth. She saw a lot of one and none of the other. Yet

Kirby acted like the entire department was cooperating to help a man who raped and murdered his daughter go free.

And worse, Kirby destroyed the case after ambushing Frank's wife shortly before her suicide. Mal had been working her for a while and felt sure she was about to spill something. Mike had to stop Mal from beating the shit out of the guy, same as he had every time she'd seen him since.

"Just please ..." Mike reminded her again. "Try not to punch him."

"I'll try to try. How's that?"

"Barely acceptable. There're cameras. Can you please just *try* to be nice?"

"Like I said, I'll try to try."

Mike sighed, shaking his head as they approached Kirby. She could feel him bracing for whatever was about to happen. A part of her enjoyed keeping her partner on edge a bit. Was it her fault if he was so uptight?

"Detective Black." Kirby turned to Mike. "Detective Cortez."

"Hey, Lois!" Mal greeted him; she couldn't have been nicer.

"Either of you have any—"

"Our PIO is preparing a statement. Until then, no comment."

"So, you won't confirm that the body in the woods is a teenage girl?"

How the fuck does he know that?

Mal kept her expression neutral. "I said no comment."

She turned away, giving Mike a *How was that?* smile.

Kirby shouted, "So are you denying that the victim is a teenage girl?"

Mal spun around, holding her smile. "I said no comment, Lois."

"*Lois?* Why are you calling me that?" Kirby asked.

"*Lane,*" Mike explained.

"Not much of a reporter," Mal said. "How about Murphy Brown? Would you get *that* reference? Probably before your time. It was the 80's. Not sure if you were a zygote yet."

"We're on the same side, Detective Black."

"You can't possibly believe that." Mal shook her head.

"I'm just looking for a comment."

"Oh, awesome! I have one."

"Mal …"

Mal ignored her partner; she was done being nice. "Reporters who impede ongoing investigations for the sake of ratings help to keep pedophile murderers on the street and should really be ashamed of themselves. In case it wasn't clear, that was totally on the record." She smiled at the camera trained on her, then turned on her heel and left.

Kirby shouted, "So, there's no comment on whether the victim's hands were bound like Jenny Grimm's?"

How the fuck does he know that?

Nobody had gotten close to the scene. And the deputy who questioned the man that found the body had told him not to talk to anybody about it. Did he tell his co-workers what he'd seen before he even called the sheriff's office? Or did a deputy tip him off?

Mal glanced around at her fellow deputies working the scene, looking for a traitor in her camp. Still too many deputies loyal to the old sheriff, who hated the new one, Gloria Bell, because she'd had the audacity to not only be a woman but a black woman in a department that was still somewhat stuck in the fifties when it came to things like progress and equal rights. Some of the deputies hated Mal because she had backed Bell. Too many "good ole boys" were still in the department, clinging to their ancient hate.

Mal spun back around, glaring at Kirby. "What part of no fucking comment did you not understand, you piece of shit?"

Immediately Kirby smiled, knowing he'd won. She felt the gravity of the camera on her, the mic in her face, and Kirby's smug expression smirking back at her. And she felt Future Mal's embarrassment at being shaken by this fool, the video making a loop on the nightly news to make her and the department look unprofessional.

And, of course, disappointing her boss.

She turned quickly and walked away.

Mike followed, exasperated, "What the hell was that?"

She refused to stop and address him while Kirby's camera was probably still trained on them. She kept walking, back toward the body, until she was looking down at the corpse again, as she choked down the rising rage.

Mike caught up to her.

She didn't turn to him. She couldn't face his disappointment. "Not now."

He stood there for a moment, then walked away, leaving her alone.

Mal couldn't wait to get home and to pour herself a stiff drink or four. Then she remembered that she couldn't drink after work today. She had a fucking movie to go to. And she would probably be late.

Fuck my life.

Chapter Seven

Frank

FRANK ALREADY REGRETTED KNOCKING.

The door swung open, and Rachel looked delighted to see him. "Frank!"

She threaded the threshold with her body while Dolly yipped and yapped behind her. This was stupid. Surely there were better ideas than taking the obnoxious chihuahua for a walk if he'd only given it a few more minutes of thought. Now he had to deal with Rachel *and* a rat dog.

"Did you come to bring me my mail?"

He handed her the stack of printed crap. "I was wondering if you needed any help with Dolly. I was just about to go out on a walk."

"Oh, you are the nicest man in this cul-de-sac. Ya hear that, Dolly? He's gonna take you for a walk." Then back to Frank. "You don't happen to have any strawberries, do you?"

"Um … no. Sorry. I haven't bought strawberries since before … in a long time."

"Would you like some strawberries?" Rachel asked while Dolly got louder behind her.

"Sure." Really he just wanted the leash.

"Wonderful!" She beamed while closing the door, leaving Frank standing perplexed on the porch. It swung open several seconds later, and Rachel was now holding her purse. "No hurry, but whenever you get them, can you grab me a couple of pints? Maybe three? I'd like to make a pie."

She handed him a five-dollar bill. For her, maybe three pints of strawberries.

"Okay." No use arguing. The strawberries would remind him of Sarah, but maybe in a good way for once. "So … Dolly?" He pocketed the fiver and held out his hand for the leash.

"Oh, of course. Be right back." The door shut again, this time staying closed for nearly a full minute before it opened all the way, and Rachel presented Dolly by her leash like a prize.

"I'll have her back in a bit." Frank tipped his head and turned to go.

"You know much about diamonds?"

"I'm sorry?" He could smell a story and wanted to run.

"I bet you didn't know that the three largest ever found in America were all from one state."

"No. I did not."

"Guess which state."

He could tell her that he had no idea and explain how little he cared, but it was much more efficient to answer. "Utah."

"*Arkansas*." She said this like it was the solution to the world's greatest riddle.

"Oh."

"And you know where the largest ever found on the planet was?"

"Arkansas?"

"That's right." She gave him an emphatic nod. "Largest on Earth."

"I assumed you meant our planet."

"Strawn-Wagner."

"I'm sorry?" But, no. "Dolly's really going crazy down there. I should be getting—"

"She's always doing that! She could be licking ice cream, and it'd be the same exact thing."

Frank had no idea what that meant. "I'm—"

"The Strawn-Wagner diamond was unearthed in 1990. Now it's on permanent display at the Crater of Diamonds visitor center. *In Arkansas.*"

Maybe there was a point. But it would be faster to ask. "Why are you telling me this?"

"Not enough people know about Arkansas." Rachel said it like a *harrumph*. He wanted to suggest she get a job at their tourism office, but he would only come off sounding sarcastic.

"I really think Dolly wants to—"

"People make fun of that state, but they shouldn't. It's a great state."

"Did you just finish watching a documentary or something?"

"I'm from Arkansas!" Rachel jabbed a thumb at her chest and stared at Frank as though he'd insulted her.

Can I please just go?

"You ever hear of the Dover Lights?"

And walk your dog?

"Um, no, ma'am."

"Bizarre phenomena in the Ozarks. Restless spirits of Spanish soldiers who died looking for treasure. I can see you're in a hurry, so look it up. You ever hear of the Fouke Monster?"

"Nope." *YOU JUST SAID THAT YOU SAW I WAS IN A HURRY!*

"Southern Sasquatch. Beast of Boggy Creek. Seven feet tall and three feet wide. Troublesome cousin of Bigfoot and a natural enemy to the Chupacabra."

Nothing was worth this.

Frank had nothing to add other than *Kill me.* The best strategy right now was to stare back in silence and pray for a merciful end to their exchange.

A full two seconds passed, so Frank liberated the third. "You got it, Dolly!"

He let her yank the leash, then followed the sort-of dog off of its porch and onto the sidewalk.

Finally.

Dolly was annoying, and Rachel even more so, but at least now he had a reason to be loitering in front of 47 Heirloom. Frank kept yanking the leash on his way to Freya's place, not letting her sniff on any of the aromatic lawns. She could take her sweet time at their final destination.

And she did. Dolly was up on the Dahl's lawn like it was her own backyard.

Frank studied the grounds, loosely looking at the house and lake behind it while appearing to take in the world around him.

The house was dark.

No one in the second-story window.

And Frank didn't feel like anyone was watching him or looking to be seen.

He made another circuit, wanting to see the house from farther away, and forced himself through three minutes of mindless conversation with Erin Duvall, a divorcée who adored using the word and stretch the *ée*. Her recent split with the former Mr. Duvall was now seven years old, and like always, she parlayed Frank's *How are you doing?* into a tirade of why her divorce from that "whore fucker" was both the best and worst thing that had ever happened to her.

Today it was the best. "I was fifty-eight. *My decision*. Not his, so what's there to regret? We'd been married for twenty-seven years. Three grown kids, and one of them with too much testosterone. He'd been sticking it into anything willing. And we were firm on that, Mikey's father and I, *No means no!*"

Erin stole a breath but didn't let her victim escape. "No one expected bliss; I figured our marriage was fine, as far as marriages go. We did it once a week and played it one for him and one for me. Good enough, right? Too bad the whore fucker had to be the center of attention at all times, using at least a few of those six days when he wasn't giving it to me to shove his cheating balls into a prostitute. *Prostitutes*. There was more than one."

Frank already knew that, of course.

"You know how much he spent paying women to fuck him in just the last year before I found out?"

Frank knew that, too.

"Five thousand dollars!"

He had done the math. For a few times a week and covering an entire year, it sounded to Frank like a bargain. "I'm sorry."

"*He* should be sorry." She huffed, then added, "And he is!"

"I'm glad he got what was coming to him." Frank

looked down at the chihuahua, still yapping like crazy but now trying to scamper away. "Have a great day."

And back to Freya's he went.

"Take your time," he muttered to Dolly, looking up at the house, using a more studious eye, noting anything unusual, searching for details he'd missed from far away or before.

Dolly was done and wanted to go, but her walker wasn't ready to leave.

The dog started making a mockery of actual barking again, but Frank kept standing there, needing to move but wanting another moment to take it in.

"Can I help you with anything?" The voice behind him was chillingly calm.

Frank turned and saw Patrick Dahl, smiling without meaning it, holding a half-full thirteen-gallon trash bag like a prop.

He might have been a handsome man. Frank wasn't quite sure since there was also something off about him. Dahl's cheeks were round without being overly full, his jaw was nicely cut, and his light-brown eyes, arresting. Yet despite the warmth of their shade, they seemed cold, and his handsome features felt like a facade. Maybe even a weapon.

"I was just waiting on her to finish her business." Frank looked down at the dog.

"Looked to me like she already did that." Still smiling. "Was there maybe some business *you* were finishing?"

Frank smiled back. "I guess that sometimes I just get a little lost in my thoughts."

"Oh yeah?" Genuine interest in Patrick Dahl's darkening eyes. "And what kind of thoughts were you having out here while looking at my house?"

"I'm just walking my dog."

"*Your* dog?" Patrick looked down at the still-yelping chihuahua.

"Rachel's from across the way." Frank tipped his chin toward Mrs. Goldberg's house. "She busted her hip and has been having a hard time getting around. I've been helping her out by walking Dolly here and grabbing her mail."

"What a wonderful neighbor you are." His smile was there, but something fierce and unrelenting kept creeping behind it. "She must really appreciate you."

He walked to the trashcan, dropped the bag inside it, then stood there looking at Frank, waiting for his neighbor to answer.

"Yes. I think she does." Frank gave him a nod and began to walk away.

"Now you want to go?"

He turned back around. "I was already on my way when you came out."

"Sure you were."

"Do you have some sort of problem with me?" Frank asked.

"Should I?"

"I'm helping a neighbor out by walking her dog, like I said. I'm sure not trying to get in your way ... or whatever *this* is."

"*Whatever this is,*" Dahl repeated with an un-neighborly nod. Then he took several steps toward Frank until they were face-to-face, not even moving when Dolly came over, barking, snarling, and snipping at his heels.

"You think I don't know who you are, Frank Grimm?"

Guilty; he did think that. "I'm not trying to hide anything."

"I hope not. But I'm new here. Let's just say that gives me a bit of fresh perspective. You haven't been walking my dog or baking me pies long enough for me to trust you. Plenty of former officers have used their station to take advantage of decent folks. Isn't that right, Frank?"

He studied Dahl instead of offering an answer.

"I hear you. Probably not a fun question to answer. Here's a second one: *How do you think the police would respond if I told them that former Officer Grimm was nosing around my fourteen-year-old daughter?*"

"*What?* I wasn't—"

"I didn't ask what you were doing, Frank. I asked how you thought the police would respond to my call. So ... do you have an answer for that?"

This wasn't the time or place to argue about anything. Not on Dahl's property, and not with Erin Duvall now looking at them from across the way.

"I'll get out of your way." Frank gave him a nod, then turned and walked away.

"Make sure that dog shits in your yard. Or the old lady you're borrowing her from. Not mine."

Frank didn't turn around, stealing a glance up at the second-story window anyway, because he wanted to see if Freya was watching, and because he needed to show Dahl that he wasn't scared of him. Of course, Frank could see how he might seem potentially threatening to the guy's daughter, but there was something else there for sure.

"What was that all about?" Rachel asked as he reached her front door, where she'd already come outside to wait for him.

Frank wanted to look behind him but didn't and wondered if the eyes he felt burning the back of his head were really there. "I have no idea."

And that was the truth.

Chapter Eight

Mal

DAMMIT.

Dammit.

Dammit.

Dammit.

That was all Mal could think over and over as she raced to meet her husband and daughter.

Ray was going to kill her. And Mal deserved whatever death she had coming.

The rest of her day had gone as precisely as well as it started. No leads on the case or even a name to match the body. Right now, she was a Jane Doe.

Mal spent most of the day getting yelled at by her bosses, first her captain and then Gloria, because not only did that punk Ty Kirby file a complaint against her, but the channel had aired her interview on TV to shame the department. It was bleeped out, but not on the online version, where it was going viral fast.

Mal would make Kirby pay for it eventually, but today

she had to take her reprimand like a good girl. Be grateful that it was only a slap on the wrist. Things could have been much worse and would've been for sure if Barry was still sheriff instead of Bell.

Ray would be pissed that she didn't text after knowing she was running late.

He would be furious that she hadn't answered a single one of his messages and would refuse her excuse that she just wanted to get from A to B as fast as she possibly could.

Mostly, Ray would act exhausted by what he would insist was an unbreakable pattern for Mal.

And really, it wasn't.

She *was* trying. Kirby knew what he was doing, baiting her like that. Mike should have kept him away from her before it was too late.

Mal swung into the Super Saver Cinema 6 parking lot, then pulled up next to her family's Outback.

Out of the car and jogging toward the entrance, but they weren't waiting outside as agreed.

Though, really, that was her fault, too.

They had *agreed* on *no later than* 5:40 — the movie started at 6:00, and that gave them a comfortable twenty minutes to negotiate which concessions they were going to get and stand in line to buy them.

It was 6:04 now.

Mal ran up to the box office window.

The teenager with long blonde pigtails and a shocking amount of acne was already pushing a ticket forward through the window.

"Mal, right?" The cashier didn't wait for her response, but she grunted agreement anyway. "Your husband said you'd be running up and to make sure you got this."

She took the ticket with an embarrassed nod, then entered the theater.

No sign of them in the lobby, so she marched directly to Theater #4, where *Sherlock Bones* was playing.

The trailers had already started but weren't yet over. At least not for the first fifteen seconds she spent trying to adjust her eyes in the dark. Then the screen flickered, and it went onto an advertisement for Coke.

Weren't the commercials supposed to come before the previews?

That was infuriating. It made Mal especially angry, landing on top of everything else.

She went down one row, then back up the other side.

Behind the very last row, against the wall, then repeating her pattern down the opposite aisle.

But still, she didn't see Ray or Ashley anywhere.

The movie was starting, and Mal still couldn't find her family. Even though it hadn't happened yet, she could hear Ray yelling at her and Ashley's mournful disappointment.

Maybe she had missed them. She was exhausted to the marrow after today. Not just Kirby, but the body; yet another dead little girl, and not enough clues.

It was too much on her mind. Hard to shift gears. Mal had to go from murdered girls to puppy sleuths that unintentionally mocked her profession. Ray was a photographer for the paper and constantly compared his situation at work to hers. But it wasn't even close to the same. He had to take the pictures, sometimes of horrible tragedies, yes, but once he was done, the photos went in the paper and online, and he was onto the next thing, maybe a local charity event or a dance or a sporting event when the sports photographers were busy. He didn't have to deal with many dead bodies and never had to snap pics of anything half as grisly as what Mal was forced to witness.

She couldn't just let the tragedies go. She had to study them instead. She had to interview the family, the suspects, and she had to study the crime scene and the photos and get inside the mind of both victim and killer.

Even after going up and down both aisles again, Mal still didn't see her husband or her daughter. Her supply of NoDoz had worked to keep her awake, but now it was making her on edge.

She tried not to panic, but they weren't in the lobby.

And their vehicle was still in the parking lot.

Her heart started beating much too fast.

She needed to squelch her paranoia. Ray was fine. So was Ashley.

They were probably in the bathroom.

Ashley was too old for them to share the same one, but they could have gone in together, separately. Bad timing … that's all this was.

The rationale was solid, but it didn't halt the parade of images. Macabre postcards sent to Mal's mind from Jenny Grimm's unsolved murder, and images of Jane Doe in the woods, violated and left for all the world to see.

She checked the girl's restroom.

Then, what the hell, she checked the men's.

But still nothing, and still no family in the lobby.

She took out her phone and looked at the screen. Her last text was from Ray, asking what time she expected to be there and wanting to know if she would like for them to wait. Mal hadn't wanted to answer because she was at a red light, and he would know she was on her phone while driving.

Damned if she did, damned if she didn't.

She wanted to text him, but if Mal had missed him in the theater and his phone light went on, he would be even angrier at her.

She went to the car, looked inside to see if there was

anything amiss, then looked frantically back at the front of the restaurant.

Then, suddenly struck by a new and logical theory, she trotted across the lot and went into the Jones BBQ Chicken next to the theater. Ashley always wanted to try it, and Mal always said it looked like they only served food poisoning. It wasn't fair; the place was probably fine. Maybe Ray decided to eat there as a way to make his wife pay for her lack of participation in their family affairs.

But they weren't in there either.

Nor were they in the lobby.

So finally, Mal sent Ray a text.

No answer, and still no sign of them.

It was now 6:13 — Ray would kill her for sure.

And Ashley would probably cry if she wasn't in tears already.

Mal went back outside and to the cashier.

"Everything okay?" she asked.

"My family. I can't find them. I've looked everywhere."

"Hmm …" The cashier made a face. "*Dragon Soup* at 6:20?"

"No. It was the puppy detective movie." She felt like such an idiot saying this shit out loud. "*Sherlock Bones* at 6:00."

The cashier shook her head. "That's not what their tickets say. Or yours."

Mal took out her ticket and checked. Sure enough, *Dragon Soup* at 6:20. "Shit … I'm so sorry."

"No worries," the girl said apologetically as if *she'd* screwed up. "I'm glad you solved the mystery."

Mal nodded, then walked as fast as she could without running inside and over to Theater #3, which Mal had passed no less than two dozen times in the last ten minutes.

She opened the door and saw her family immediately.

Left side, halfway down, tucked slightly in so the aisle seat was left for her, Ashley tapping on the cup holder as if expecting Mommy's hand.

Mal made her way over and sat.

Ray didn't look at her.

Neither did Ashley.

"I'm here," she whispered.

But neither of them spoke, or so much as glanced her way.

* * *

Mal turned uncomfortably on her couch, unable to sleep.

She desperately wanted to and kept trying everything possible to make it happen, from counting backward to alphabetizing a list of dickheads who deserved to die, but nothing was working. Ray could fuck her to sleep if his fury with her wasn't part of the problem.

Her mind was still marinating on Grimm and his possible connection to the Jane Doe case. Not to mention his own daughter. Mal wasn't sure she'd ever stop thinking about that.

But right now, she was pondering her argument with Ray after the movie. Or specifically, after Ashley went to bed when he could really let it go and tell his wife exactly how disappointed in her he was.

"Why didn't you tell me you were seeing a different movie?"

He shook his head. Couldn't even look at her. "We picked something that started a little later, figuring that you might get in before we started. Ashley's idea. She chose a crappy movie that she didn't even want to see, hoping you'd be there in time. It seemed like a reasonable expectation. But so did assuming that you'd look at your ticket."

"I was just—"

"I know what you were *just*, Mal. But if you gave a shit about seeing the movie with us, you'd have been there on time."

A beat of heavy silence followed, then he finished with the line she couldn't stop thinking about.

"I'm sorry that your family is such a distraction from your job." Another heavy breath, then, "It doesn't have to be that way."

Mal had asked what he meant, but Ray hadn't answered. Instead, he went to watch ESPN downstairs. On the smaller TV in his office. With the door closed.

She tried again once more before bed about two hours later. She knocked, then knocked again, and only entered after nearly three minutes of being completely ignored.

"How can we go to bed feeling better about this?"

Ray turned from the TV. From his expression, he could have been watching nothing at all. "You could start with being more present."

And like a reflex hammer hitting her knee, she said, "*You're* not all that present, either."

A tired, defeated smile, then Ray had said, "We've already acknowledged that we both have work to do. The difference is I changed my hours so that I could be around more. It's your turn to do the same."

But then she made things even worse. "It's easy for you! Other people can snap a pic, Ray. I'm one of the best detectives in Creek County."

"Congratulations. It's good to know what you're best at."

"Fuck you." Then immediately, "Sorry. I didn't mean that."

"It's the lack of sleep." For a second, Mal thought he was being understanding, but then he clarified his thought. "Maybe you should pop a few more caffeine pills so you can have a proper argument with your husband. You know, minus the swearing."

It hurt a lot more than Mal had wanted to admit.

She had nothing to say after that.

So Mal slipped out of his office, retreated to a dark corner of the living room, and waited for him to retire. Then, once Ray was upstairs, she made herself a bed on the couch.

That's where she had been ever since, thinking about all she had done wrong and all that she needed to do better.

She was dying for sleep. Her alarm would go off soon.

She wanted to wake up early and greet Ashley in the morning with a delicious breakfast and another chance at getting things right.

Mal made it halfway through her list of dickheads for the third time, stuttering through Gorman Karr, who murdered an old lady to "see how long it would take" before hearing the first of her own snores.

Chapter Nine

Frank

FRANK ALMOST HAD to laugh as he closed the back door of 47 Heirloom behind him. He adjusted the ski mask to ensure it was covering his face as he imagined himself falling to the ground with his back pressed against the wood, heavily panting, just like he'd seen and not believed in so many movies.

But nobody did that in real life.

And yet, Frank was fighting not to do that exact thing now. He had broken into every house on Heirloom except for this one. Not once had he ever felt so near the edge of panic. There was something deeply unsettling about this place. An aroma he couldn't identify, but it riled something primal inside him, and he didn't need to be inside the house to catch a whiff.

Frank had finished off a whole pot of coffee by the time he could finally make his move.

Both cars were finally gone. Freya rounded the corner on her way to the bus, Patrick roared off in his Impala, and an hour later, Irene left for her job at the craft store in an old Volvo.

The cul-de-sac was quiet on his way over, and despite using his same subtle approach, he still couldn't shake the sense of being watched.

Or expected.

The lights were all off, but the windows were open enough for Frank to see his way around.

The house wasn't what he had imagined, but after a seven-second survey of the living room alone, he no longer felt surprised. The place was void of personality, decorated with the approximate character of a mid-range hotel.

From the living room into the dining room.

A home office, then the master bed and bath after that.

And still, not a single personal item that might speak to the people that inhabited this place.

The sterile surroundings were unsettling. Frank kept wanting to tell himself that maybe the Dahls had busy lives that had kept them from fully unpacking in the last half-year. But expression might as well have been illegal. There was *nothing*.

Frank didn't want to believe it, for Irene and Freya's sake. But even if Patrick Dahl wasn't a killer, he might very well be a monster all the same. The kind who had to exercise control over those he saw as beneath him. And if Dahl was anything like the few people — men, always men — Frank had known to strike a similar chord inside him in the past, that meant pretty much everyone in his way.

The home wasn't naked, just nude of personality. The colors worked, and the generic art was perfectly placed to frame the entire facade with a unifying appearance.

Still, it was an empty aesthetic without any soul.

Frank hadn't just been to every home on Heirloom.

While working as a sheriff's deputy, he'd been in more houses than he could count. This was the least lived-in place he could ever remember seeing. Like the owner had ordered one of everything in the Masquerading as Normal catalog. Even the home office didn't really look like a place where any work was done. It seemed more like a collection of staging furniture in a model home.

He withdrew his phone and used the app that detected infrared signals of hidden cameras as he went from room to room. No cameras, though he kept his mask on — just in case.

Frank went into Freya's room, and that tiny world felt instantly different.

Every stuffed animal in her collection appeared *exactly* the same vintage, with the same amount of wear and tear. Not a single one looked loved like a stuffy should. But other than that, the room had obvious hints of personality, even though it was easy to see how little was allowed.

A covering on the lamp made it look like a cage.

A sky-blue pillow on her bed. It had a girl with no face and big black sunglasses.

The room had no posters, but the single area rug said a lot—pure black with vibrant flowers popping off the fabric, as if in flight from the darkness itself.

All three items looked like they had come from the same catalog. As if her father had shoved it into her hands and barked at her to *Order from this.* Then she did her best to scream into the silence.

And that was before Frank found her drawings.

Her treasure (Payless ShoeSource) box had just two precious items: a fat folder full of her drawings and an envelope stuffed with something even more curious.

The drawings were a wonder, especially given the limits

of her medium. They were all made on wide-ruled note-book paper. Every bit as cheap-looking and feeling as Frank would have pictured. Same for the markings. Patrick probably acted like boxes of pencils from the dollar store were still too expensive, yet that didn't detract from the drawings.

There were faces and buildings, trees, and lonely roads, but in every sketch, the light was clearly clawing against the dark as it tried to escape.

Like the flowers on Freya's rug.

The envelope was full of business cards. An indie book store (Present Tense), a gelato shop (Cherry on Top), a comic book store (The Comic Vault), one of those joints with a bunch of overpriced makeup and accessories (My Cherie Amour), a nail salon (Pinkies), a place he figured by the name and look of the card sold sparkly junk jewelry (Glitterati!), a guitar studio (Mojo Dojo), a college prep tutoring center (Aced It!), a pizza place (Stuff You!), plus a trio of chains: The Inside Scoop (ice cream), Hill of Beans (coffee) and even one for Provisions (an overpriced "organic" grocery store).

Business cards? Such an odd thing to collect.

Unless it was the only thing you were *allowed* to collect.

Or the only thing you could *afford* to collect. Business cards were free, even if Patrick controlled every red cent. Each one was probably a place she sneaked in and visited. Frank wondered if she would get into trouble if Freya's father knew about her little envelope and how much trouble if so.

She'd certainly never bought anything in any of those places that was in her room now. No books, comic or otherwise, no makeup or accessories, and no sparkly jewelry. Maybe she'd nabbed a slice of pizza or a scoop of ice cream once or twice, but he doubted it.

Frank returned to her treasure box so he could see her drawings again before putting the thing away. There weren't many hiding spots in her room, but Freya had buried her drawings and the shoes underneath an old pair in the box, and that box underneath a second identical one.

He studied all of her drawings again.

One of them captured his full attention, then held it, prisoner, for minutes.

Because, yes, Frank was certain: The man in that drawing was supposed to be him. Freya didn't have a lot to work with, but even with only the cheapest of ingredients, he could recognize the scene. A house looming behind him, the man hunched over, trying to make himself invisible.

But obviously, he hadn't been.

Frank had been seen by Freya.

And she wanted him to be here right now.

He turned the note over and swallowed hard in surprise.

She wanted him to be here for sure because the note scrawled on the back with that same cheap pencil on that same awful paper must have been for him.

My father is raping me.

You're the only one who can help.

I need you to kill him.

73

Chapter Ten

Mal

"Why don't we start over," Mal suggested.

By the time she got to work in the morning, things were looking up. They had a name for their Jane Doe, Rory Day, a sophomore at Ellison High School. And by lunchtime, they had a person of interest sweating in the box, Phillip Waite, the girls' volleyball team coach at the school.

Mike took the ball as he sat at the small square table across from Phillip. "But this time, when you tell us all about your special relationship with Rory, we won't act like we don't know what all the other girls on the team have said."

Mal, walking behind the suspect to keep him nervous, nodded. "And you don't have to pretend like you didn't rape and murder the poor girl."

The man looked devastated, but it was early in the interrogation when the whole thing could still be an act. "I didn't touch her," he blubbered. "Not like that ..."

"*Not like that?*" Mike repeated, making a big deal of looking at Mal.

"I heard it, too," Mal said, still nodding.

"That's not what I meant!"

Mal leaned across the table. "So, what *did* you mean, Phil?"

He swallowed, his bottom lip twitching, taking too long to answer a simple question.

Rory Day had played as a defensive specialist. After news went out identifying the victim this morning, a few students had called in saying that Coach Waite had been acting weird around the girl, with some of them saying he was stalking her and others that he was sleeping with her. The detectives had to determine what was gossip and what was fact and where the hell Coach Waite had been the night of Rory's murder.

"I just meant that I wouldn't ever harm her." Then, in case he hadn't made himself seem sympathetic enough, he added, "I would never hurt anyone!"

"Except the other team, right?" Mike offered Phil a smile, but even playing good cop like he always wanted to — mostly because Mal was so good at the other side — it seemed a bit much.

"How would you describe your relationship with Rory?" Mal asked, now standing at his left. He was unable to meet her eyes. Was it the fear of an innocent man caught up in something? Shame? Guilt?

He shrugged. "Same as it was with any of the other girls."

Mal shook her head. "Not according to the other girls."

"Could you be more specific?" Mike seemed genuinely curious.

"What do you mean?" Phil asked.

So he clarified. "If your relationship was the same with Rory as her teammates, why don't you go ahead and describe what your relationship is like with them?"

"You mean all of them?" His fear was ramping up — not a good look on him.

"Sure. Or one of them. Start wherever you'd like. Who was your favorite?"

Mike's voice had the slightest edge, veering ever so slightly away from Good Cop. An indication to Mal that he was seeing this like she was, that this really might be their guy.

Phil swallowed and started in on his defense. "You know, I wanted all the girls to be competitive, so that meant promoting competition while also teaching them compassion."

"For each other, or the other team?" Mike asked.

"Well, both, I guess …" Phil sounded unsure of his answer, just like Mike had wanted him to.

"What else did you teach them?" Mal asked.

"How to be confident. It's important for players to believe they will win."

"Is that working for you right now?" She gave him a smile. He looked up and quickly back down at his hands, fingers folded in front of him on the table. His left leg was bouncing.

"What do you mean?"

Mal asked, "Are you playing a game, Phil?"

"No, I'm just trying to—"

"Do you think you can win?" Mal finished, cutting him off.

"I imagine you really have to push some of your players," Mike prompted.

"Sure. Of course."

"Must get intense," Mal added. "All that … *togetherness*."

"How would you describe your team culture?" Mike's question came fast, keeping the coach off balance.

"The girls are close. Expectations are high in every part of our program."

"Can you be more specific?" Mike looked at him, waiting for an answer Mal knew he didn't really care about.

"Athletically, academically, on and off the court?"

"Is he asking us or telling us?" Mal asked Mike.

"Sounds like he's asking us," Mike said.

She shrugged. "Maybe he doesn't know the answer."

The phone buzzed in her pocket. She silenced it without looking.

"I gave everything to those girls. You can ask anyone."

"I bet you did," Mal said.

"That's the thing, Phil … we have been asking around. And, boy, it does not look good for you." Mike sighed. "We've already talked to most of the parents on your team. What do you think they had to say about Ellison's volleyball coach?"

Stubborn pride swallowed his face. "If they're saying the same things to you that they've been saying to me for years, then they probably told you that Phillip Waite is a great coach who cares deeply for the health, well-being, and success of his players. He's demanding, but he always has their backs and knows how to mix tough love with genuine praise to get the best out of his girls. Maybe that he teaches them valuable life lessons and makes them feel like they're part of something special."

Her phone buzzed three times in a row.

"And, did you make Rory Day feel special, Phil?" Mal asked instead of checking her texts.

There was no way to answer that question correctly.

But Coach Waite gave it the old college try anyway. "Of course I did."

"Of course you did," she repeated.

"Caring about the girls on my team doesn't make me whatever it is you think I am! Not every adult that cares about kids is a goddamned pedophile."

"You're right," said the Good Cop. "Caring doesn't make you bad. And right now, we don't *think* anything. We're just asking you a few routine questions, so we have a place to start. Our job is about ruling suspects out so we can find the person. You want us to find Rory's killer, right?"

"Of course."

"You spent a lot of time with Rory, right?"

"I was her coach. I spent a lot of time with all of the girls."

"Must be nice." Mal nodded in mock approval.

Her phone buzzed again, and Mal knew she had to answer. It almost for sure had to be someone on the emergency list to make it through her *Do Not Disturb*, which was always on during an interrogation. Ray, almost for sure. And if he called and then texted before calling again, something important was up.

"I need to take this," she said to Mike with a glance at the coach. "Why don't you ask him more about how he made Rory feel special while I'm gone? Then you can catch me up on how he tripped all over his story, soon as I get back."

Mike nodded, and she left the interrogation room. It was Mike's job to "understand" the suspect, to make Phil feel like Mal really wanted to believe the worst, but he could confide in the more compassionate detective among them. Mike would probably give Phil some lines to get him to think his deviancy was normal, or at least understandable. *They grow up so quick. They did not look like that when I was in school, believe you me, buddy. And they're way more aggressively sexual. She was a pretty girl. Who could blame you, right?*

He'd suggest that maybe there were some extenuating circumstances that could explain what happened. Maybe he killed her accidentally. Maybe she overdosed or hit her head, and he just slit her throat to stage a murder scene. Of course, evidence would prove otherwise, but no reason to tell Phil that. Give him an out that might come off as sympathetic to a jury, but also something that would serve as an admission of guilt, something he couldn't talk his way out of once they came back at him with more facts that blew apart the lie surrounding his bits of admitted truth.

Her missed call was connecting before the door closed behind her.

"Good afternoon, this is—"

"Hi. This is Mallory Black. I'm—"

"Yes, Mrs. Black. This is Desiree at the front—"

"Is everything okay with Ashley?"

"That's why I'm calling. Ashley is sick."

"What's wrong with her?"

"She's been throwing up."

"That's terrible." Something in her own stomach somersaulted. What if she'd made Ashley's special breakfast with spoiled eggs? "Where is she now?"

"She's in the nurse's office. We need—"

"Can you please tell her that I'm so sorry she's sick and that I'll pick her up early from school? As soon as I can?"

"That's what I'm trying to tell you, Mrs. Black: we need you to pick her up now."

"I can't pick her up right *now*, Desiree. I shouldn't even be taking this call."

"Your child is vomiting, Mrs. Black. We can't have her around other—"

"Have you tried calling her father?"

"We've been unable to reach him."

Goddammit, Ray! He's playing Jimmy Olsen while a potential child murderer might be wiggling away.

"I'm just finishing something. I'll be there as soon as I can."

"I understand that—"

"I said I would be there."

Mal hung up.

She drew a deep breath, then went back inside the interrogation room, ready to tear their suspect's head from his shoulders. She glanced at Mike for a signal to stand down in case he was on the cusp of something. But he made no such indication.

Mal dragged her chair across the floor with a loud scrape, even though it didn't need to be moved at all, then she sat, her posture aggressive. "So, what did I miss? Coach Creepyfingers didn't give you a confession yet, did he?"

"I don't have anything to confess to." Phil crossed his arms in defiance. She guessed he was seconds away from lawyering up. Why he hadn't done so immediately, she wasn't sure.

Mal looked over at Mike, trying not to shake her head. There clearly hadn't been enough Bad Cop after she left the room. She needed to make up for lost time and hurry this interrogation way the hell up.

She barked a laugh, knowing how unsettling it sounded.

But then she said nothing. Instead, she just kept looking at the coach while shaking her head.

Mal expected him to take the bait like they usually did, but he didn't.

Time was short, so she kicked their back-and-forth forward. "Wanna take a guess at who just called me?"

The question rattled him. For the first time, Phil seemed to lose some of his cool. But his answer came fast. "I hope it was your boss ordering you to give me an apology for wasting my time and throwing accusations my way."

"Nobody's accusing you of anything," Mike said. "In fact, the door is unlocked, and you can leave here at any time you wish."

He didn't look at the door, but she could tell he wanted to, that he was thinking about it.

"She is." Phil jabbed an angry finger at Mal.

"I was just asking if you'd confessed. An innocent man shouldn't have a problem with that."

"Bullshit," Phil spat. "An innocent man can still take an accusation personally."

"Are *you* taking this personally?" Mal gave him a smile she knew he hated.

"I—" He was about to ask for his lawyer, and then they'd have to stop.

Mike interrupted with a voice so calm he could put a crying baby to sleep.

"Listen, I know what you're thinking. You wanna lawyer up. But let me tell you, the minute you ask for a lawyer is the minute we can't help you. Right now, we're just asking a few simple questions to rule you out as a suspect."

"*Accusation*," he corrected.

"Again," Mike said with perfect delivery, "we're not accusing you of anything."

"She is!"

"Well, she's just really upset. She's got a little girl, so she's taking this case personally. She really wants to find the person who did this. And, being Rory's coach and caring about her as much as you seemed to, I'd think you want to help us. You call a lawyer in here, that slows this thing *waaaaaaay* down. And it means that much longer that we can't move on to our next person to talk to. You want us to move on, for this to just be over, right?"

"Yes," he said with a nod, his eyes hopeful that he might just walk out of this room soon. "I didn't murder anyone. I could never do anything like that."

Mal raised her hand. "Can I ask you something without you getting all defensive?"

He nodded.

"I'm just curious about your 'very special relationship' with Rory Day."

"The way you say it sounds so ... *wrong*. It wasn't like that."

"So, what *was* it like? Did you give her one-on-one lessons?"

"I gave all the girls lessons."

"Did you ever touch her inappropriately?"

Judging from the distaste in his expression, maybe he *was* innocent — maybe.

"What was it that made her so special?"

"She was bright and hardworking. She had talent."

"Was pretty, too, right?"

He wasn't sure how to answer. And, to be fair, it was a loaded question. She was trying to unnerve him. "I don't know. I don't see the girls like that."

"You can't tell she's pretty? Bullshit." Mal laughed, then continued needling him. "What did your girlfriend or wife think of you spending so much time with these pretty teenage girls?"

He stared down at his hands. "I don't have a wife or a girlfriend."

"Really?" Mike said, picking up her cue. "Why's that? A good-looking man like yourself and a stable job."

"I dunno."

"Maybe he doesn't like girls his own age," Mal said to Mike. "Is that it, Phil? Girls your age just can't compare to them teenagers? Is that why the kids call you Coach Creepyfingers? They know, don't they?"

He looked up at her, his eyes tearing up. "I want my lawyer."

Fuck.

Mal was about to talk him out of it, but Mike stopped her. "You're free to go, Coach. Like I said. We just wanted to talk."

"Well, if you want to talk to me again, I want my lawyer present."

"As is your right, sir."

He got up and, not meeting either of their gazes, headed toward the exit and turned the knob, probably half-expecting the door to stay closed. When it swung open, Mike said, "Coach?"

He turned, looking like he was expecting to be handcuffed and told to sit the hell back down.

Mike put on a friendly smile. "Just don't leave town anytime soon, eh?"

Phil swallowed and nodded, then left.

Once he was out of the room, and the door swung shut, Mike said, "Creepyfingers? Kids called him that?"

"Nah, I made it up."

"Why Creepyfingers?"

She shrugged. "It was the first thing I thought of. I was just saying shit to see how he would react."

"And, what do you think?"

"I think he's worth bringing in again, but I want to interview the kids and parents who know him before we try for a warrant."

"I'll get on that."

"Can you start without me? I need to head out for a bit."

"What's up?"

"Ashley's school called. She's sick, and I've gotta go pick her up."

"Shit. Sorry. Yeah, I'll do the interviews."

"Thank you, Mike."

"Tell her I hope she feels better."

"Of course."

* * *

Mal was pulling up to the school twenty-three minutes later.

She got out of her car while trying to stifle a heavy agitation that had only worsened with every traffic-filled mile between the precinct lot and this one.

Mal wanted to get in and out of the school with a minimum of shit, but everyone seemed intent on shoveling some on top of her anyway.

The receptionist gave her shit, even if she only did it with a dirty look. The nurse gave her shit, also with a look, but more pointed, clearly asking Mal what kind of a mother she thought she was.

Even Ashley gave her shit for "taking so long."

But Mal was proud of how well she held her cool. Even riled as she was, the receptionist and the nurse both got a smile. She smothered her daughter with sorries and kisses.

That all changed once they were back in the car, and Mal could tell that Ashley wasn't really sick.

"Do you think it was something you ate?" she asked while pulling out of the parking lot.

Ashley was evasive, and Mal, a master of interrogation. It took less than a minute before Ashley admitted that she had only been faking. Easiest thing in the world to tell a teacher you threw up in the toilet. Then flushed all the evidence.

"I was doing something important!" Mal yelled at her, knowing that Ashley had only wanted attention. Hers, specifically. "What the hell is wrong with you?"

"I was feeling anxious."

"About what?"

"I … dunno."

"Goddammit. Not this again."

Ashley was crushed and instantly crying. Mal felt like shit. She wasn't sure what the hell was going on with her daughter, but it felt like attention-seeking behavior. And she hated rewarding it. Hated more that she was the one that had to stop her day investigating a murder. Why the hell was Ray's job, probably taking pictures of a ribbon-cutting at yet another fucking bank today, somehow more important than hers? Because he was a man?

Mal drove back to their house in silence because her speaking would only make Ashley feel worse.

She hated the position she was in. She hated snapping at Ashley. And she resented Ray. But none of that anger equaled how much she hated herself at the moment for losing control.

She wanted to apologize, yet words felt hollow. So she said nothing as she continued the drive home.

Chapter Eleven

Frank

CHICKEN MARSALA FOR DINNER AGAIN.

Not that there was anything wrong with that.

Especially now that Frank treated dinner as a ritual.

He never had that ritual with Sarah, but at least now he understood why she had always pleaded with him to make family dinner more of a priority. She constantly argued the merits of a predictable time to connect with each other while unplugging from the world. Dinner was a time to focus on their past, present, and future together. His schedule couldn't be as routine as she wanted it to be, and he'd realized too late that he should've made his family a priority. He'd thought he had been, providing for them just as the men in his family had done for generations before them.

If there was any lesson he wished he'd learned sooner, it was that work would always expand to take up your time, but time with your loved ones was truly finite, and you never knew how much you'd get in this life before Fate stepped in.

After they lost Jenny, those dinners turned silent. Then eventually, every dinner descended into an argument.

But now that Frank had lost both of his girls, he finally saw what Sarah had always longed for him to do. A dinner ritual gave him a sense of belonging, even if he was eating alone.

And so marsala it was.

The dish Sarah had been eating the night he proposed, and coincidentally, the night they discovered she was pregnant. Marsala made him remember Jenny's first day of kindergarten (Sarah's first day back at work), every anniversary, and two Thanksgivings when Sarah "just couldn't do turkey."

"Mine's not as good as yours," Frank said to the empty seat across from him. "But I'm getting lots of practice ... I wish you could taste it." He took a bite and finished the thought with a mouthful of chicken. "I think you'd be impressed."

I'm sure I would be, he imagined her saying.

"Freya, that girl down the street from us ..." He took another bite but now chewing more slowly. "She needs help."

Frank refilled his merlot.

"She's about Jenny's age ... or the age she was. I don't know what to do."

Another bite, followed by a long and thoughtful quiet. On Frank's part. Sarah offered the same silence she always did. "The girl says that her father is raping her, and she wants me to kill him."

Sip.

"I'll bury Jenny's murderer alive less than twenty-four

hours after I finally figure out who he is." Sip. "But this is something else. A specific target doesn't make me a murderer any more than my work as a deputy." Sip. "I guess we were never going to agree on that, but maybe you could still help me work this out."

Screw sipping. Frank took several gulps in a row.

"The girl could also be lying about her dad. Everything points to a controlling narcissist, and I'm sure he's a nightmare to live with. But that doesn't mean Patrick Dahl is actually doing what his daughter is accusing. Maybe she just hates him for suffocating her. Lots of kids hate their parents and wish them dead for a while, right?"

Another long swallow, then he returned to slowly chewing and sipping.

"But if he is doing … that, then maybe he does deserve to die."

The marsala had lost most of its taste. He chewed through another mouthful anyway. "Even so, it's not my job to pull the trigger." He thought and sipped. "I should see what I can figure out on my own, then turn it over to the sheriff's office."

He drained the glass, shaking his head.

"But that's just the thing. I shouldn't be anywhere near this girl. If Mallory so much as *thinks* I'm sniffing around her, everything could fall apart. She'll for sure think I'm looking for my 'next victim', and it'll be like a wrecking ball. Our neighbors were mercifully forgiving. They knew I couldn't have done it because they know me. But still, there's always that doubt, right? And you know half of them will start thinking that all this smoke must mean there's fire."

He sighed and emptied the rest of his bottle into the glass. "Maybe our neighbors will start locking their places up tighter and looking at things more closely. You'll be glad to know that my investigation is over, but that reality won't work for me."

Frank finished the final bite of his marsala.

"Even if the neighbors don't turn on me, Kirby will for sure. He'll get most of Creek County believing the worst of me." He choked. This next part was so hard, but he wanted it out of him, so that meant saying it out loud. "Just like he got you wondering if I could really have ever hurt Jenny like that."

A long pause and Frank didn't even fill it with wine.

"I know you didn't wonder long. But you wondered enough." He took a sip and pushed his empty plate away from him. "So. What do you think I should do?"

Frank had taken to asking Sarah for her counsel during dinner, always hoping from somewhere deep that she'd find some way to answer him. He longed for a sign. Something that could help him to believe she was still out there listening, watching him, making sure he was never truly alone.

If Sarah was out there, then Jenny might be too.

But Frank never saw any signs. At least, not really. He could have convinced himself if he tried hard enough. The shadows, the noises, the sudden flood of memories. Any of it could have been manufactured by him.

Tonight was different.

The lights flickered, then they flickered again.

That would have been enough, but then the microwave beeped, and a car alarm began braying outside three beats after that.

"Sarah?"

No answer.

But Frank was still calling it a sign.

He stood from the table, took his dish (and Sarah's) to

the sink along with his glass (she wasn't much of a drinker), then a minute later, he was outside and on his way to Rachel's.

"Knock, knock." Frank smiled when she opened the door. "Sorry I missed your mail today. I just checked the box, and it looks like you grabbed it."

"I can get my own mail, though I appreciate it when you do. Did you come by to take Dolly on a walk? She sure seems to think so."

"Only if that's helpful."

"What do you think? Dolly's small but yanks on me like she's tied to a Volkswagen. Just give me a minute, and I'll get her leash."

The door closed.

Again Frank wondered if it was only paranoia or whether there really was someone staring at the back of his head. He forced himself to keep staring at Rachel's closed door, knowing it would be a mistake to turn around.

Her door opened again, but only enough to shove words through the gap.

No leash for Frank.

"What do you consider old?" Rachel asked.

Surely the most loaded question he'd heard in a while.

But then he thought of something. "The wrong attitude."

"How old do you think I am?"

"Oh … I wouldn't know how to …"

"You're not gonna insult me."

She looked seventy-five. "Sixty?"

"I'm seventy-five! You know why I still look sixty?"

Seventy-five. "Because you think young?"

"Because I put the right things in my body. I stopped aging at sixty." She laughed. "I *really* should have started paying more attention earlier. If it wasn't for this damn hip, I might be doing the Roger Rabbit right now."

"The Roger Rabbit?"

"That's a dance, isn't it?"

"Maybe when I was in high school."

"Look at you," she laughed, "sounding older than me!"

The dog was throwing itself against the door.

"I should really take her." Frank showed her his empty hand, waiting for her to fill it with Dolly's leash while feeling an acute sense of déjà vu.

"You're getting old now, and it happens fast." Rachel ignored him. "Take my word for it. Most of my friends lost their minds a long time ago, and they also look like mummies. I have to show people my driver's license to prove my age because they never believe me."

Now she was flat out lying. "How old are you, *really?* That's what they ask me. You should see their faces when I show them! Last year I was changing a tire — before all this nonsense with my hip — and this man came up to me. You wanna know what he said?"

No. "Of course."

"I bet you do. He said, 'You won't be doing that when you're my age.' So I asked him how old he was. Guess what he said?"

"Sixty-five?"

"He was seventy-three!"

Dolly was now impersonating an alien on the other side of the door, making sounds Frank had never heard. And he'd been feeling stared at for a while now.

"Wow. That's a really great story." He shook his empty hand, still waiting for the leash.

"You should have seen his face when I told him I was

older than he was! Only by a year, but still. Impressive." Rachel handed him the leash and opened the door, but only after Dolly was yapping so loud that she could no longer pretend to ignore it.

"Okay, okay! I hear you!" Rachel shook her head like it was the chihuahua's fault for not wanting to be teased with a walk before being held like a prisoner.

Dolly ran outside and raced in a circle around Frank's leg. "I'll have her right back."

"My point is, it's good that you're always going on walks. Use it or lose it isn't a cliché so much as a fact. That's my secret."

"It's a good one," Frank said, already racing away as quickly as he could without appearing rude.

"That's why I'm sharing it with you!" Rachel called after him before closing the door with an audible *THUNK*.

Frank was finally facing the right direction, but Freya wasn't in the window like he had been hoping, and in the glimpses he managed to steal while slowly making his way around the cul-de-sac, no one appeared to be looking out their window at him.

But Freya's light was on, and Frank kept hoping her silhouette might appear.

He was closer to her house, enough to look right at it without being suspicious when she finally did.

Freya was staring directly at Frank.

He stared right back at her for a long and frozen moment.

Even Dolly cooperated. Far away as he was, Frank imagined he could see the teenager's brittle pleas in her eyes.

But then Freya's mom entered the room.

She startled away. Seconds later, her room was doused in shadows.

With the house gone dark, every second spent outside 47 Heirloom felt even riskier. So Frank focused on giving Dolly a great walk, making the dog love him in case he needed to use her again, then returned her to a grateful — and still too talkative — Rachel.

Then back inside his house and right to the pantry.

Frank unscrewed the false bottom in his jumbo canister of generic oatmeal and added Freya's note to the gun, cash, and trio of fake IDs — just in case — that were already in there.

"I saw what you bought."

Frank could still hear the accusation in her voice, still feel the way it chilled him to remember that argument. He didn't have the IDs yet, and though he'd already started stashing some cash, Sarah didn't know. But she found his new gun and knew it wasn't his official piece, that he'd not gotten it through normal channels.

"And I know why you bought it."

"It's not what you think," Frank had insisted.

But it was exactly what she thought.

And Sarah knew he was lying.

She found the cash two days later. That argument should have been worse than the one before it, now that she had proof of her husband preparing for a Plan B, just in case he wasn't careful enough with his Plan A.

They barely fought, their arguments reduced to echoes. And that night, for the first time, he could see that Sarah had finally given up.

"I don't think you killed Jenny, but I know for a fact that you're killing us."

She was right.

He hoped she was watching him from a better place and still would be when he finally made everything right. Maybe it was Sarah from the beyond, or more likely, Freya, her father, or perhaps even Mallory Black, but Frank felt that *someone* was watching him.

And he felt it every time he went outside.

Chapter Twelve

Mal

MAL SAT in her home office, staring at the monitor, bracing herself for whatever she was about to see.

She got excited whenever Grimm left his house.

Sure, every time was another opportunity for her to see what the creep was up to, but she still didn't have much to go on. It was a tedious process, fast-forwarding through all that footage to study his comings and goings. And she had to cover all twenty-four hours because who knew what that creep might be up to in the middle of the night.

The department had software that could automatically tag movement on the cameras to simplify the process of scrubbing through the footage. But this wasn't department-approved surveillance. She'd bought everything online, using a prepaid credit card that even Ray didn't know about.

It wasn't like she was using the card to cheat on him. Everyone was entitled to a certain level of privacy. Mal wasn't being dishonest. She was doing her job.

95

She could find similar software if she took the time to look. Mal increasingly realized that not only should she have done that before starting to scour the video, stopping now would likely save her a lot of time in the future. But she kept making the argument without changing her behavior, always plowing forward, not wanting to stop as she moved through the timeline, increasingly confident that when Grimm next stepped off of his porch, she would finally see what he'd been up to.

Mal would be in a world of shit if she got caught putting cameras across the street from Grimm's house, but it was still the right thing to do. She wasn't worried; she'd gone out of her way to make both the purchase and their placement untraceable.

Grimm could suspect and even publicly blame her, but he wouldn't be able to *prove* shit.

But so far, neither could she.

There was plenty to be curious about, but Mal could only draw the loosest of conclusions. Grimm did leave at odd times, without any apparent pattern. Even if that meant something, it wasn't evidence. To anyone who didn't know what happened to his daughter, Grimm could be a guy on early retirement, enjoying several walks throughout the day. But Mal knew he was probably circling his little cul-de-sac while thinking about how he didn't have to work now that he could live on his daughter's life insurance. Sarah's policy hadn't paid out since she'd killed herself.

Grimm was supposedly working as a Private Investigator. He had a license, but Mal hadn't seen or heard anything to make her believe he actually had clients.

He was up to something. But her cameras only showed three different views. None of the angles were especially good, and her footage had yet to reveal anything significant.

But there was a common denominator with every excursion. A couple of times, he had a chihuahua, though Mal had no idea where the dog came from. It would just appear in the frame a long time after Grimm left his house, then disappear before he went home.

Chihuahua or not, Grimm was always looking around like an addict hoping to score.

She finally saw something in the footage. Mal didn't know what it meant, only that it chilled her.

A girl — about Jenny's age, and yes, that clearly mattered a lot — had stopped in front of his house that afternoon. It was only for a moment, and she appeared to be *maybe* gesturing at something behind her. The action seemed to be decisive, whatever it was, and whoever it might have been meant for.

Except, of course, it was intended for Grimm.

Because something was going on between him and the girl.

And could anything aboveboard be happening with an adolescent girl and Grimm, a suspected child killer? Of course not. He ought to be viewed with as much trust as you'd give a registered sex offender.

She finished the footage but didn't see the girl again.

After watching it all, Mal only knew that she needed to know more.

Like what Grimm was doing every time he left his place.

Like who that girl was and what she was doing with him.

Like whether or not a monster was planning to come back out of his lair.

Mal grabbed the last of her cameras — another two bought *just in case* that she really should have installed already — then got in her car and started driving toward

Heirloom, where she would place the other cameras at the front of the street to get a better view of what was going on.

That way, she could see everything and finally get some—

Chapter Thirteen

Frank

ANSWERS.

That's what Frank needed.

And he knew exactly where he should go next to get them.

But it wasn't an easy drive to make, knowing he'd have to face Sarah's former best friend, Marcia. She was a teacher at Freya's school, and even if Marcia hated him for what happened to Sarah, she would put a child's welfare in front of her grudge.

At least he hoped so.

But Frank was full of doubt as he clutched the steering wheel, looking over at the exterior of Andrew Jackson Middle School, hoping that Freya might magically appear so the two of them could have a conversation.

Although that was risky, too.

Frank was tired of feeling so out of his skin.

Ever since Sarah's suicide, he'd had one plan with

exactly three steps: find Jenny's killer, make the monster disappear, then vanish himself if needed.

The cash wouldn't last long, and the passports might or might not work. Frank was ready to eat a bullet from either of his guns if the situation went wayward.

But none of this was part of that plan.

He waited for the lunch bell to ring, then went to Marcia's classroom without checking in at the office as a visitor. He'd never been on the campus before, but she was easy enough to find. The first student pretended not to hear him, but the second kid looked Frank right in the eye and told him that yes, he knew where Mrs. Madison's classroom was, then walked him halfway there while giving simple directions to take him the rest of the way.

"What are you doing here?" Marcia asked, sitting at her desk and looking up from her sandwich.

"I thought maybe we could talk."

"What could you and I possibly have to talk about?" She looked back at her sandwich as if he didn't exist, just like she probably wished.

"It's not about me."

"Is it about how you abandoned my best friend?"

"I didn't—"

"How you abandoned my best friend?" Then in a lower voice, "*To chase after Jenny's killer.*"

"I was dealing with things in my own way."

"I'm sure you were. Is that also why you cheated on her?"

"I should never have—"

"Damn right, you shouldn't have!" Marcia dropped her sandwich on the desk. Meat and cheese went everywhere. She looked down in disgust, then up at Frank with repulsion. "How long were you fucking another woman who wasn't your wife again?"

"I'm sorry about that."

"So you've said."

"We both made plenty of mistakes."

"You and Sarah? What mistakes did *she* make, Frank? Are you referring to the number of pills she took? Because I'm pretty sure her miscount was intentional."

He refused to let that one hurt as much as she wanted. "I was referring to my infidelity. You don't know the whole story."

"Of course, I know the whole story. Asshole." Marcia grabbed a piece of meat, and a slice of cheese, then shoved them both into her mouth and started chewing with a grudge.

"We hadn't had sex in months."

"Boohoo, Frank. I'm sorry you had to jerk yourself off."

"We weren't communicating at all."

"I hope you never gave Cyrus any marriage tips during one of the hundred barbecues we invited you to. Sometimes he and I have problems communicating, and I wouldn't want him putting his dick in a waitress or—"

"She wasn't a waitress."

"Whatever," she finished.

"Did it ever occur to you that maybe Sarah might have abandoned me?"

"Oh? And how is that, Frank?"

"She didn't understand that the only way I could find closure was to find who did it. To bring them to justice. I tried to talk to her about it, but … she just lost faith in me."

"What did you expect her to do? Indulge in your little fantasy? Help you plot the murder? Pretend to be your getaway driver? She tried to talk you out of it."

"No." Frank shook his head. "She told me I was turning into a monster."

"Weren't you?"

Frank didn't know how to answer Marcia without pissing her off.

"Why are you here?" She made it easy for him. "And what do you need from me so you'll go away?"

"Do you know a girl named Freya Dahl?"

"Why?" Pure hostility; the specific question clearly bothered her.

"She lives on my street."

His answer seemed to make things worse.

"AND?"

"It's good to know you think the best of me." He should have known better. "I was just wondering if you've seen any signs of abuse."

Her face twitched. It looked like she was considering another insult, but then her expression shifted into something no more or less serious but very suddenly centered.

"Why?"

"*Have you?*" he pressed.

"No." Marcia shook her head. "I mean, Freya seems like a sensitive student, and she definitely does the emo thing, but that's what alienated kids do when they're trying to find something to fit in with. I've not seen anything out of the ordinary. Again, *why?*"

"It's related to a case."

"Finally started that P.I. work?" she asked, knowing he hadn't. "Or did you go back to the sheriff's office where—"

"It's a private case."

"On your street?" Marcia raised her eyebrows and finally stood from her desk.

"If you see any signs of trouble at home, can I trust that you'll let me know?"

"You can trust that I'll alert the proper authorities. Same as I would if I saw any student who seemed to be suffering abuse at home."

"So, you won't help me help this girl?"

"Are you saying I *shouldn't* alert the proper authorities?"

"I'm saying you should stop treating me like an enemy. I'm saying that you should stop holding what happened between Sarah and me against me, or at the very least, don't let it keep you from doing the right thing."

"The 'right thing' is alerting the proper authorities."

"Assuming they can help, and in this case, I'm not so sure."

"Then I'm sure you'll be happy to tell me why this case is different."

Frank shook his head. "I shouldn't have come here."

"Damn right. I hope you remind yourself of that epiphany the next time you consider a visit."

"If you don't still have my number in your phone, then you know where to find me if you reconsider. Please, give Cyrus my best."

He turned to go and even made it halfway to the door before Marcia called out to him.

He turned back around.

"Is it her father?" she asked.

"Isn't it always?"

"You didn't like it when people said that about you."

"I'm not Patrick Dahl."

Now stone sober. "Do you think Freya's in danger?"

"I don't know. It's like what you said about kids doing the emo thing to fit in. Maybe it's all an act. I only see her walking home from the bus, so there's not a ton to go on here, but I was a detective for a long time. And it's fair to say you develop a sense."

"Is it possible you're taking it personally … after what happened to Jenny?"

"Of course, I'm taking it personally."

"Oh." Marcia seemed surprised by his answer.

"I think Freya's father has threatened her at the least, but maybe done something much worse. Same for the mom. I've seen it with guys like him plenty of times. They're great at keeping their abuse under wraps. And if I'm right about the little things, then that almost for sure makes me right about the bigger one."

"And what's that?" Marcia asked with a hard swallow, obviously needing to hear the answer more than she wanted to.

"That the two of them are terrified of him."

She looked at him, assessing.

"Will you let me know if you see anything?"

"I'll report it to the proper authorities," she answered, though Frank could tell that despite her answer, they were finally sharing a side.

"Thank you." Frank gave her a nod. "I'll let you get back to your sandwich."

She didn't answer or look up, but he thought it possible that Marcia hated him fractionally less than she had just a few minutes ago. Maybe that was something.

He milled around the middle school, killing time until lunch ended and hoping he could casually run into Freya. But five minutes after leaving Mrs. Madison's classroom, Frank felt like he had a radioactive glow.

He shouldn't be here, and everyone knew it.

He found Freya seconds ahead of a ringing bell. She was talking with another emo-looking girl, and both were standing in front of a teacher, a rotund man with a thin mustache, a tie that looked like it might have been made of cardboard, thin and greasy hair, and beady eyes that were fixed on Frank.

Freya glanced up and over. She might have seen him, but maybe not. Frank was usually great at determining such things, but the girl might have been even better at hiding them. Just a flinch, then her eyes were back on her friend or whoever it was standing beside her.

Two emos in a pod. Both dressed all in black. But Freya was in pants and long sleeves, and her pale skin had no makeup. Closer, he saw a lot of acne. The other girl was in a skirt that might reveal too much if she made the mistake of sneezing and a tank top that was at least one size too small. Her face looked like she might have gone to that Cherie Amour place and asked to sample one of everything.

"May I help you with something?" Cardboard Tie asked, walking over.

"I was just visiting Mrs. Madison." Frank tipped his head, then walked past the man and Freya, still not knowing if his neighbor was ignoring him or not.

* * *

Frank was all out of marsala and in no mood to cook.

He'd come home feeling defeated. He didn't expect any easy answers, but the more he thought about his moment of seeing Freya at school, the more he couldn't stop worrying about her.

Because *yes*, she had seen him.

And *yes*, she was terrified that he would call her out.

She wanted his help, but the fear of getting caught asking for it was clearly haunting her.

Frank could no longer believe that she was making it up. Not seeing her eyes up close … or at least as up close as he could get across the middle school hallway.

He checked on his security footage from the four cameras he had installed around the exterior of his house, hoping to see something but expecting little like always.

But this time, he did see something.

Fifteen minutes after he started watching the sped-up footage, Frank found something that managed to stun him without being much of a surprise. He paused, rewound, then stared at the screen.

Mallory, setting up a camera — or maybe two — at the entrance to Heirloom.

Today. And not all that long ago.

From the looks of it, this was still Mallory acting off-book and not Detective Black following orders.

And if she wasn't following orders, that meant she was probably disobeying them.

Frank left his house and walked directly to where he saw Mal placing the camera(s).

Sure enough, he found two of them.

They were put there shortly before he got home, so there was no way she could have seen anything incriminating. But if she'd installed those two, Frank wondered if there were others he didn't know about. Ones that might have been there for a while and perhaps prompted the placement of another two.

He had to calm himself. And think.

The most Mallory could have seen was him walking circles around the neighborhood and maybe casting suspicious glances around. She couldn't have cameras everywhere, and if she had evidence of Frank's breaking and entering, she would have already knocked on his door and put him in cuffs.

Unless.

Maybe Mallory had seen him going into Freya's backyard. Maybe even through the back door if she'd had the foresight to plant a camera on that door. But that was highly unlikely.

If she had seen what he was up to, then maybe she was waiting to catch him doing something worse.

No. If Mallory had seen him breaking into a house with a girl Jenny's age, it would be game-over already.

Frank walked faster. He opened his front door, closed it behind him, then pulled out his phone and made his best move.

He dialed.

By the end of the day, Captain Wilson would be tearing Mallory a new one.

Chapter Fourteen

Mal

CAPTAIN WILSON GLARED AT MAL, letting her feel the heat of his stare before speaking.

She was seated in front of his desk while he stood up and over her, arms crossed, steeping in the moment before starting his obvious reprimand.

"Would you like to know who I just got off the phone with?"

She had a pretty good idea, but it wouldn't be wise to admit. "Mr. Dogget, wanting to thank me and Mike for our excellent work on—"

"Frank Grimm." He stopped. Stared. Waited. Then continued when Mal had nothing to add. "Would you like to know what he said to me?"

She needed to be careful. There were more than a dozen responses, right on the tip of her tongue. But every one was sarcastic. Grimm and Wilson were friends. This time Mal had stepped in it.

She nodded. "I'm sure he thinks I've been giving him a hard time."

"*Thinks.*"

"It's not a secret that I think the guy did it."

"No," Wilson agreed with disdain. "It is not."

"Am I in trouble for my opinion? Sir?"

"No, detective. You're in my office right now because of some specific behavior on your part."

"*Alleged behavior,*" Mal attempted to correct him.

But Wilson wasn't having it. "Nothing alleged about it. Grimm has you on tape planting cameras on his street."

"Oh." She swallowed.

"*Oh* is right, detective."

The best defense here was — no doubt — a superior offense. "I'm doing this off-book."

"Damn right you are."

"I mean, the department isn't responsible," she tried. "I'm doing it as a private citizen."

"So is that what we're doing now? You're just going to keep telling me things we both already know?"

"I'm following a lead. On my time. You know, above and beyond what I'm doing for Rory Day and everything else."

"Were you working the Day case when you were planting these cameras?"

Mal wanted to scream but managed not to. "Goddammit, Captain. He's guilty! Why can't any of you see that?"

"Maybe because those of us who believe in his innocence know him a lot better than you."

"Maybe that's the problem."

"Is *this* your version of an apology? I had Frank on the phone rightfully asking me if this was a department thing or if 'Mallory Black has gone rogue.' What kind of a position do you think that puts me in?"

"I'm sorry if my looking into Grimm is making things difficult for you, but if this was anyone else, you would be patting me on the back and telling me that Creek County needs more of my kind. Isn't that what you said to me last time I was in here? After the Martell fiasco?"

"You're absolutely right. *If* this were someone else, I'd encourage you to keep investigating because if this were anyone else, you might actually be onto something. But Frank Grimm is not a murderer."

"Don't you see the flaw in your logic?" Now she was yelling.

And that was too much.

It felt like Wilson was about to lose whatever anger he was holding back. "You got anything else to say, detective, you better say it now."

Mal looked back up at him, intimidated by his offer but not wanting to refuse it. She drew a breath, used half of it to think, then said, "I don't understand why Frank Grimm gets a pass."

He nodded at Mal, then unleashed. "Frank Grimm 'doesn't get a pass,' Detective Black. Frank Grimm is an innocent man who was questioned by this office out of routine—"

Exactly. Routine.

"—and cleared almost immediately. Do you know why?"

Because Frank Grimm is one of the good old boys.

"Because Frank Grimm is one of the good guys. His record is exemplary, and—"

Sociopaths can be great at their jobs.

"—what happened to him is a goddamn shame. We lost an excellent detective, and he's been through enough.

So *that's* why Frank Grimm is to be left alone. Why you, of all people, aren't willing to see he's not a bad guy is beyond me."

"What's that supposed to mean?" She seriously had no idea.

"Grimm always had your back when you were coming up."

"He absolutely did not." The idea was offensive.

"He absolutely *did*." Wilson glared at her like a disappointed grandfather. "Plenty. And he was one of the only ones."

"How do you know?"

"How do you think I know?" Still glaring at her. "I was one of the people who *didn't* like you. You're a fine detective, and I understand you, but you're not always easy to get along with."

"That's what my husband keeps telling me."

"Ray is right. I don't even need to know the details." He finally sat on his side of the desk and gave her some space. "You don't know how to be wrong."

"Yep." Mal nodded. "Those were his exact words."

"You often use humor to avoid direct confrontation, especially when you're being corrected."

"Let me guess … Ray made you some sort of a cheat sheet?"

"I predict big problems in your future if you can't get this part of your personality under control."

She smiled. "If you know tomorrow's lotto numbers, could you maybe let me know? Winning that would change everything for me. Then I could be like everyone else in this county with money and break all the rules I want to."

"You're out of line, detective," Wilson said.

"Sorry." It came out almost as instinct, a pure response

to his flare of anger. "I genuinely had no idea that Grimm ever had a nice word to say about me."

His face relaxed. "He thought you had the makings of a great detective. He liked a lot of what he saw. And you were easy to defend because the two of you were so alike."

"Ha!" She shook her head. "We're *nothing* alike."

"You don't even know him. You're both stubborn as hell. You're just more …"

"Thorough?"

"Vulgar."

"Well, then." She looked toward the door.

"Can I trust that we understand one another?"

You mean trust that I'm not supposed to investigate someone who might have committed the most heinous possible crime?

"Yes, sir."

"I need to hear you say it."

"Frank Grimm is off-limits. He's been through enough. I should really know better."

"I need you to take this seriously."

"I understand that, sir."

"Other people on this force will not take kindly to the sort of accusations you seem to be making, implicit and otherwise."

Mal didn't respond.

Wilson added, "A lot of people owe Frank a lot for the things he's done for this department."

"I hear you. Really. I'm sorry. Grimm is off-limits."

"Are you bullshitting me right now, detective?"

She shook her head but held his gaze. "No, I am not."

"Are you just telling me what I want to hear?"

"Absolutely not. I do understand the seriousness of this discussion."

"I am willing to let this go with a warning. But this is the only one you get. Is that understood?"

"Of course."

"The next time we talk about this, that conversation will include the sheriff. Is that also understood?"

A vigorous nod. "Absolutely."

And that was her ace in the hole. Mal didn't mind that because she was pretty sure Sheriff Bell would be on her side.

"Then we're done here. Keep me updated on the Day case."

"Yes, sir."

It was nearly the end of her shift anyway.

So what if she felt like her every action was going to be scrutinized? Mal could take an evening or two away from watching Grimm. This would all die down in a couple of days. In the meantime, she could make Ray and Ashley happy with a night at home.

The longer she worked, the more Mal liked the idea.

She deserved a night away from Grimm. Wilson had done her a favor.

Not much new on the Day case, no new suspects. The girl's dad died six years ago. The mom worked two jobs to make ends meet and was absolutely distraught. No new suspects. And their only person of interest so far, the volleyball coach, wound up having an alibi that checked out.

So they were back to square one while their tech guru, Aanya Batra, was going through the girl's phone, computer, and social media accounts, searching for any suspects.

After trading notes with Mike for nearly an hour, without bringing any of her theories into the conversation even once, Mike asked what Wilson had wanted. She confessed what she had done with the cameras and that she was done watching the guy.

Mike said, *"Good."*

They bid their farewells for the evening — Mike was much more religious about making it home in time for dinner; he blamed his punctuality on his wife, Gina, but Mal knew he wanted to be there for her and the kids even more than they wanted him to be there.

She considered picking up ice cream but figured Ray and Ashley would both want her home sooner. She pulled into her driveway, earlier than she'd been in more than a month.

But it was already too late.

Mal found a note on the counter.

Hey Mal,

We weren't sure if you'd be home for dinner, and we hadn't heard from you. So Ash and I are going out for some daddy/daughter time.

See you tonight.

Gobble gobble gaga monsters.

(Ashley made me promise to write that last part)

She crumpled the note, got into her car, and drove to Heirloom Cove.

Chapter Fifteen

Frank

FRANK OPENED his freezer and realized he'd need to restock the chicken breasts soon.

Eating chicken marsala and little else kept everything from shopping to cooking and general inventory management about as simple as it could be. He liked simplicity. It meant barely needing to think as he strolled the grocery aisles, stood over the stove, or made his lists before a trip to the store.

Freeing up his mind from minutia, Frank could focus on his ongoing work of finding Jenny's killer. Not that he'd had many leads, but he did enjoy imagining what he would do once he got something solid.

Then everything would change.

Thinking about Jenny was better than thinking about Sarah.

Jenny had been taken away from them both, but in his darkest moments, Frank knew that in the end, he was responsible for what happened to his wife.

He tried not to think about that now while making his marsala, but it wasn't easy to keep the thoughts away for too long.

As he pounded the chicken breasts, he remembered watching Sarah cook, talking about how she wanted a bigger kitchen with a nice fancy island. She'd always watch those home improvement shows, too, asking him, "Don't you want to do something 'different' with the place?" He never understood the need for change. He liked the house as it was. Besides, he'd been too busy with work to commit to any real home improvement projects.

He thought about Jenny while slicing the mushrooms, how she'd sit on the couch and read books for hours at a time, especially on the weekend. She wanted to be a writer someday.

He wondered what kind of stories she would have gone on to tell.

Then he thought about Freya while adding flour, a three-quarters teaspoon of salt, and a quarter teaspoon of pepper into a Ziploc bag, wondering if she was going to reach out to him again or was she waiting for him to come back? She couldn't just expect him to act, even if he were going to kill her father, without some evidence.

He thought of Mallory while heating the oil and adding two tablespoons of butter into a large skillet over medium-high heat. Why was she so consumed with making him into a bad guy? It didn't make any sense.

And he thought about the big mess he might have made of everything by calling Captain Wilson while shaking off the excess flour and dropping the dusted filets into his pan.

He was too agitated for planning, so Frank tried clearing his mind.

But it stayed occupied as he turned the chicken, slightly

golden and barely cooked through. It was mostly Mallory he was worried about.

Or, not *worried*, Frank kept telling himself. *Appropriately aware.*

And that was exactly how he needed to stay until he figured out what she was after or what she already knew. Melting more butter in the pan, adding mushrooms, stirring until brown, Frank finally acknowledged an inescapable truth to himself.

It didn't matter that Captain Wilson made a promise that Mallory would back off; that wasn't a pledge he could make on her behalf or one that Frank could believe she would keep.

He added the shallots, garlic, and salt.

Then he added the broth, wine, heavy cream, and thyme.

He really should've left it alone, not let Mallory know that he'd seen the cameras. Now that she knew that he knew she was watching, she might change up her game.

Unless she actually listened for once and gave up.

The meal was almost done. Frank only needed to use a wooden spoon to scrape any of the brown bits from the pan into the liquid, then bring the whole thing to a boil and reduce his sauce to medium heat.

But Frank suddenly lost the will to finish his dish.

He didn't want to cook or eat. Especially not marsala.

Probably not ever again. Maybe he should—

A soft knock from the back door just past the kitchen nook where he usually ate dinner. His heart made a joke of the next two beats, then he checked the flame and went to see who it was.

Who knocks that softly?

He already knew and wasn't surprised to see Freya

standing on the other side of his door, looking terrified to be there.

He opened his door all the way and ushered her inside.

She was talking before he closed it. "I don't have a lot of time, Mr. Grimm."

"It's Freya, right?"

She nodded, not seeming the least bit surprised that he knew her name, too. "I only have a minute. If I'm not home in—"

"I understand, Freya. Why are you here? What do you need?"

She didn't want to say it and made Frank wait a long moment ahead of her first attempt. "I need to know if you're going to do it."

"Do what, Freya?"

Another long moment, then, "You know …"

"Maybe I do. But a person wants something like that done …" Frank gave her a decisive nod. "Then, at the very least, they should be able to say that thing out loud."

Freya nodded, found her courage, and said, "I need you to kill my father."

"You know about the difference between needs and wants?"

"Of course I do."

"What is it that makes you think I might be willing to do something like that? Murder a man, *for you?*"

"I know what happened to your daughter."

Not too big of a shock. Even if she didn't learn that on her own, Patrick could have informed Freya with a warning.

"And I know you break into other people's houses."

Of course, she knew that; she'd caught him red-handed at least once.

"So you must be hunting the killer … right, Mr. Grimm? You think that maybe he lives on this street."

But he was definitely surprised that she'd so neatly filled in the blanks. From the moment she first saw him leaving the Jhasti home, Frank assumed that she thought he was a thief, or a pervert or something, sneaking into people's homes and looking in their underwear drawers or through their porn collection.

He nodded. "I'm looking for evidence."

"My dad is like the man who murdered your daughter."

"That's a big accusation to make, Freya. You know for a fact that your father has killed someone?"

"I didn't say that." She shook her head, looking suddenly mad. "I said he was raping me — isn't that enough? Your daughter was …"

She didn't finish the question, and he didn't answer it.

Instead, he said, "You're talking about ending a man's life, your *father's* life."

"He ended mine a long time ago." Her entire face seemed a sneeze from collapsing. "I should go."

She turned toward the door.

"Freya, wait."

She turned around, but her eyes weren't especially hopeful.

"I want to help—"

"But you won't. I get it."

"Can you get me any proof?"

"He films it."

"*He films it?*" Frank's response was involuntary; he *had* to repeat her words. That really did change everything. "Do you know where he keeps the recordings?"

"I think he uploads the videos somewhere." She swallowed, now clearly wanting to cry. "I think he shares them.

He said something once about a guy who wanted to see me in a red nightie."

Frank had definitely lost his appetite now. He had to help her, no matter what. Frank opened his mouth, but she started talking again before he could say anything.

"I overheard him talking on the phone once and thought about checking a site that I think he was talking about. But I'm not allowed to use the computer at home except for schoolwork. It logs everything, so he always knows exactly what Mom or I do on it. Same for the school computers. They have filters that don't let you look at anything inappropriate for kids. So no, I can't prove anything. But maybe I could use your computer?"

"It's not that simple. I'm sure it's on the dark web, and it's not going to be like using Google or Forage. This won't be fast. Have you told anyone about—"

"Mom knows. But she can't do anything about it, or he'll kill her. Same for me." Freya blinked. Of course, the girl was already well-versed in the dangers of her conversation with Frank right now, yet the realization seemed to strike her anew and flush Freya's face with a hideous fear.

"You need to call the cops, Freya. If there's evidence, they'll find it. Trust me. They've got canines that can sniff out thumb-drives and stuff."

"No way." An emphatic shake of her head.

"I get it. He has you scared. Terrified. But the law will protect you. If he's doing what you say and has threatened your life, then—"

"You're just saying that because you used to be one of them!"

Her fury was intense and immediate.

Frank stopped in case she had more to say.

And she did. "Mom called the cops one time when I was little. He was *beating me*. And they *took his side*."

He swallowed. "I'm so sorry about that, Freya. Sometimes there's nothing the police can do in that moment, but—"

"Exactly. They won't believe me and then—"

"If we go in with proof, then they'll have to act immediately."

"*We?*" she repeated.

"I'll help you get the evidence."

"How?"

"I have surveillance equipment. You can use that equipment to film your father when he's filming you. The minute we have something solid, you and I can go to the police."

She shook her head, looking less scared and much more of something else.

"What is it, Freya?"

"I don't want a video of me out there!"

"Without tangible—"

"Everyone will think that I wanted it!"

"That's not true, Freya. Did your father tell you that?" Of course, he did. "He's only poisoning your mind with as many ways to keep you quiet as he can possibly think of. Even if you did want it, you're a kid. You can't consent. Nobody would take his side. *Nobody*. He will go to prison, and you and your mother will be safe. Do you understand that?"

After a while, she finally nodded.

"I really have to go, and I can't look like I've been crying."

Frank wished he could say something more to ease her mind. For now, they'd both have to be patient. "I'm going to help you, okay? We just need proof."

With a glimmer of hope, she said, "So what do I do?"

"What's the best place to hide the equipment, somewhere outside of your house? Maybe—"

"There's a decorative bucket right by the plum tree. Put it there. I'll leave the house with an empty backpack and grab the stuff on my way to the bus."

"That's great. But—"

"I really need to go."

"Just one more thing. Okay?"

She looked at him: *Go on.*

"Why don't you call the cops right now?" Frank pulled the phone from his pocket and handed it over to her. "You can stay here until they come and arrest your father. Or if you're not comfortable here, I'll find you a safe place to stay. I have friends. I can get deputy protection for you and your mom."

"You don't know him." She was definitely going to cry again if he pushed.

"I understand." He walked to the door and made her exit easier by opening it.

She left in a hurry and without a goodbye.

Frank dialed his phone, wanting to call the sheriff's office himself but wasn't willing to betray her.

"Yo, bitch!" Stan answered.

"Is it possible to use facial recognition software to find porn with someone's face?"

"Well, *hello there*, you kinky bitch."

"I'm serious," Frank said.

"You think I have that kind of software?"

"I think you know people with that kind of software. The same people who spend all their time on the web. Do you want to help me?"

"Will you finally try Sloppy's?" Stan asked.

"No."

"That means yes. It's a fair trade. So, you're looking for some celebrity porn …"

"This is a real person."

"Ah, so something a little closer to home? Maybe the MILF down the block has been—"

"Would you please stop? It's nothing like that. An underage girl might be in trouble."

"Oh." Stan went sober. "Sorry, bitch. Shooting straight, sure it's possible, but it'll probably take a while. I assume a video or videos are being uploaded somewhere on the dark web?"

"Right."

"You know the site it's posted on?"

"No," Frank said. "But I can get a starting point."

"If the person you're looking for is distributing the videos through a private network, we might never find it." A beat, then, "Probably won't. Just get me a pic to start with, and I'll get Marco on it right away."

"I'll see what I can find."

"Sorry, bitch," Stan said again.

Then the call went dead, and Frank went to the computer to search for a photo of Freya he could use for reference.

He spent an hour looking, knowing he wouldn't find anything but needing to tick that box, anyway. Of course, there weren't any pictures of Freya online because Dahl kept her away from every form of social media. But after surrendering that search to a smarter one, Frank did find *one* picture of Patrick. Whether the monster liked it or not, his photo was right there on his employer's website. And he was wearing a polo shirt, of course.

Frank dragged the pic to his desktop.

A long shot, for sure — odds were slim that Dahl

would have ever been dumb enough to allow his face on camera.

But everyone made mistakes.

And it was possible that he might have erred at least once.

He called Stan again.

"You got something?"

"Maybe," Frank said. "You'll have to tell me."

Chapter Sixteen

Mal

MAL KEPT STARING at Grimm's front door, willing it to open.

But she'd been doing that for more than an hour now, and nothing had happened.

She should get home. Ray's alone time with Ashley wouldn't last all night, and they would definitely go at it after she went to bed if Mal wasn't there when they got back from whatever little adventure they decided to go on.

And even though she'd only been sitting at the edge of Heirloom for an hour now, Mal had been out twice that long. Renting the car took a lot longer than she expected it to and at least twice as long as it should have. Another necessary evil. Grimm knew her car, and Wilson couldn't catch wind of this. Mal needed to be more discreet when it came to catching this guy, and that included more of the old prepaid credit card and hiding her rental from Ray.

No harm, no foul, so long as Grimm finally left his house and she could catch him in the act of something.

Tonight would be a great time to make his move. He might feel emboldened after his whining to Wilson. But the captain hadn't even come close to convincing her. Wilson, like most of the Creek County Sheriff's Office, had a bad case of collective cognitive dissonance. They didn't want to believe that one of their own could ever do such a thing, so they simply refused to follow logic. She didn't want to believe it either, but Mal would rather face that terrible truth than allow other innocent girls to get hurt.

If Grimm wasn't guilty, then how the hell did he know she put cameras up?

He had to be monitoring the street, and focused paranoia probably fueled that behavior. Why would Grimm be paranoid if he wasn't doing anything?

Mal had done some basic recon to see if there had been any new residents to the cul-de-sac. Maybe a fresh face to spark the ex-detective's interest. She was slightly surprised and immensely excited to see that there was indeed a family of newcomers to Heirloom Cove.

The Dahl Family, living in a two-story Victorian at the end of the cul-de-sac.

Of course, Mal had run records on the family and was chilled to see that the couple in that house had a fourteen-year-old daughter named Freya. The same age as Jenny had been when her father did what he'd done to her.

Was Frank planning to strike again? And if so, would it happen soon?

Time to go. Nothing to see here. Mal was just feeding the addiction.

She checked her texts, secretly hoping that she'd see something from Ray giving her the grace of another hour or so. But there weren't any messages from him or anyone else.

Mal imagined Mike at home with his family, smiling

without work on his mind. Part of her felt envious, but the rest felt resentful and bordered on angry.

But that rage should only be directed at herself. This was all her fault. What was she doing, sitting in front of Grimm's after being ordered not to, when she should be missing her family and waiting for them to come home?

It was probably already too late.

She pressed the button to start her rental, then immediately pushed it a second time to kill the engine. Karma had other plans for Mal tonight. The second she was finally ready to go and had proved it by punching the engine, Grimm opened his front door and then set something — she couldn't see what — on his porch before walking briskly down the street.

Of course, she had to see where this went.

No looking furtively around. Grimm walked fast and in a relatively straight line to a smaller cottage with an abundance of roses out front.

He knocked on the door, and it opened right away.

Mal couldn't see who was on the other side, and it felt like he was standing there for an eon. Five minutes at least, but each of them was driving her nuts with nothing else to look at.

Grimm finally left, and sure as shit, he was holding a leash when he did.

So *that's* where he got the chihuahua.

He walked the dog, pretending to amble but slowly making his way back home. Once there, he went to his porch and grabbed whatever he'd set there before. A box by the look of it, though Grimm appeared to be doing his best to conceal the thing.

She was gripping the steering wheel, leaning forward, dying to see what he might do next.

Same as on the trip back to his place, Grimm's dog

walk appeared almost performative. Especially when he got to the house at the end of the street.

She wanted to pound the wheel, pump her fist in the air, scream, *I GOT YOU!* out loud to no one.

There was zero doubt that Grimm was paying more attention to that place than any other home on the street. Not only was he about to go down, but Mal would also finally be vindicated for not giving up on her gut instincts.

It was only a matter of time before the man fucked up. He couldn't behave himself forever.

Now she would be preventing him from doing something to Freya — or finally stopping him if the unthinkable had already begun — and every other little girl after her.

Mal could barely breathe. She was about to catch this sick bastard red-handed. She wasn't sure what Grimm was up to, but she couldn't wait to figure it out. He was crouched next to a plum tree, probably hiding whatever sick little thing he had in his box.

Even crunching her brain, Mal had no idea what that might be.

With the item placed, Grimm made an about-face and started back toward the chihuahua's house. Nothing ambling about his gait now — he made it from Freya's place to the dog's in less than a minute.

He knocked on the door, and it opened immediately, same as the last time.

Whoever it was on the other side of that door appeared to be talking Grimm's ear off, also same as the last time.

But now, when he turned from the door, Mal could read Grimm's expression, and she was sure she had just seen it go from *man on a mission* to *mission accomplished*.

She waited a full five minutes after he was back inside

his house before she dared to get out of the rental. She couldn't remember the last time she'd felt so excited.

She casually walked the cul-de-sac, making her way toward the girl's house with her head low.

Nothing to see here, just another neighbor on Heirloom, out for a stroll. Mal really only cared about one resident of the cul-de-sac seeing her, but she couldn't afford to get caught.

What would a guy like Grimm put into a box outside the house of a teenage girl he was apparently fixated on? No matter how hard she scoured her mind, Mal still had no idea, which further drove her curiosity.

She looked around as she approached the two-story Victorian, saw nothing of note, then walked to the plum tree and crouched in its shadows.

She found a small bucket — not for actual use, more like something one might find at Pottery Barn — and sure enough, there was a small box inside it.

Mal grabbed the box with a feeling like stealing a leprechaun's pot of gold from the end of his rainbow, then concealed it in her jacket and walked swiftly back to her car.

She got in the car and closed the door. Her heart was racing as she looked down at the box on her lap, taking a moment to savor it.

She would never have this again. The cold case she couldn't stop caring about would finally see justice. Soon, everyone in Creek County would know that Frank Grimm had always been guilty.

She opened the box and …

Didn't know what to think.

She knew what the items were, but not what they meant. A tiny audio recorder and a couple of miniature cameras; curious more than condemning.

She could draw a loose conclusion, sure, but it wasn't anything she could take to Wilson, Bell, or anyone else. Mal couldn't even tell Mike about this. Not yet.

Both the recorder and the cameras were small enough that they were obviously meant to be hidden. But who was Grimm hiding them from?

Or the better question: *Who did he want* Freya *to hide them from?*

Because he must have left that box behind for her.

And if he wasn't spying on Freya, then maybe he found some way to get the girl spying on herself. Maybe he was paying her to record some porn for him to get off to, the sick fuck.

Mal needed to get home, and she would soon, but right now, nothing was more important than this. She had to figure out what was really going on.

She used her phone to look up things she should have investigated later. Maybe at home, maybe while on the toilet pretending she had acid reflux again, or tomorrow at work like a good girl, even though she had been ordered off the case, so even that wasn't really so good.

Mal might as well do it now.

The lead would never get any fresher.

But her research wasn't showing her much. Or anything. No one in the family had any web presence whatsoever, except for a one-paragraph bio and a pic of the dad on his company website.

Nothing on Facebook or Instagram or LiveLyfe for any of them.

Not even a relatively ancient MySpace page for either of Freya's parents.

And what kind of teenage girl didn't have at least one social media account?

There was something very, *very* wrong here.

Tonight wasn't the time to figure it out, but fuck Wilson in his sour face — she had never felt more sure that Grimm was guilty than she did right now.

Mal wondered if she should return the box so that Grimm wouldn't know she was onto him.

But it didn't take long to decide that she didn't really care.

This was the end of the hunt. She would be bringing him in soon.

She *wanted* him to know it.

Mal checked her messages but saw nothing.

It was now an hour past the last time she'd checked after she told herself it was probably already too late. She needed to get home.

She started the car and drove with no radio, thinking about what she would say to Ray. Constructing her arguments ahead of time and hating that she had to, hating that he didn't support her in trying to do her job and protect an innocent girl, hating that she constantly had to explain herself to someone who had seen the worst of what humanity could do from behind his own lens. He should understand and not need convincing. But mostly, she hated herself because Mal knew that despite her many justifications, Ray was right that she always did things the way she thought they should be done and steamrolled over everything and everyone else.

Tonight she would make peace, no matter what.

There wasn't any reason to fight. She could surrender for now.

Because soon, everyone would know the truth.

Chapter Seventeen

Frank

FRANK SHOVED another disgusting forkful of lukewarm chicken marsala into his mouth as he stared longingly out the window from his dining room table, wishing he could be in any house other than his own.

He wondered if it was too early for wine.

Breaking into one of his neighbor's homes would soothe his nerves. But he couldn't afford to do that now. Couldn't even really afford to think about it since that's what Frank was doing now, and it was only driving him crazier.

It would be easy. He did it all the time. Frank had a strategy for getting in and out of every house on Heirloom unseen, and he'd been using them for months. Most of the homes had spare keys that he made copies of before returning them.

He hadn't left the house all day. It didn't feel worth the risk.

Frank felt watched. It could easily be paranoia, but that

truth didn't diminish its strength. He felt bad; Rachel was probably expecting him to knock on her door at any minute. She needed someone to listen and walk her dog, in that order, and today he didn't want to be there for either one.

He was selfish, using her and that irritating little chihuahua whenever he pleased.

But Frank had no desire to talk to Rachel or spend another second with Dolly right now. If he did leave the house (and he desperately wanted to), it would be on his own, using one of his tailored strategies to slip inside Arlo's oversized bungalow, or maybe Mrs. McCord's undersized two-bedroom.

He longed for the fix of breaking in and the dopamine rush of pilfering secrets.

Yes, Frank had started because he was hunting Jenny's killer. But he knew that it was now sometimes about feeding his own curiosity.

Today that would be enough.

But today, Frank couldn't afford it.

Today, he would just have to wonder what was happening with Arlo in 51 Heirloom and his boss. Arlo was among the messiest residents. His place was too big for him, and he left his stuff scattered everywhere. He did his dishes once a week at most. But he was also compelling in that he printed all his emails and responded to each one in red pen, occupying the margins and available space between paragraphs. Lately, he'd been having crimson-inked arguments with his boss, and Frank had been following the saga.

Mrs. McCord's story was even more interesting. She had been happily married for fifteen years until she happened to find her high school sweetheart on LiveLyfe. The flirting started casually, then escalated over a year and a half until they were meeting in person once a month, ninety minutes out of town for her and ninety for him, to bridge the three agonizing hours between them. Mrs. McCord had a memory for details and a desire for color. The password for both her computer and her journal app was Suzy11, her daughter's name and the year she'd been born.

Maybe Mrs. McCord thought that was a good password, but part of Frank felt sure that she wanted to get caught. That might also be why she never cleared her browser history. Her fetish did little for Frank, but he did find it interesting how often Mrs. McCord was looking at taxicab porn from the UK. She didn't bother to hide that or her hotel queries.

Frank should have stopped looking long ago, the moment he knew there was no chance that the McCords were connected to what happened with Jenny. But he loved the entertainment provided by Mrs. McCord's browser and journal. He enjoyed both and missed them today.

He'd get a chance to catch up with everyone at the Heirloom barbecue on Friday. But it would be different this time. He usually asked questions to amuse himself, inquiring about things he already knew the answer to, just so he could see how often his neighbors were lying.

It never ceased to amaze him the way people would spin the most unnecessary of yarns. Most of the time, it seemed like they were only doing it to see if they could get away with it. Mostly, though, Frank enjoyed seeing the differences between the public and private faces his neighbors wore.

He liked knowing their secret selves, the parts they hid from even their closest loved ones.

Frank pushed his half-empty plate away from him. Freya would be home soon, and then maybe he wouldn't feel so on edge. Or feel an unrelenting urgency to get out of his house and into someone else's.

And then maybe he wouldn't have to keep reminding himself that it would be a mistake to leave right now. Mallory was watching. Or, if Wilson had effectively scared her off, Frank could see her getting someone else to keep their eyes on the cul-de-sac on her behalf.

No matter how many times he tried to argue otherwise in his mind, Frank knew it for a fact: he had to stay away from Freya's place right now, no matter what, because if Mallory Black so much as caught him glimpsing her way, she would assume the worst and refuse to drop it until she discovered something unrelated that he really didn't want her to know.

So for now, Frank was stuck in front of his window, staring out at the street while waiting for Freya to come home, even though her arrival wouldn't be for another twenty-two minutes or so.

He wouldn't be so on edge if not for this morning. But the reality had him rattled. Frank had left his box in the bucket exactly as promised.

Problem was, Freya couldn't pick it up on her way to the bus because her mom had driven her to school instead. Frank saw it all while watching at his window. She cast him a glance like a fishing line into water before yanking her head back and climbing into the passenger side of her mother's car.

The most cancerous thought, now living inside his brain: *What if Freya's father found the box?*

His eyes had been on it all day, but what about before then? What about when Frank was sleeping? What if Dahl had seen him placing it last night, waited until early morning, retrieved the box, then ordered his wife to take their daughter to school?

Frank had no idea. Watching was the only thing she could do.

Seven minutes to go.

They all eventually passed, each of them excruciating on its way out.

He heard the bus and watched Muriel, Tabitha, Peter, and Capri all amble onto Heirloom, but Freya wasn't among them.

Frank stayed rooted in his seat, planning to stay in front of the window for as long as he needed to. All night if that's what it took. He'd piss in his pants and go without eating until he saw Freya again, or someone knocked on his door to—

Her mother pulled onto Heirloom, with Freya sitting in the passenger seat.

She didn't dare to glance over as the car passed in front of his house.

Then pulled into the driveway.

Freya got out, waited for her mom to take the lead, then stumbled toward the plum tree. She dropped her backpack close to the bucket.

Then she kneeled down, though Frank couldn't see what she was doing.

Freya stood, her face creased in worry.

She stole a glance at Frank's place, then scurried inside.

The door closed, but Frank had no idea what had just happened.

* * *

Two days later, Frank was sitting in his same seat, staring out the same window, waiting to see something — *anything* to soothe his agitated, worried, and increasingly terrified mind.

He needed to know that Freya was okay.

It was Thursday, and he'd been occupied ever since seeing Freya disappear into her house on Tuesday. Of course, he hadn't stayed sitting. He'd walked around the house, and he'd made more marsala. He'd spent hours staring out the window. He'd gathered Rachel's mail and taken Dolly on several walks, but he'd steered clear of his hobby and still didn't have a clue what was happening with Arlo's boss, or whether Mrs. McCord was any closer to getting nailed *for*, rather than just *in*, her affair.

Two days later, and he was still in the dark about so many things.

The only things Frank knew for sure was that Freya hadn't been going to school and that the cops hadn't knocked on her door to investigate. But he had no idea what was happening inside that house or if the girl was even okay. And he didn't know what was up with Mallory. The fact that he couldn't see or hear her meant nothing.

Frank had only dared get close to 47 Heirloom the one time, late Wednesday night, to see if his box was still there. While taking Dolly on a walk, of course.

It was gone, and yet that revelation wasn't relieving at all.

Dahl could have found it.

And that could be why Freya hadn't seen the outside of her house for the last two days.

Maybe she's dead …

Frank told that thought to go the hell away like he always did. The thought wasn't welcome because it couldn't be true. If a man like Dahl was planning to kill his daughter, then he would make it look like an accident and give the world an Oscar-worthy performance as the grieving father. That meant he'd have to call it in, then look the camera in its eye with his tears.

But there hadn't been any ambulances or reporters. If

there were cameras on this street, they were tiny and hidden. Frank had been watching her house in a daze, but he hadn't seen a single sign of activity since Wednesday when she got home.

No one coming or going. Not Freya or either one of her parents.

It was Frank's fault if something happened to her.

He'd handled this all wrong. After making a big mistake on Tuesday by not calling the situation into the sheriff's office when she'd left his house — *after begging him to help her* — Frank kept worsening the blunder with every hour he kept refusing to make the call.

He told himself over and over that he was honoring his word and doing his best to protect her.

But was he really just protecting himself?

Was he secretly worried that she might be making it all up? Even if her father was a controlling narcissist, that didn't make him an evil incestuous pedophile rapist. Frank could be throwing a lot of lives away if he was wrong about this.

He could see the fixated blindness when it afflicted Mallory because he was on the other side. But was this the same thing, and he just couldn't see through it?

Maybe he was a coward, constantly thinking about what he might do instead of actually doing something. Breaking into people's homes just so he could keep telling himself that he was looking for Jenny's killer.

Freya didn't even have to call this in herself. She was obviously frightened, and that was clearly too big a leap for her. He could have called this in without giving his name. The police got anonymous tips all the time.

If he'd had the balls to do that, then Freya would be safe right now.

Instead, Frank might have led an innocent girl to Jenny's fate.

Maybe he should make the call right now.

But, no. He hadn't seen anything to trigger his move. Maybe they were all staying home sick.

So Frank would wait, as excruciating as that would be.

Tomorrow was Friday, and the neighborhood barbecue.

Maybe with everyone out, Frank could finally get some answers.

Chapter Eighteen

Frank

FRIDAY AFTERNOON.

Still no sign of Freya.

Still no signs of anyone coming or going from the house.

Still the ever-growing certainty in his stomach that something was amiss. Something had happened to Freya. Same as with Jenny, Frank had been unable to stop it.

And just like with Jenny, this was going to haunt him for the rest of his life.

Neither car had left the driveway. Frank had spent most of his time in front of the window and hadn't seen their door open or close even once. There was no way to be sure, but Frank would have bet every dollar stashed in his canister of artificial oatmeal that Freya was locked inside that house.

And that was the best-case scenario.

He wanted to believe that Dahl would never be so bold as to murder his daughter outright, but men like that would do anything to protect their secrets, and the juice might have been very much worth the squeeze once he found her with all that spy equipment, and knew she meant to tell.

A daughter without any social profile whatsoever was the kind who could disappear without a surplus of questions. And a man like that knew where to hide the bodies. Frank could imagine:

"What do you mean, *where is she?* She was right here a minute ago. Maybe she went for a walk. Of course, she hasn't been to school for three days. She's been sick. No wonder she needed fresh air. Now, what are you all standing around for — isn't anyone going to help us get a search party together?"

Us. Assuming he didn't kill Irene as well.

Frank had been counting hours to the barbecue all day, but now Frank was counting minutes until seven o'clock.

Forty-eight to go.

He spent them looking out the window, pacing, shaving, pacing, looking out the window, using the restroom, pacing, checking the fridge and freezer for needed ingredients before making a list, looking out the window, and finally, pacing.

He was hungry and definitely wanted a beer or few. But that's what the barbecue was for. He should be starving when he got there. Really look like he was enjoying the food.

It was finally time, but with cases of Corona in hand and his feet halfway out the front door, Frank realized that he didn't want to appear overeager. So he walked to the kitchen, went ahead and cracked open a beer from the fridge, spent fifteen minutes drinking it while looking out the window and watching his neighbors shuffling to the block party, then finally tossing the bottle in his recycling and going outside to join them.

Mrs. McCord was standing next to her husband.

"Hey, Frank!" Abbot waved to him.

"Hey, Abbot." Then to Mrs. McCord. "Hey, Marianne. Ready for all the meat?"

Frank glanced over to the smoker, where Javier was preparing pounds of burgers and brisket.

"Oh, yeah." Abbot made several slaps at his swelling belly, then glanced over at his wife. "She'll only pick at her plate these days, so that means I'll be having seconds."

"Not hungry?" Frank asked, already knowing the truth.

"She's always watching what she eats lately," Abbot said.

"I have to be careful. The older I get, the harder it is to keep the weight off."

Frank wasn't really listening. He'd had this same conversation with the two of them before, and right now, he just wanted to see if anyone from the Dahl family was at the picnic yet as he went to one of the two large coolers and started dropping the bottles of Corona into ice.

So far, the Dahls seemed to be a no-show.

"It's all the traveling you've been doing this year." Abbot was more right than he realized, just not in the way he was thinking. "All that eating out."

"I still think it's the hormones. It feels like my body is always doing something to me."

"Or you're doing something to it," Abbot joked, again missing his proximity to the bullseye.

Mrs. McCord laughed and made a joke about how *somebody needed to.*

Frank used the moment to excuse himself, but he didn't get more than a few feet away before Harriett Sanders started walking over with her mute husband Raphael in tow. She always did all the talking for them both, but not nearly enough of it. Harriett was just as exhausting as Rachel but in the opposite way. The elder of the two launched a verbal blitzkrieg, leaving her victims with little to no chance of making an exodus from the one-sided exchange, whereas Harriett's volleys were more like a trapdoor one fell into, instantly regretted, then immediately plotted their escape from. Though Harriet asked a lot of questions, rarely did they ever belong to a specific conversation. It was like she was always going through a new roll of "conversation starter of the day" toilet paper or something.

"Hey Frank," Harriett called out in a monotone.

The timing was terrible. He had just turned away from the McCords, and there was no way to simply wave without looking rude.

"Hey, Harriett. Hey, Raphael."

They walked over in tandem. Raphael offered Frank a nod but no words. Harriet waited a long moment before adding to her original greeting.

Trapdoor, now fallen into.

Awkward, table for three.

"So …" Then, an hour (a few seconds) later, "How's your week been?"

"It's been good." Frank gave her his best *you're totally not boring* smile. "Yours?"

"Good." Long pause; Raphael filled it with a very slow nod. Frank scanned the area, but still not a Dahl in sight. "So … what's your favorite number? And why?"

And why? Was that on the toilet paper too, or was Harriett improvising?

"Twenty-four." Frank had seriously never considered it before. "I guess I like how even it feels."

"Good answer," Harriett said.

Raphael nodded.

Long silence, still no Dahl.

"Do either of you—"

"If you could replace all of the grass in the world with something else, what would it be and why?" Yes, Harriett actually interrupted him to ask that.

Frank said, "Tomatoes."

Because *why not?*

And, of course, Raphael said nothing.

"Excuse me." He gave the Sanderses his friendliest smile and abruptly excused himself. After catching sight of Patrick (sans family), Frank determined that the action wasn't rude so much as responsible. "I just remembered something I needed to do."

Who cared if they saw that the thing he needed to do at that moment was grab a beer from the cooler before he made his way over to where Dahl was talking to Darius Russell, an accountant who usually stayed indoors and seemed allergic to fun. He also happened to live right next door to Dahl.

Frank got close enough to hear their conversation, then raised his bottle. "Cheers to the weekend."

Both men looked over. Neither were drinking.

"What are we talking about?" Frank asked.

"I was just asking Patrick if Irene and Freya would be joining us. I haven't seen them."

Dahl gave Frank a sinister smile. "And I was just telling Darius that my wife has a migraine, and my daughter is grounded."

"Oh. I'm sorry to hear that. What did she do?" Frank asked.

Dahl stared back, eyeing him like a combatant. "It could be too much caffeine, but I think some things are just genetic."

"No." A light laugh while returning his smile. "I mean, what did your daughter do to get grounded? Freya … is that what you said her name was?"

"It is, and no, I didn't." Dahl glanced at his neighbor with a barely perceptible *I'll get you later* etched into his face. "She got caught in a lie. I've told that girl over and over that fabrications are dangerous, but she just can't seem to stop."

"At that age" — Frank was staring right into the monster's eyes — "kids need consequences. If you don't teach her, who will?"

"Exactly." He turned to Darius. "You mind asking Javier when he thinks the burgers might be ready?"

Darius nodded — *sure thing* — and walked away.

Dahl obviously wanted a moment alone with Frank, as much as Frank wanted a moment with Dahl.

But they didn't get it. He heard the chihuahua yapping before he saw it.

"She misses you!" Rachel called out behind him.

Frank turned around, gave her his best smile, thin as that was, and said, "I was just talking to Mr. Dahl. You wouldn't mind if—"

"Of course I wouldn't!" She turned to her newest neighbor. "I'm sure Frank has probably been telling you all about Dolly."

"He doesn't need to," he replied without missing a beat. "I know quite a lot about chihuahuas."

"You do?"

Frank had never seen anything delight the woman more.

"Sure. Like, did you know they're really little geniuses?"

"What makes you say that?" Rachel asked. "I say the same thing all the time, but no one ever believes me."

Frank knew exactly what Dahl was doing and hated him for it.

"People think small means dumb. But it doesn't. Relative to their little bodies, chihuahuas actually have the biggest brains in the world."

"That makes sense." Rachel nodded in vigorous agreement.

"Quick-witted and easy to train—"

"Not when it comes to house training this guy." She laughed.

"Yeah, well, how do you think you would do with a tiny bladder and a willful personality?" Dahl asked.

Rachel laughed, beaming at him.

Frank wanted to murder the man, maybe more than before.

He needed to get this monster alone.

That was the only way he could get to the truth.

Of course, Irene and Freya weren't sick. Had Dahl caught his daughter with the recording equipment and beat her badly enough that she needed to stay out of sight? Was her mother slowly nursing Freya to health while praying the same fate didn't come her way? Or maybe she was also tending to her own wounds?

Was Dahl onto Frank, and thus playing a game?

They all felt possible. But that last one felt like a certainty.

Darius had started talking to Bill Jhasti. He and his family were at a table to Frank's right, and Erin Duvall was standing equidistant to his left. Dahl was still making nice with Rachel, right in front of him.

Erin saw them and started walking over. If Frank had to hear about the whore fucker right now, he'd have to break someone's leg.

"I bet Dolly's just going nuts smelling all that meat.

And I'm sure Javier'll be happy to give her a little taste," Frank interrupted the exchange just as Erin approached. Then he barreled on before Rachel could get going with another story. "I bet Erin would love to help you two over there. You should go *now*; Javier's never happy with his first burger. Oh — Erin was also telling me a story about Ross that you're going to love."

Erin brightened. "Which one?"

"The one in Mexico." Frank was sure there were at least a couple there.

"Oh yeah." Erin walked over to Rachel. "Let me help you."

Then they left.

Frank and the monster were finally alone.

The air felt suddenly dangerous. Freya was right, and he could smell it. This man had done terrible things, committed atrocities upon his daughter, and his wife, and certainly others. This man really did deserve to die.

Frank knew it in his gut.

But Mallory Black felt the exact same thing about him.

Dahl was still wearing his smile like a mask. "If I didn't know any better, I'd almost think you were trying to get me alone."

"I was," Frank admitted; there was no other way to play this.

"And why is that?" Still smiling. "Is there something you wanted to talk about?"

"Your daughter."

"What about my daughter?"

"She looks familiar."

"Oh, yeah? How so?"

Frank shrugged. "I'm not sure. I guess that's what I wanted to talk about. Maybe you could help me figure out where I remember her from. Could I have seen her on the internet?"

"Maybe you shouldn't be asking around about fourteen-year-old girls, considering what happened to yours."

"I know how it looks." Frank nodded, holding his gaze. "But I figured you'd understand. That *is* why I thought this conversation was better between just the two of us."

"Good thing Darius started talking to that family over there."

"Good thing," Frank agreed. "So does she have her own YouTube channel or anything? LiveLyfe maybe? I just know I've seen her somewhere."

"My daughter isn't allowed to post anything of herself on the internet. There are some real sickos out there." Dahl's smile didn't fade; his expression disappeared like it was never even there. "You must have seen someone who looks similar."

The corner of Patrick's mouth started twitching. Twice and only barely, but enough for Frank (*it would probably be enough for Mallory, too*).

This monster was raping and filming his daughter.

Frank needed to flee this conversation, get away from the barbecue, go home and hop on the phone with Wilson.

Except … this call should come from an anonymous tip line.

"I'm sure you're right." Frank forced a friendly, knowing smile onto his face, just as Rachel returned with Erin and Darius trailing behind them. He turned a beat before Rachel was standing in front of him, holding out his hand for the leash. "She looks like she needs a walk."

"She sure does." Rachel beamed at him. "Here you go."

Dahl was looking at him, the smile back on his face.

"Thank you." Frank took the leash, then excused himself from the group.

Then he walked the chihuahua, knowing that Dahl was watching.

Frank made nice with his neighbors — though he didn't trade another word with the monster — ate plenty of burgers and brisket, and even polished off another beer while bantering with the Jhastis and yet another while talking (listening) to Erin about her ex-husband and all his whore-fucking ways.

He left before the barbecue ended, but late enough for no one to notice his early departure. Dahl was already long gone, perhaps watching Frank from his window.

But Frank didn't care.

He went home, closed the door, and made a call that should end Freya's suffering.

Chapter Nineteen

Mal

MAL HAD every intention of making nice with Ray, but it didn't matter how hard she tried, he refused to make nice with her.

Daddy-daughter time was a movie. *Sherlock Bones,* since "Ashley still really wanted to see it" and the film "didn't seem like anything Mal would be making time for in the immediate future."

They only beat her home by five minutes, but considering they'd grabbed dinner and a movie — on a school night, which Ray would have had a massive problem with if things had been the other way around — her arrival felt later than it actually was.

Mal honored her commitment and steered clear of a fight. She didn't even try to stick up for herself. Ray treated her with indifference while Ashley was still awake, then something closer to an arctic chill once she'd gone to bed. Mal might as well have slept on the couch. He wouldn't even let her say sorry with sex. Not that she asked outright; she didn't need to be a detective to see that he wanted nothing to do with her.

Not last night, and not this morning.

Mal had been in the kitchen the entire time he was making breakfast and tried to make conversation throughout the entirety of their little interlude, but the few times she got responses to her comments or queries, they arrived one lonely word at a time.

She was sipping her coffee when Ashley came charging downstairs.

She swallowed with a flush of relief. It was always harder for Ray to act like an asshole in front of their daughter.

You're the one being an asshole, Mal had to remind herself.

"It's Saturday!" Ashley announced, climbing up onto her favorite barstool.

Ray brightened as he turned from the coffeemaker — already starting on the second pot — to look at her. "That's the one that comes between Friday and Sunday, right?"

"It's the one where we're going to play at Swingers!" Ashley was almost yelling.

Mal had forgotten that they were planning on spending an afternoon at the inappropriately — according to Ray — named miniature golf course.

Daddy agreed for the most part. "*Tonight.* You and Mommy will have to do something else fun during the day. I got called in for an after—"

"On a Saturday?" Mal said.

"It happens," Ray replied without looking at her.

"But I might have to work tonight, too."

Ray turned to her, his indifference warming to mild

anger that Mal didn't want to see get any hotter. "No. You don't. Are you saying that you *would like* to work tonight? That you *choose to work* instead of going to Swingers with your family?"

That was much more pointed than he usually was in front of Ashley.

But Mal still wanted to play nice. "Of course not. I'm responding to my responsibility, same as you are by——"

"Showing up for my assigned shift?"

"We have different jobs."

"We sure do," Ray agreed.

"You're always working, Mommy!"

"I know. That's because——"

"And you NEVER want to do fun stuff with us!" Ashley's face was starting to change.

"That's not true, honey." Mal circled around to the bar and sat on a stool beside Ashley, now uncomfortably close to Ray, considering the way he was glaring at her. "I always *want* to do fun stuff with you. It makes me so sad when I can't. But it's like when you have to do your homework. You don't *like* doing it, but homework is something you have to do so you can understand the information and get good grades in school."

Ray was chewing his bottom lip to raw burger but not interjecting.

"Your dad and I have really important jobs."

"I know that, Mommy."

"We just do it differently. Your dad is great at what he does——"

"No one needs you to do this right now, Mal."

"——bringing news to the people so they can understand the world around them."

"I like when Daddy's photos make the front page."

"Me too, honey. And the news doesn't always work

with our schedule. Just like crime doesn't. Kinda like Puppy Detective probably doesn't get to have a normal—"

"Your mother's job is nothing like the Puppy Detective's."

She nodded. "Your father's right. It's way harder and much scarier."

"Mal …"

"Do I interrupt you when you're trying to communicate something important?"

"You try not to." Ray rolled closer to a boil.

She turned back to Ashley. "I'm working on a very important case right now."

Ray was gritting his teeth.

"Have you heard of Rory Day?" Mal asked.

Ashley scrunched her face; a familiar name, but she didn't know why. "I don't know … who is she?"

Mal didn't pause to check Ray's face, but she could feel a withering heat from his staring. "She's a little girl, just a few years older than you, who was brutally murdered."

"Mal!"

Ashley flinched, but her question came a split-second later. "What happened to her, Mommy?"

She looked interested, not scared, regardless of what Ray would surely claim later. But Mal was protecting her. She was sick of him treating their daughter more like a dandelion instead of a daisy.

"We don't really know." Mal sent a cascade of worry onto her face; it was important that Ashley understand the severity here. She'd been bold enough to open the door a crack, so now Mal needed the courage to open it all the way. "That's what we're trying to find out."

"But a bad guy killed her?" Ashley still looked interested more than scared.

And for the moment, Ray was holding his silence.

"He sure did. We think it was someone Rory knew really well. Someone she trusted. And do you know what that someone did to her?"

"No." Ashley shook her head, now seeming less certain about this being something she wanted to know.

But the door was open, and mother and daughter would walk through it together.

"A bad man abused her. And when he was all done doing what he wanted to, he killed her so that no one would ever know—"

"Mal!"

"—and we found her body getting eaten by bugs in the woods."

Ashley started to cry.

Ray was already holding her and wanting to know what the hell was wrong with Mal.

"I help to catch people like the man who killed Rory Day so that—"

"Just. Stop." Ray was back to glaring at Mal, Ashley's face pressed to his chest.

She did. And Ashley calmed in no time.

No big deal, even though Ray was about to turn it into one.

"Are you all finished with your breakfast?" he asked.

Ashley nodded.

"Why don't you go upstairs and brush your teeth, then finish getting ready, okay?"

She nodded again, then scampered out of the room.

"Are you going to chew me out now?"

Ray shook his head. "I seriously don't even know what to say."

"How about something like, 'It's a really fucked-up world out there, Mal. Thanks for doing the hard work of preparing our daughter for it while I sit on the sidelines and judge you.'"

"*That's* how you see this?"

"That's the conclusion the clues in this very difficult case have led me to, so yes, Ray. That's how I see this."

"So you can't see that you just dragged our daughter into your world?"

"It's not *my world*. It's *the world*. She's old enough to understand, and she *should* understand. You've seen a lot of the same things I have. You just can't admit that we're doing her a disservice by being—"

"*Brutally murdered?*" Ray cut her off, about to make one of his lists. "*Abused her body? Doing what he wanted to it? Eaten by bugs in the woods?*"

"You're acting like I graphically described her rape and how he slit her throat, probably while ejaculating, and how—"

"You're right. What you said was totally appropriate, Mallory."

"It was age-appropriate language, *Ray*."

"But not age-appropriate subject matter."

"Says you."

"I am the one talking." He ran an angry hand through his hair. "Can you please acknowledge that you just terrified our daughter?"

"Sure. Now it's your turn. Can you acknowledge that maybe a little terror in the right place isn't such a bad thing? Which way prepares her for the world better, yours or mine?"

"There's a time and a place, Mal."

"Like right now, here in this kitchen."

"It's bad enough that you abandon your family for this work." He shook his head. "I'm not going to let you drag

Ashley down with you, scaring the hell out of her so she won't ever trust anybody ever again."

"I'm not 'dragging' Ashley anywhere."

"You're right. You'd probably have to spend time with her for that."

"Fuck you, Ray."

"There it is. I love when you start swearing at me."

"Ashley should know that the reason I'm not around as much as we would all like for me to be is that I'm trying to make the world a safer place for her."

"Should she also know that another reason you're not around so much is because your ego is attached to your job and that it feeds you more than being a mother?"

Ouch.

"Should she know that her mother has an addictive personality and that her current addiction is catching Frank Grimm doing something no one else thinks he's guilty of? Because — and this one is super important for her to understand, Mal — her mother doesn't know how to be wrong?"

"Fuck—"

"You said that." He clenched his fists, then relaxed them. "I think spending so much time around corpses and murderers has killed your perspective."

"That's cute."

"I'm not trying to be cute. I'm trying to—"

"This is who you married. *I* haven't changed."

"I disagree. You *have* changed." Ray shook his head, and Mal couldn't remember the last time she'd seen him so sad. "And I think you've changed for the worse."

No more words.

Ray left the kitchen, and Mal to her thoughts.

She had a lot of them, but they were all just screaming in tongues about how much she hated herself. She wanted to pour a nice stiff drink, but the thought of Ray coming back down as she was drinking and proving his point about her addictive nature soured the idea.

So she just stared out the window, wondering when and where things had gone wrong.

Chapter Twenty

Frank

THE WEEKEND WAS a month long as Frank waited with his stomach in knots for something to happen with Patrick Dahl.

On Monday afternoon, Frank paced in front of his living room window, watching the street and wondering what was taking so long.

Whether his impatience was born from worry over Freya, an eagerness to see Dahl get what was coming to him, or an atrophied memory that failed to recall the many miles of red tape that had always wrapped everything during his time at the sheriff's office, he really had hoped to see something happen after he'd phoned in his anonymous tip.

And now, the suspense was about to give him a heart attack.

Frank had been watching the house ever since Friday night. At least he was no longer worried that Freya was locked up, beaten too bloody for a public appearance, or dead. He'd seen both Freya and her mother coming and going — maybe to the store, Frank had no way of knowing — but no deputies pulling onto Heirloom and knocking on the family's door.

Freya left the house this morning alone, in a furious march toward the bus.

Frank wasn't worried that his tip would go nowhere, but the lack of movement over the weekend told him something he didn't want to know. He had been hoping that the first official move would hit Dahl directly. But now, they would go to Freya first and unintentionally give her tormentor an escape hatch.

A man like him would be prepared, and this greatly increased the odds of his squirming away.

If the sheriff's office didn't send any cars out over the weekend, then that was probably because the State Attorney's Office was planning to act on Monday by sending a Child Protection Team to Freya's school. They would call her out of class and request her presence for an intimidating exchange that would pull all her triggers and push every one of her buttons.

Sure, the child psychologist would be well trained and say all the things she had been taught to get a victim like Freya to open up enough to admit what was happening to her. But that one-size-fits-all approach wasn't going to work here.

Not with Freya.

Meaning the State Attorney's Office and the Child Protection Team might simply be stabbing an open wound.

It was possible that Frank was worrying about nothing. If all went well, they would either go and arrest Dahl directly or — if they felt that there was little chance of finding evidence at the house — they might have Freya participate in a control call. She would either call him from the police phone and get him to admit something over a recorded line, or they would put a wire on Freya and get her father confessing in person.

But that was all assuming she would talk or cooperate.

And from what Frank had seen so far, she wouldn't. She was too frightened. He'd seen it too many times, victims who feel like their tormentors have godly power over their lives, that there is nothing they can do to escape. Rarely was that the case. There was almost always a way out.

But sometimes, men were too far gone, the kind that would rather burn the world than surrender, even if that meant taking out their family. Frank feared that Patrick Dahl might be just that kind of guy.

And, it was quite possible that Frank had only made things worse for Freya with that phone call.

The school bus would be pulling up to the edge of Heirloom in just a few minutes. The best he could hope for was seeing her missing from the group of kids walking home, which would mean that someone had taken her into custody, that she was safe. Soon after, deputies would move on her father.

Those last couple of minutes were the hardest. Frank felt like he was chewing through nails. But then he heard the bus hissing and held his breath. Moments later, he saw the usual crew rounding the bend, Freya included.

He almost wanted to swear. And not just one word, but a string of them. Maybe Stan had been right all along.

Freya broke from the pack and began walking right to his door.

He opened it to her, already screaming.

"WHAT WERE YOU THINKING?"

"You have to stop yelling." Frank grabbed Freya by the arm and yanked her inside the house before any neighbors could see if they hadn't already.

The only thing riskier than pulling her inside was leaving her on the porch.

He kicked the door closed, then let her go. "Calm down and tell me what happened."

"You calm down!"

He didn't respond.

"How could you do that to me?"

"I don't know what you're talking about, Freya. If you tell me what happened, I'm sure I can—"

"You promised you wouldn't call the cops!"

"I didn't—"

"Some shrink showed up at my school, wanting to interview me!"

"That's because—"

"For like two hours!"

Frank waited to see if there was anything more, but Freya was apparently finished for now. She was angry, but maybe that was a good thing. Pus leaving the wound. "And? What happened? Did you tell them?"

"Of course I didn't tell them!"

Unbelievable.

"Why not, Freya? That was your chance to—"

"I already told you why not, Mr. Grimm! You don't know my father. *He's going to kill me, and my mother!*"

"He's not going to kill you," Frank said, making a promise he intended to keep, heart pounding against his ribcage. "I won't let that happen."

"*You* can't stop him. If he wants to do something, then he does it. There's only one way to stop him, and I told you." Freya turned to him, her fury giving way to desperation. "Please, Mr. Grimm … can't you just kill him?"

"That's not how the world works, Freya." Now pissed, he stepped away from her and started pacing his living room.

"People kill people all the time."

"Of course they do. Those people are called murderers, and folks like me are in charge of finding out who they are and putting them in jail."

"Folks like you *used* to be. You're not a detective anymore, right?"

"Once a detective, always a detective. And detectives aren't murderers."

"But they break into people's homes?"

He didn't respond.

"What if my father murders me?" She meant the question. Freya's terrified eyes were about to start leaking. And still, he couldn't squelch his anger at her.

"Why didn't you tell them? I gave you a way out. If you had just answered their questions, this would all be on its way to over by now. Don't you understand how much worse you've made things?" He hadn't intended to hurt her and instantly wished he could take back the accusation.

"How much worse *you've* made things. Everyone already makes fun of me at school. They call me *Voodoo Dahl.* A bunch of people know the police were there today. Tomorrow everyone will be talking!"

"It's not too late. You can still call the sheriff's office. Tell them you were scared, that you were terrified of what would happen if your father knew you'd talked." He pulled up the proper contact, then tried to hand her his phone. "Ask for Captain Wilson. You can—"

"No way." She shook her head, refusing the phone.

"Freya."

"I said no, Mr. Grimm. He'll kill me."

"He won't—"

"You said they need evidence, right? Otherwise, they'll have to let him go."

"They can get a warrant and search—"

"I don't know where he keeps his … things, so—"

"With guys like this, there's usually someplace in the house that's off-limits to everybody. Where does he spend the most time?"

"He goes into the office every night, and I can hear him … doing gross stuff … in there all the time."

"Great. That's a starting—"

"We need more than a starting point, Mr. Grimm."

"Agreed. What happened to the surveillance equipment I left you?"

Freya gave him a look that was equal parts annoyance and confusion. "You didn't leave me any equipment. I looked where you told me, and it wasn't there."

He drew a breath, considering what this might mean. "I left it there."

They looked at one another until her lip started quivering. "I never got it." She shook her head wildly. "The box wasn't there." Shook it harder. "You didn't leave me anything, I swear!"

She started to hyperventilate. "Oh my God … oh my God …"

She turned toward the door and took two long steps toward it.

There were only four at most, so Frank reached out and grabbed her arm again. "Wait!"

"No." She shook herself out of his grip and made the final two steps toward the door.

He grabbed her again.

"LET GO OF ME!"

Frank flinched back, but he couldn't let her leave looking so upset. He imagined a neighbor or her mom or dad home early, seeing her leave in such a state. Plus, he needed to calm her down for her own benefit before she went home, and her face gave everything away, leading to questions, and ultimately disaster.

He raised his hands, palms up, falling back in retreat. "Please. Just don't open the door yet."

"I need to go home."

"Just hear me out," Frank begged her with his eyes.

She said nothing.

He took that as permission. "I know you're afraid, Freya. But I promise, your best shot is, to tell the truth. Call this in. Let me take you to the sheriff's office. They can do a rape kit and—"

"That won't prove it's him. I know you don't believe me, Mr. Grimm. But he really will kill me. The second he gets a chance."

Frank did believe her. More than ever. That's why he couldn't let her leave.

The girl might melt right into her misery. Somber clothes, conservative like always. No makeup, nail polish, or jewelry. Not even sneakers. Though she often wore black and wore her hair in her face, gray was the closest thing to a color in Freya's ensemble. Looking at her now, Frank realized something that he hadn't noticed before.

Freya was dressed like a sad doll.

A doll that belonged to a beast.

He tried to hand her the phone again.

And again, she shook her head in refusal. But this time, she opened the door. "I have to go."

"Please. I promise this is what's best for you."

"I already told you what was best for me, Mr. Grimm. I understand that you can't help me now."

She opened the door and practically threw herself out of it. Then she ran down his porch and down the street toward her house while sobbing.

Reckless and risky and rash — Freya had made things worse at school, then multiplied the problems by coming over to his place in broad daylight while her peers were all still walking home from school, and leaving looking as upset as she was, without making any effort whatsoever to hide it.

He looked outside. Not just through the window but down the porch and into the street. If someone had seen her, then it didn't make any difference if they saw him looking out his window. He might as well survey the cul-de-sac.

Freya was already inside her house, and so far as Frank could see, there didn't seem to be a single neighbor looking at her house or his.

Back into the house and right to the key rack.

He grabbed his hat and fob, then was in his car, backing out of the driveway, hard into the road, forcing himself to go slow and not accelerate, even though he wanted to tear the hell out of there.

Frank was in one of his few indulgences, bought as a narcotic in the aftermath of Sarah's passing. A 2013 Chevy Avalanche. The last year they made them. A tank with a little enclosed cargo bed. Tons of lockable cubbies and storage spaces. High 300's horsepower, but nothing fancy. Didn't stand out. The mechanical systems were easy to work on, and parts were easy to find. A luxurious interior and an AC that knew how to whisper. The perfect car so far as he was concerned.

There was only one place that might possibly soothe

him right now, and he needed to get there an hour ago. On the open road, he allowed his instincts to take the wheel. He would get there in time and think hard through the drive ahead of his arrival.

But he didn't cry, holding his release, wanting to leave the catharsis in his car where it belonged.

He parked.

Got out.

Then crossed two sprawling lawns and an untold number of forgotten bodies to find himself in front of the saddest, loneliest place in the world, a place *he* should've been long before his daughter or wife.

He looked down at the headstones, then quickly away.

A long second was all he could bear of it.

Frank took off his hat and held it against his chest.

"I'm sorry, Jenny." His tears were already falling. "Whatever happened to you, I should have seen it coming. I just know I could have done more for you if …"

He needed a moment to cry and nothing else.

"I never should have quit the force. But your mom was on me even before I got shot. She pressured me to leave the force because you guys never saw me. And I knew she was right, even though I wanted to stay. I never wanted to be a P.I. like your mom wanted me to, and it was hard to give up being a detective with the sheriff's office. But I did it for you, then …"

Another moment.

"Then what happened happened. You got kidnapped before I could get the business started, and that put me on the sidelines instead of heading the manhunt for your kidnapper. By quitting the force, I left your rescue to others. Pure torture for two days until they found your body. Then the autopsy …"

No way to tally the numerous rapes.

He swallowed and turned his attention to Sarah. "That was such a hard time for us both. We should have been there for each other more. I expected to get questioned and that I'd become a suspect by default. The department had to do its job, after all. But it was still a shock that people I had worked with for years could believe that I'd do something so heinous. You were with me, and I felt your support all the way until Kirby got in your ear. Why did you let him do that to us? Why did you believe him even for a minute?"

More crying.

"I know little lies lead to big ones, but how could you think the worst of me, especially when I was already at my low?"

Crying harder.

"I'm sorry for everything that happened after that. I know so much of it is my fault. But you were just as much a ghost as I was. I still read your goodbye letter every morning, and I understand why you left me. I wish we could have trusted each other more …"

That was enough for now.

Frank wiped the tears away, quietly collecting himself, thinking about all the mile markers of misery on his long road here. To this lawn, to these headstones, to the new and singular goal that swallowed everything else.

The sheriff's office ultimately concluded that Jenny had probably been randomly grabbed by a predator who spotted opportunity while passing through the county.

Frank didn't agree. Or couldn't.

He wasn't willing to acknowledge that his daughter's death was just one of those things that happened. Jenny had always been special, and he had to believe that the killer chose her for a reason.

Frank could discover that reason if he just looked hard enough.

Maybe he was wrong. Maybe he couldn't. And maybe he could never have done anything to save his baby girl from her fate.

But there was something he could do to save Freya.

And he was damn well gonna do it.

Chapter Twenty-One

Frank

FRANK FELT BETTER the next day.

But this was still taking much too long.

It had been a week since he had planted the surveillance box. Life had been raw nerves ever since. Whether he meant to or not, Frank had put this into motion, and it was now his responsibility.

If Freya hadn't caught him breaking into the Jhastis, none of this would be happening. She had probably been watching him for a while. Or perhaps believing that was better than her guessing his patterns and motives immediately.

Frank was tired of sitting on his hands.

So despite still feeling watched and knowing that if he got caught breaking into the Dahls' place, everything else might spiral away from him, and that monster across the street was probably actively waiting for him to make an idiot move exactly like this one, Frank finished picking the lock to their back door, then slipped inside the kitchen and closed it behind him.

He just needed to find some evidence. A thread to pull, anything to go on. Something he could lob to Stan. Nothing from his buddy Marco so far, but Stan worked property crimes, and if Frank tipped him with the right lead, he could kick the information forward.

Frank shouldn't be anywhere near this. He had to be careful not to create a fruit of the poisonous tree situation where the court excluded legitimate evidence because it was illegally obtained.

Same as before, Frank entered every room, checking for camera signals. Nothing yet.

Same as before, the Dahl residence was the least lived-in he'd ever seen. Most houses he broke into, or had been invited into, told its family's story. This was like one of those model homes, waiting to be filled with memories.

And same as before, the reek of something wrong permeated the house.

But this time, Frank's mission was more defined. He gave the entire place a cursory once-over, excluding Freya's room for now, since the kind of evidence he was looking for was least likely to be there.

He saved the home office for last, wanting to spend the bulk of his time there.

Freya said that her father went into the office every night to jerk off, so Frank figured Dahl must keep something in there. But his office was the only one he could remember ever having seen without a computer, at least in the last twenty years.

It was an office with nothing digital. Dahl kept meticulous records of everything, but all on paper. There were two filing cabinets, plus folders filling two-thirds of the desk drawers.

Frank had no idea what he was looking at, and there was no way he could go through it all. It would take who-knew-how-many hours just to photograph what was here. And Dahl probably had the placement of every item memorized.

He did rifle through the drawers of each cabinet after taking time to pick their locks but found no photos. Just white paper with lots of numbers and confusing catego-rization, receipts, written documents, contracts, letters — but it all looked like boring accounting information.

He wondered if phony files and documents could be ordered from the Masquerading as Normal catalog just like the furniture.

Or maybe more like Frank's canister of oatmeal.

Next, he investigated the room itself, searching for any visible seams in the wall; there had to be a hiding place or somewhere for Dahl to keep his stash.

The bookcase yielded nothing, and neither did the naked walls. He considered unscrewing outlets to see if anything was hidden in any of them or perhaps find a false one from those catalogs of stupid "spy" shit, but first, he'd cover the more obvious places.

Frank had already given the closet a glance but surveyed it further.

He didn't get far, hearing something the moment his fingers brushed the wall.

Back out of the closet, he heard something else. And the second sound was unmistakable.

The front door finished opening, then swung shut.

If Irene, or Irene and Freya, were home, that would be bad.

But if Daddy was home, then that would be a whole lot worse.

It didn't matter who it was if Frank could slip out of

the house without being seen. If Dahl was coming home, then he might head directly to his office. But if it wasn't him, then the office was the safest place in the house.

For now.

"Are you sure it wasn't something you ate?" He heard Irene from a couple of rooms away.

"How many times are you going to ask me that?" Freya replied.

"I'm sorry for being concerned."

Freya sighed.

"I had to leave work to go and get you, Freya. Your father is going to give me a hard time."

"Do you think he'll use his right or his left fist this time?"

"Can you please not do that?"

"You're right, Mom. What you're doing is so much better."

He opened the door a crack.

"You need to stop this." Irene's tone sharpened to a sudden and dangerous edge. "He'll be home any minute."

Why's he coming home early? He isn't usually home before five-thirty.

Frank's heart might have been beating loudly enough for them to both hear, even two rooms away.

"You're right," Freya said. "I should never say anything and just give up like you."

Frank slipped out of the office.

Freya continued. "Haven't you ever considered that telling the truth might be our best shot?"

"Of course I have."

Frank crept down the hallway, ears perked and ready to pivot.

His right foot was raised halfway above the hallway carpet. He took an eon to softly lower it.

Then he waited.

But in his mind he heard, *He'll be home any minute.*

He dared a step.

At exactly the wrong second.

Irene turned the corner and screamed.

"Wait!" Frank raised his hands in instant surrender. "It's me, your neighbor, Frank Grimm!"

Irene screamed even louder.

But Freya was yelling, too. "It's okay, Mom! He's here to help us."

She wasn't buying it. Irene grabbed Freya by her wrist and dragged her toward the kitchen.

Frank followed, wanting to leave but knowing he couldn't.

Irene was back out of the kitchen before he arrived, brandishing a knife in front of her. He wondered if she'd ever done the same thing to Dahl before he taught her *never again* with a beating or whether she was now acting out a fantasy she'd rightfully had for years.

"Mom. Mom. Mom." Freya's hands were all over her. "It's okay. Mr. Grimm is my friend."

Irene turned to her daughter, horrified. *"Your friend? What?"*

"He's trying to help save us from *him.*"

Irene lowered her weapon, but not her resolve. With a voice dry of both moisture and warmth, she said, "He can't help us." Then she looked him in the eye and added, "There's nothing to be done."

"I have friends that can—"

"It doesn't matter who you know. My husband knows people too, Mr. Grimm. You need to leave before he—"

"Just hear him out, Mom." Tough as she'd been with her side of the volley a few minutes before, Freya was all tears again now. "I'm sick of having to pretend this isn't happening. I'm sick of *you pretending, Mom.* It's not just the control and the beatings." She choked on a sob. "*I know you know what he's doing to me.*" Then a guttural, terrible, unforgettable wail. "I KNOW YOU KNOW HE'S RAPING ME!"

"FREYA!"

"No ..." Now Irene was shaking her head, falling slowly to her knees, burying her face in her palms while shaking her head.

"Are you going to deny it?"

Irene sounded like an animal dying.

"FUCKING SAY SOMETHING!"

Frank couldn't move his gaze from the unfolding nightmare. The house had been stone-cold silent just minutes ago.

Irene looked up, still manically shaking her head. "I didn't want to believe it ... I didn't want to see it ... I tried to leave him once ... it wasn't ..." She couldn't finish, and even trying might have been enough to end her. "It's not important why. But he shoved a gun in my mouth and pulled the trigger twice ..."

Irene needed another moment.

Freya had been stunned into silence and was now staring at her mother spellbound.

"I lost two teeth when he yanked the gun back out of my mouth. Then he showed me that the third bullet was ready for me." The memory seemed to weaken her further while simultaneously making her stronger. "He told me that pulling the trigger would be the easiest thing in the world, next to getting away with it. He knew people that would help him with 'every part of the process.'" She let that sink in, then looked at them both. "He meant everything from 'getting rid of the body' to 'making sure that no one ever said shit.'"

"I'm so sorry, Mom," Freya said, still crying. "I remember when you lost your teeth … from the car door." Then more choking.

"I know how hard that must have been for you." Frank dared to touch her gently on the shoulder. "And I can understand your reticence to get help now."

"You need to leave." She shook her head. "Before he gets home."

"I can get you the police protection you need to stay safe, as long as you're both willing to testify against him."

Another furious shake of her head. "I need a *guarantee* that he'll go to jail. Otherwise, we'll both end up dead."

"You give me proof, that's as close to a guarantee as you can get. And I promise it's a lot better than what must be happening now. For you, I'm sure, but especially for Freya. We can't let him keep doing this to her." Frank could see she was breaking. He looked from Freya to Irene and back. "Do either of you know where he might be hiding his stash?"

They both shook their heads.

"He must have a laptop, right? Where does he keep it?"

"He always has it on him," Irene said, then added, "That thing never leaves his side."

Good news if Dahl kept the laptop handy because it had all his dirt.

Bad news if he had some uncrackable encryption or kept things encrypted remotely. Frank wasn't a cybersecurity expert, but he knew enough to know that people like this had ways of hiding their filth. But the sheriff's office had their own people, as did the FBI, with tools the average person didn't have access to, including backdoors in many of the popular encryption programs.

"Even if you don't *know* where he keeps his stash, can you think of any part of the house where he might keep something he wouldn't want anyone to see?"

Two shaking heads.

"Maybe your bedroom?" Frank pressed, looking at Irene.

Freya's head suddenly stopped shaking, her expression struck by a sudden, sickening realization. "If we find his stash, then won't that mean the videos will be used as evidence in the trial?"

He nodded. "Almost for sure. But they'll be handled with—"

"No!" Panic hit her like lightning. "Everyone will see that I'm being forced to do those things that—"

"It's not like that." Frank tried to soothe her. His hand found her shoulder, same as it had for her mom. "I—"

"What if they get leaked?"

"That's not how this kind of—"

"I know that evil people have already seen them. But what if they get out there into the real world? What if kids at school see? What if this follows me around for the rest of my life?"

She was breathing too hard, getting hysterical.

His hand firmed on her shoulder. "Nothing will leak. I won't ever let that happen to you. There's a good chance that if he knows the evidence is piled up against him, he'll plea so this wouldn't ever get to court." He probably shouldn't say this next part, but there it went anyway. "Even if it did somehow leak, your life won't be over. You can fight, Freya. You can reclaim your life, become a victim advocate. Believe me ..." He turned to her mother. "And Irene. Anything's better than living like this."

Her expression had cracked in half, and for a moment, it looked like Mom might finally acquiesce. But instead, she retreated. "I'm sorry, Mr. Grimm. Thank you for your concern. It really means a lot. I promise to reach out if we find something. But without any evidence, we really can't risk it. And you need to get out of—"

"I'll help you hide."

"I'm sorry?" Irene asked.

"Fine. Don't testify. Let me help you disappear. But you have to get out of this house right now."

"He'll find us," Irene insisted, still frantic.

"Where will you hide us?" Freya asked.

"We can—"

Frank didn't finish. Dead quiet, so they could all agree on the sound that had frightened them into silence.

"*He's home!*" Irene whispered urgently.

Freya repeated her mother's mantra. "*You have to get out of here!*"

Frank thrust a hand into his pocket, pulled out a small pad of paper, then scribbled his number and handed the small sheet to Irene. "Don't lose that or let him see it. Text me when you can, and we'll come up with a plan. *I am going to help you.*"

"You have to go," Irene repeated.

"She's right." Freya grabbed Frank by the wrist and pulled him behind her.

She opened the kitchen door and practically shoved him out of it.

Then it closed without a goodbye. He took a second to survey the clearing, then rushed toward the street.

"Hey there, Grimm!"

He turned to see Dahl beaming at him from the driveway with his sinister smile. "Mind if I ask what you're doing nosing around my yard?"

"Of course not." Frank pretended to look around.

"You seen a chocolate-colored labradoodle anywhere around here?"

"Is that what you're looking for?" He smiled wider, ugly and knowing. "It's not a chihuahua this time?"

Frank laughed, light but friendly. "I'm walking Dolly later. This is for Erin Duvall."

"The divorcée?" He looked surprised. "I didn't realize she had a dog."

She didn't. "Oh yeah. Erin loves that thing."

"You sure she has a dog?"

"Pretty sure," he lied.

"You sure you're not really here perving on my daughter?"

"Hey." Frank raised his hands. "That's not—"

And again, his smile fell like snow off the side of a mountain, and Frank found himself looking at an ugly, angry man. "I better never see you anywhere near my house again. You understand me, Grimm?"

"I—"

"You probably don't want to answer me with anything less than a *yes sir,* right now." He looked around, was apparently satisfied by what he saw, then lifted his shirt enough to give Frank a glimpse of his gun. "Just so we're on the same page."

"I believe we are." Frank gave him a nod, then turned and walked home, feeling his furious stare all the way.

And he now knew without a doubt, and no matter what: *Patrick Dahl would have to die.*

Chapter Twenty-Two

Mal

MAL SPENT all weekend wanting to hit things and doing her damnedest not to.

It was a near-constant impulse. Right now, while driving, she wanted to pound her fist on the steering wheel over and over until her knuckles bruised. That was the main reason she missed Mike and wished he was sitting next to her in the Explorer. Driver, passenger, it didn't matter. Whether her impulse control came from a desire to avoid embarrassment or from the distraction of frivolous banter with her partner, Mike had a way of keeping her mind away from places it didn't need to be.

Like Frank Grimm.

Like Ray and Ashley.

Like all the ways she kept on fucking things up.

She made a right, headed nowhere in particular. Mal had chased a dead lead on the Rory Day case, a homeless guy people had seen hanging around the woods near the shopping center, but she'd already been through there a few times and hadn't seen any homeless people, let alone a toothless old man with long gray hair and only one eye. So driving and thinking seemed like a better way to while away her afternoon.

Mike had a dentist's appointment or a doctor's appointment, or maybe a dance recital — some bullshit she was pretty sure started with a *D*.

It was neither a coincidence nor something Mal would want to answer questions about, but she happened to be driving awfully close to Heirloom Cove when a call came in from dispatch. Someone had phoned in to report a possible predator.

On the same street as former detective Frank Grimm.

So what if she showed up on the scene before anyone else. She happened to be in the neighborhood. It would be irresponsible to fall short of her stated duty to serve and protect.

She stepped on the gas, glad that her birthday was coming early. Christmas and New Year's, too, by the look of things.

Mal pulled into the cul-de-sac and drove slowly by Grimm's house, not surprised in the least to see him standing by his window, staring out at the street as she passed.

If only she could go slower and take more of it in.

Or better, if she could just cut to the chase and drive directly to Grimm's. Knock on his door and put the ex-detective in cuffs. Let him look into her eyes and know that she knew what he had done. Mal had always seen through his act to the monster inside.

No surprise. The complaint came from 47 Heirloom. Freya Dahl's place.

The girl Jenny's age.

Motherfucking pedophile creep.

Mal was going to make him pay.

Grimm would regret every goddamned second he'd ever spent so much as thinking about hurting a child. But Mal couldn't mention the history.

And can you remind the court again, Detective Black: How did you know he left a box of surveillance equipment in the bucket in front of the plum tree at 47 Heirloom Cove?

But she knew, and that was enough.

Patrick Dahl was out of his house and approaching the Explorer before Mal finished parking. She hopped out of the driver's side and met him halfway down the drive. "Patrick Dahl?"

"That was fast," he said. "Why aren't you in uniform?"

"I'm sorry." Mal took a moment to flash her badge and hand him a card. "I'm Mallory Black, a detective with the Creek County Sheriff's Office. I just happened to be a block away when I heard this call come through dispatch. How can I help you?"

He studied her, apparently decided that Detective Mallory Black was on the level, and nodded. "I'd like to file a report."

"I can help you with that." She took out her notebook. People always started talking faster once they knew you were writing it down. "Your name?"

"Dahl. Patrick Dahl."

"Thank you, Mr. Dahl. Now, I understand that you've spotted a possible predator in the neighborhood."

"I'd say it's more than a *possibility*."

"What can you tell me about this person? Is it someone you've seen before?"

"Of course I've seen him. He lives right over there." He tipped his chin to somewhere behind her, vaguely toward Grimm's place.

"Do you know this individual's name?"

"He's been lurking around my house, and he seems to have taken a particular interest in my daughter."

"Do you know his name?"

"A keen interest, if you know what I mean."

"I understand—"

"She's only fourteen. Can you tell me one thing a man in his fifties needs to be having a conversation with a middle-school girl about?"

"I'd like to look into that for you." Then, third time: "Do you happen to know the name of this potential—"

"I think his name's Frank. We haven't lived in this neighborhood long, and I only just met him. And I keep seeing him sniffing around my house."

"Okay," she prompted, "tell me what you know."

"I saw my daughter walking away from his place yesterday. She seemed awful upset. You know the kind of crying I'm talking about. Deep, like she just broke up with a boyfriend or something. But our girl's not like that. She doesn't date, dresses modest, respects herself."

"Did you ask her what happened?"

"Of course I did. But she wouldn't say anything more. No matter how hard I tried, she just wouldn't open up."

"When did you say this was?"

"Yesterday. Right after school. She got off the bus, then walked right over to his house."

"What happened after your daughter refused to talk?"

"I went over there. I knocked on his door, but nobody answered. I'm positive he was inside, hiding like a coward. But if he wasn't doing anything wrong, then why does he need to hide? From a fourteen-year-old girl's father, knocking on his door, after she came running from his house?"

"That's what I'm here to find out."

"What's it going to take to get this guy to stay away? A restraining order? Do I need to—"

"Slow down, Mr. Dahl. Let me help you. What happened after this Frank guy didn't answer the door? Did you call the sheriff's office? Think about calling us? Talk to your wife?"

"I thought about calling the cops, but it's not like I had anything concrete to say. Same as today. But I'm finally sick of it. I know a pattern when I see it."

"What kind of pattern are you talking about?"

"He was in my front yard when I came home this afternoon. A few minutes after my daughter came home early sick. Seems like an awfully big coincidence."

"What sort of interest has he been showing in her?"

"I know it's a big thing to make an accusation about, so I'm not saying he's sick or anything like that, but he probably is. Definitely not the kind of guy I would ever want around my daughter. You have children?"

She nodded. "Is there anything more specific you can tell me? Did you ask him what he was doing in your front yard?"

"Of course I did. But he just made up something about how he was looking for one of our neighbor's dogs, except I'm not sure that neighbor even has a dog." He shook his head. "It's just one too many things."

"What other things?" She needed a nail to pound Grimm into the coffin.

"He's been walking his neighbor's dog and acting like he's Mr. Nice Guy, but I think he's doing it so he can nose around my place. Around my daughter, more specifically."

"Anything else?"

"We had a neighborhood barbecue last Friday."

"And?"

He looked uncertain. But then, "Let's just say he said a couple of questionable things."

"Look, Mr. Dahl, this Frank guy is probably looking out his window at us right now. If he's a danger, and you want to protect your daughter, I'm going to need you to tell me what he said."

"He was acting weird the whole time and sort of trying to corner me. So I asked him if he was trying to get me alone, making a joke about it, you know? I'm usually not sure how to act in those situations where the person is making me uncomfortable. But he said that, yeah, he had been trying to get me alone. I asked if there was something he wanted to talk about. He said, my daughter."

"Your daughter?" Mal repeated.

Even more brazen than she could have imagined.

He nodded. "Was asking if my daughter was online, had a YouTube or LiveLyfe channel or something like he wanted to see more of her. I don't know. It was real odd."

Mal, still surprised: "And what did you say?"

"I told him that maybe he shouldn't be asking around about fourteen-year-old girls. It's not a good look if you know what I mean."

Frank could no longer control himself. He had to satisfy his evil urges again, but this time she would be there to catch him. To stop him. To make sure that he never harmed another innocent child again.

"Have you had any other interactions with this man? Or observed him talking to your daughter any more than what you've already told me?"

Patrick appeared to think, squinting his eyes and touching his chin. But then he shook his head. "No, nothing more than what I've already said. But the guy just *seems* like a creep."

Yes. He did.

"It's always the quiet ones you've gotta watch out for," he added.

Mal nodded, then feigned ignorance. "Can you direct me to where this Frank guy lives?"

"Gladly," Patrick said.

Chapter Twenty-Three

Frank

FRANK HAD the feeling that the monster had called the sheriff's office the moment he saw Mallory Black swinging onto the cul-de-sac.

She slowed by his house and looked over. For a single cataclysmic second, it felt as though the two of them were staring right into each other's eyes, across the distance, and with two panes of glass between them.

Zero surprise, she pulled up to 47 Heirloom and got out of her Explorer.

Dahl approached her.

He gestured toward Frank's, but Mallory didn't turn back to look.

Not that she needed to; the detective knew why she was here.

Frank kept watching, kept breathing, and kept telling himself that everything would be fine. He couldn't go down for anything because he hadn't done anything wrong. Dahl was the monster.

He kept calm, reminding himself that Mallory wasn't a bad person. She wasn't his enemy. It hurt like acid on a wound to think that anyone could ever think such a terrible thing about him and worse that the accusation would come from a fellow detective. But it wasn't personal. He genuinely liked her and wished that she wasn't so hell-bent on taking him down.

They finally finished talking.

Mallory offered the demon what appeared to be a decisive nod, turned around, got back into her Explorer, then backed out of Dahl's driveway and traded it for Frank's across the way.

He closed the curtain and went to answer the door. No reason to delay the inevitable. She was on the porch when he opened it.

"Detective Black."

"Grimm." His surname described her bearing.

"What brings you to Heirloom Cove? Let me guess … you think I raped and murdered my only child, and now you're here to make sure I don't do the same thing to my new neighbor, who just so happens to be the same age as Jenny was before I killed her. Do I have that about right?"

"You're one bold son of a bitch, Grimm. But yes, that's about right."

"So let's talk."

"You know we will." Mal stared into his unflinching eyes; he might not have blinked since he opened the door. "I'd like you to come with me to the station."

"What do you want to ask me? I'm sure we could handle this here."

"No, Grimm. We can't. And you know how this works. So are—"

"You're right. I do know how this works. I want to have a conversation, but you want this on record. You need to handle this carefully because you're under the impression that other detectives and general personnel in the department are covering for me. You need witnesses for whatever it is you want to discuss. You want to make sure there's someone else in the room so you can't be accused of going off-book or making anything up. Do I have that about right?"

"Like I said, you're one bold son of a bitch."

He sighed and offered her a knowing nod. There was only one way out of this, but Frank didn't mind. Getting away from Heirloom and Dahl was a good thing for what had to happen next.

"Mind if I use the restroom first?"

"Am I going to catch you climbing out the window?"

"A man my age? Are you kidding?"

Frank closed his front door, leaving Mallory on the porch.

But he didn't need to use the bathroom. Instead, he grabbed Freya's original note, just in case, then walked back into the living room, plucked his hat from the rack, then donned it as he opened the door.

He plopped the hat onto his head and said, "After you, detective."

She gave him a look that was pure poison, then turned without a word and walked down his porch and over to the Explorer.

Mallory had already started the engine by the time Frank was sitting in the passenger seat and closing his door.

"I'm surprised you're letting me sit up front."

"You didn't ask," Mallory said.

"And no cuffs." Frank raised his free hands to show her.

"I'm just taking you in for some questions. As you surely know, you're free to leave at any point."

He smiled. "Of course. But you've already decided I'm guilty, right, detective? Damn the evidence."

She didn't respond.

The ground was littered with too many landmines, and Frank had few available moves. He had already admitted to knowing why she was taking him in, yet that seemed like his smartest play. Feigning ignorance wouldn't get him anywhere with Mallory, but nothing would. Frank was more interested in covering his bases for anyone else who might interrogate him.

Surely she could feel his nerves, but Mallory would also for sure misdiagnose them. He was in no way worried about getting into trouble. There was zero evidence, and Freya would never say anything to hurt him—

Unless that is the only way to save herself.

—or violate his side of the story. But Frank had to keep any of his direct links to Freya or her family graveyard silent because there was a better than decent chance that Irene, Freya, or both might change their minds. And if that was the case, then Patrick Dahl would have to die by his hands.

The cabin was silent until she pulled into the sheriff's office parking lot and killed the engine with animus.

"Just taking me in for some questions," Frank said, half to himself and half to unseat her.

"You know where to go." She got out of the car.

So did Frank, following her inside, offering a friendly wave to all the *Hey Frank!*s and *How you doing?*s. But nothing verbal. Agitation wafted off of her already; he saw no reason to make that any worse.

Until he did.

After she'd finally had enough of her colleagues' well-wishing her suspect, she grabbed Frank by the arm and pulled him toward the interview room.

He turned to a deputy, smiling as he passed. "Tell Captain Wilson I said hi!"

"Sure thing, Frank." The deputy nodded. "And it's good to see you!"

Mallory shoved him into the room.

Chapter Twenty-Four

Mal

MAL FINALLY HAD HIM.

If only Grimm would cooperate.

Fifteen minutes so far, and *nothing*.

"You have a much better idea of why you brought me down here than I do," he said. "So why don't you just ask me whatever it is directly, then maybe we don't have to waste so much of one another's time?"

"You know how this works. I won't pretend that I'll ever be on your side, but there are plenty of people around here who will swing for you, no matter what. You also know that the more you cooperate, and the earlier you do so, the easier you'll make it for those most inclined to help you."

"What is it, *exactly*, that you're asking me, Detective Black?"

But Grimm was really asking the camera in the corner of the room.

The door swung open. Captain Wilson barged in and

marched over to the interview table. "You want to tell me what the hell's going on here?"

Grimm didn't look over, holding his stare on Mal instead. He wasn't smiling, but she could practically smell his smug satisfaction.

"We got a complaint, sir," she said.

"Keep talking."

"One of his neighbors called in a complaint about a possible predator on the street, and that potential predator happened to be Grimm. I thought it would be best to bring him in for some questions."

"You did, did you?" He looked from Mal to Grimm and back. "Did you also just happen to be a few blocks from his street when the call came in?"

"It's all a misunderstanding," Grimm said.

Like hell it was.

"You had your turn," Wilson said to Mal before turning to his buddy. "What happened?"

Grimm finally broke his gaze and turned to Wilson. "A guy who lives down the street, name of Patrick Dahl, is trying to cause a problem for me. But given our history, Detective Black has chosen to focus on my possibly being up to something I shouldn't be — I'm assuming that something has to do with his fourteen-year-old daughter."

"Are you really going to listen to this?" Mal asked.

But of course, he was.

Wilson ignored her and kept talking to Grimm. "Why would this Dahl guy want to do that?"

"No idea," he lied, no doubt about it. "I think he knows I'm an ex-detective, and I think he sees me as a threat to either discovering or stopping whatever he might be doing behind closed doors."

"You've gotta be kidding me!" Mal slapped the table, shaking her head.

"*Detective*." Then back to Grimm. "What is it you think he's doing?"

"Not sure." A performative shake of his head. "Could be something with the mom, or maybe the daughter. The guy has given me some bad vibes. I let him know my feelings at the neighborhood picnic, and now I think this is him getting back at me, maybe trying to ruin my credibility as a pre-emptive strike."

The captain nodded, seeming to consider. He may not like the reality, but Grimm's little anecdote was gossamer-thin.

"Wait here," he said to his old friend before turning to the room's only subordinate. "Black, you come with me."

Grimm kept smiling, watching her stand and follow Wilson out of the room.

Mal couldn't wait to take the fucker down.

She wondered where they were going, but not enough to give Wilson the satisfaction of her asking. She had a decent idea and would know soon enough.

No surprise, Wilson stopped in front of Sheriff Bell's office.

He knocked, she told him to come in, then he opened the door and said, "She's all yours."

"Sheriff Bell." Mal nodded in greeting and made her way to the chair as the door closed behind her.

Wilson had just made a big mistake. Mal had held off on going to Bell thus far, but it had always been her planned first stop once she found hard evidence. Gloria was one of the good guys, an enemy to former Sheriff Barry and the old boys' network, including both Barry and his buddy, Grimm.

"Mallory." Full stop. Gloria just looked at her.

Mal wasn't sure what to say and took a moment to do

nothing more than inhale and exhale while waiting. Then, "I was only trying to do my job."

Gentle but firm: "And would you define your job as harassing Frank Grimm?"

"I wasn't *harassing* him. I was responding to a call and—"

"Are you really going to sit at my desk and try to convince me that you haven't been up that man's ass for the last year? Or that you weren't close enough to his house when that call came in to make it look like you were — and why the hell are you even answering a call like that? You work Special Crimes."

"Yeah, I was in the area, following a lead on the Day case, and heard the call come in, and I took it. I'm trying to be proactive."

"Do I need to remind you of what your job actually is?"

"What does that mean?" Mal asked.

"It means a one-week suspension, effective immediately."

"You can't do that."

"Not to sound like a cliché, Mallory, but I just did."

"This isn't right." She shook her head. "You really expect me not to question Grimm because he used to be a cop?"

"Of course not. But you could have handled this situation at his house without the embarrassment of dragging a decorated deputy into the station like a common criminal."

"I brought him in for a conversation! It's not like he was in cuffs."

"You shouldn't have brought him in at all."

"I can't *believe* you're taking his side!"

"I'm not taking anyone's side — I'm doing my job."

"But Grimm was one of Barry's guys. He—"

"No, Mallory. He wasn't. Frank was one of the few old-school detectives who always treated me with respect, from the moment I got here until well after I was running against the former sheriff. Plus, he was supportive of me during the transition, telling the guys that *weren't* so kind to me to back the hell off a bit."

"I didn't know that."

"Clearly. Nor did you know that Frank helped me out whenever he could behind the scenes. He stuck up for me publicly a few times but always knew his true value was in listening. Even more relevant to this conversation are the times he went to bat for *you*, Mal. He's a good man. You're wrong about him. I hope you use this time off to think about some things."

She already was.

Something the size of a Chevy was making itself at home on her chest.

Mal mumbled an apology and a thank you, she wasn't even sure of the order, then pushed her chair back from the sheriff's desk and fled her office as fast as she could without running.

Suddenly, everything hurt.

The way everyone was staring at her as she walked through the department, heading outside for refuge in her Explorer.

She got inside, gripped the wheel, and pressed her ass into the seat.

Then she sighed, and she thought, and she doubted herself.

For the first time, Mal wondered if maybe she really did have it all wrong.

Could Frank Grimm be the good guy that everyone thought he was?

If so, then she could never trust her own gut again. Not after it had proven itself so thoroughly wrong.

And a fucking weeklong suspension on top of it all.

She started the engine, shuddering at the thought of having to tell Ray.

* * *

Mal was still counting the ways to avoid telling her husband what happened.

She could just walk over to the stove where he was cooking dinner, tap him on the shoulder, and confess.

Hey honey, just so you know, I got a one-week suspension today. It was for following up on the Grimm case again. Right, against orders. And yep, I did take him in for what amounted to a public interrogation.

It was more distracting, and therefore more temporarily constructive, to pretend that the problem didn't exist — only for now, just for a little while — and think about ways to make it feel like her husband wasn't as mad at her as he actually was. She could suggest they all play a game or maybe take him into the bedroom and let him do whatever he wanted.

Except that lately, he didn't want to do anything.

Maybe he was cheating on her?

And maybe that would be a good thing, something to take the focus off of her for a while.

"Mommy. Look." Ashley pointed at her paper. "I still don't understand."

She glanced down at Ashley's homework, pretending she wasn't distracted. "You're supposed to carry the two."

Ashley studied her problem.

Mal looked over at Ray, wishing she could avoid telling him. Yes, she was embarrassed about what happened, but she mostly didn't want him to know because doing so might impede her privacy. And it wasn't like she could pretend to go to work and somehow keep him from finding out. They crossed paths too often, him showing up at scenes she was working. If he saw Mike alone, he'd know something was up.

But the next week was what mattered most.

A forced vacation seemed like the perfect time to follow up on every possible lead. Grimm would think he had the upper hand after getting her suspended. He might lay low for a while, but he could also make his move.

Especially if he was trying to blame whatever he was doing on his neighbor. And Grimm's actions in the interview room with Wilson made it clear that he was. She needed a conversation with Freya and Irene. Maybe—

"MOMMY!"

Mal looked over.

So did Ray.

Ashley was jabbing her finger at the paper again. "Carrying the two still didn't work."

"Um …" Mal blinked at the page, trying to focus on simple math that shouldn't be giving her a problem.

"You're not doing a good job helping me," Ashley said.

Wow. Blunt. "I'm—"

"I want Daddy to help."

"Daddy's cooking dinner right now."

His back was to them, but still, Mal felt like she could hear what he was thinking. And fuck him for that.

"Just give me a second, okay, sweetie?" She put her hand over Ashley's and gave her daughter a smile.

Right as her phone loudly buzzed on the table.

She grabbed it without thinking but honestly would have anyway.

A text from Mike.

Hey. You wanna tell me what the hell happened today?

Mal did her best to explain the situation in a quickly tapped-out reply, without coming across as defensive or casting any blame, while using the fewest possible words, feeling both the heat from Ashley's stare and Ray's silent judgment in the kitchen as he cooked.

"That was Uncle Mike," Mal explained, dropping her phone back on the counter and returning her attention to Ashley's problem, feeling like she had turned into such an under-performer in every part of her life that she was now getting stumped by elementary school arithmetic.

Mal used to be at least decent at everything and occasionally felt like the best. Now it seemed like everything was a struggle.

She was failing to be the wife Ray deserved and kept reminding her she wasn't. She was failing to be the mother she always imagined herself to be, and that Mal longed for Ashley to see her as. And she was failing to avenge Jenny — *or worse*, protect Freya from the same thing.

"Do you almost have it, Mommy?"

"Almost." This was ridiculous.

"Maybe finish after dinner." Ray had finished plating their meal while Mal was staring down at her unsolvable problem. He set the first of the serving dishes down on the table as her phone buzzed with Mike's response.

They both looked at the message in unison.

Why would you do that, Mal? You should have called me. Now you're on everybody's shit list, and I'm here having to defend you?

"Why are you on everyone's list?" Ray asked. "And why is Mike having to defend you?"

"We can talk about it after dinner," Mal told him, reaching for her phone.

"Or now," he said.

"What's happening?"

"Nothing, honey." Mal gave Ashley a half-smile and texted back.

So then, defend me.

"Mal. I'm right here."

She looked up at him, but then it buzzed again, and her eyes reflexively jumped to the screen. His next text was devastating.

That's kind of hard to do right now.

"Mal." Ray was decisive.

She looked up from the carpet bomb of a message and saw both her husband and her daughter waiting with expectant eyes.

"What happened?"

Might as well be honest with her husband and get this over with. "I was suspended today."

"For what, and for how long?"

She couldn't stand the way he was glaring at her. "A week, for bringing Grimm in for questioning."

Ray shook his head, clearly too disappointed in her to offer a verbal response. Still staring at Mal like a foe.

"Does this mean Mommy will be home for a week?" Ashley asked, sounding hopeful.

"It looks that way." Ray finally turned away.

And Ashley yelled, "YAY!"

Chapter Twenty-Five

Frank

FRANK HAD JUST FINISHED MAKING his latest batch of chicken marsala when he heard a knock on his back door and knew who it was immediately.

Not just because the knock came from the kitchen, but because the sound was small yet determined. A lot like Freya herself. He could hear her fear in that knock, but also her resolve.

He wiped his hands, then rushed to the door.

Freya slipped under his arm as he opened it and was in the kitchen before he could say anything.

"Where's your father?"

"He and my mom went out to dinner."

"How do you know he's not setting you up right now? Waiting for you to come over here?"

"I don't," Freya admitted with a shake of her head. "But it's their anniversary, and that's one of the few times where he sort of pretends to be nice to her."

Frank was already out of the kitchen and on his way to the front window.

Freya trailed behind him. "I told you, they went to dinner. I'm sure he thinks I'm too scared to do anything. Mom begged me not to, and he knows I listen to her even if I hate him."

"She begged you not to in front of him, or when it was just the two of you?"

"Both."

"So she's out?"

She shook her head, looking haunted and scared. "She's too afraid to do anything."

"Are you?"

"I might be."

"You're here. That's a start."

"I want to …"

"*But …*" he prompted.

"But he was so mad … I really think he could kill me."

"I promise I won't let that happen."

"You can't promise me that." Her face was brave, but she lost a tear anyway.

"*I promise you.*"

"He kept wanting to know why I came over here, and I told him it was because you were good at math, that I met you a couple of weeks ago while you were walking your dog. You offered to help me, so I was asking if you still meant it after a bad day in algebra. He didn't believe me and kept getting madder and madder until Mom finally talked him into leaving for their dinner and 'dealing with me later.' She never would have been able to do that if it wasn't their anniversary. Now I'm really scared about what's going to happen tonight when he gets home." She swallowed hard. "At bedtime."

"I understand why you're scared. But you're safe now. Are you okay to keep going?"

She nodded.

"What else are you worried about?"

"I'm afraid that no one will believe me."

"Of course, they'll believe you."

"You don't know him."

"I've known men like your father before. I've put men like him in prison before."

"He's too careful."

"Everyone makes mistakes."

"He says, 'Life isn't perfect, but you better be.' And he says it all the time."

"You're not alone, Freya. I'm sorry your father's a monster and your mother's too scared to protect you. But I will. Do you believe me?"

She swallowed and nodded, but the knot in her throat looked heavy.

"Your father's too careful … let's stay with that," Frank said, thinking. "What if he doesn't keep the videos at all?"

"You mean on a hard drive at home? He just uploads them somewhere, then deletes the originals."

"How often does he replace his computer?"

"I'm not sure because his laptop is covered, but I think there are new ones all the time. I know he found something secondhand off one of those local sites at least a couple of times. The first time I knew because we were out together, and he made me wait in the car while he handed money to some guy in the parking lot of a Thai Charcoal Pit. He put a bag in the trunk, and I knew not to say anything about it one way or the other, but when I asked Mom later, she said he was probably buying a computer. So the second time, I just assumed."

Frank nodded. "He doesn't trust the erasure and wants

to reduce the risk of forensics picking anything up. Buying the computers secondhand gives him plausible deniability, and paying cash helps him to eliminate much of his trail."

"I don't think he would keep anything in the house that could get him into trouble."

"Are you sure you won't consider calling this in right now and just—"

"No, Mr. Grimm. And if you're going to help me, then you have to stop asking me. Especially when my mom is still with him. I told you, he'll kill her."

Whether he really would or not, Freya believed it.

"Well, then I see two ways we can attack this simultaneously. I have someone looking into sites to see if he can find anything with you or your father. But if you let me take your picture, I can use that as a lead. It only needs to be your face, and I promise I'll only give it to one person who can help us find—"

"Okay. What's the second way?"

"We need to put surveillance equipment in your room. Right now is a good time since your parents are out, and they haven't been gone all that long."

"What kind of equipment?"

"Like the first stuff I tried to leave for you. A small spy cam we can stick inside a stuffed animal."

She shook her head. "There aren't any stuffed animals in that room, and I'm never allowed to take anything in with me."

"There will be an air vent or a smoke detector or something. Are you okay with that, Freya?"

She thought about it. Looked an awful lot like she wanted to say yes. But spent a half minute chewing her bottom lip to something that looked like sausage spilling from its casing before she straightened her shoulders and asked, "How do I know *you* won't be watching me?"

He held her gaze and shook his head. "I'll never see a thing. It'll all be uploaded to the cloud. You can make up your own account and keep the password a secret. I promise the only thing that footage will ever be used for is nailing your father."

Freya nodded, still scared but now willing, then waited for Frank to gather the equipment and meet her at the back door.

Ten minutes later, Frank was standing on a ladder Freya had pulled from the garage after leaving a marker to show her *exactly* where it was prior to its removal. He was unscrewing the vent, ready to place his miniature camera in the duct.

"What happened to Jenny?" Freya asked, breaking the silence.

"I need to focus on this right now."

"We won't be able to talk about it later."

"You can ask me whatever you want once your father's in jail."

"Or he'll kill me and my mom, and I will never talk to you again."

He stopped and turned to Freya. "Don't say that."

"I read they found her a day or two after she went missing. Do you think you know what happened to her?"

"Something unthinkable," he finally said.

"But you think about it all the time. Don't you, Mr. Grimm?"

Frank finished placing the camera. He slowly screwed the vent back into place. Then he climbed off of the ladder, collapsed it in his arms, and checked the camera's placement on his phone to make sure it captured her bed. He then turned to Freya.

"I barely think about anything else."

They stared at each other.

Until she broke the silence again.

"I'm sorry someone took her away from you. I wish you could kill him."

He might as well have had an arrow sticking out his neck. For a long moment, breathing was only something he used to do. Then words followed thoughts that thus far he'd kept to himself.

"I keep telling myself that the darker the tunnel, the brighter the light on the opposite side. But I'm just not seeing it." He was crying quiet tears, same as she was. "Instead, I've learned that grief doesn't feel all that different from fear. Sometimes it seems like I might actually bleed from the agony."

He drew a breath, then dove back in. "They say that anger doesn't solve anything, but I keep trying to outmaneuver common sense because getting angry keeps me feeling sane. I want to break things. To break people. Because doing so will make me whole."

He paused but quickly realized that, like his tears, his words weren't quite finished.

"Bad as the grief and the fear and the anger are, the guilt might be worst of all. Even though it's constantly eating at me, it's still always hungry."

Frank stopped again. For a while this time. They should go, but the current between them was insistent that neither of them leave.

"How do you go on?" she asked.

"I don't really … I think about Jenny all the time. I'm thinking about her and Sarah both right now. I'm mostly a ghost, even standing here, talking to you."

"What happened to your wife?"

"She was too heartbroken after losing Jenny, then losing me right after that."

"Losing you?"

He shook his head. "I wasn't the same after we lost Jenny. Neither of us was."

Frank looked down at Freya, feeling more than he could process. They needed to go, and yet the emotions were flooding him. This was the cosmic edge of redemption. A few of his deepest truths were out, like poison gone from his body.

"I'll never forgive myself for failing to save her. I have nightmares of what it must have been like for Jenny in those last few hours. I picture her bleeding and begging the monster who stole her to stop. But I'm always locked in a big metal box, the walls thick enough to imprison me but thin enough that I can hear her screaming."

Freya put a hand on his arm, slow and gentle, then followed that comfort with another. "When he's hurting me … I go to another place in my mind … and when I go there, it doesn't hurt so much. I bet Jenny figured out how to go there, too."

Frank nodded because nothing else felt quite right, then replaced the ladder just so.

She was standing too close in the garage, so he took a step back from her before reaching into his pocket. Then he handed her the flip phone.

"I don't have to tell you to hide that."

"You just did." She smiled.

"And keep the ringer off."

He smiled back, took a blink to appreciate the moment of warmth, then continued. "If anything happens, if anything goes bad, my number is in there. It can't be traced to me, but I'll get the call. Better yet, call 9-1-1. Whatever keeps you safe."

"Thank you."

Another nod, then Frank made to leave.

"Mr. Grimm?"

He turned back around, asking *What?* with his eyes.

"Have you found anything on this street?"

"No." He shook his head. "I don't think anyone living on Heirloom did it."

"So why do you keep breaking in to people's houses?"

He thought, then told the truth as he knew it. "I look at other people's photos, and they feel like family to me. Or at least, it feels like I'm touching that sense of family I no longer have and never will again." Frank shook his head, looking at the floor, ashamed. "I know it's wrong, but it's all I have."

Then Freya surprised him.

She had been looking up at Frank through his monologue; now, she fell against his chest and wrapped her arms around his body.

He stood there for a moment, paralyzed, unsure of what to do.

Then he hugged her.

"I should go," he said.

"I know." Then, "Thank you."

He left without another word, hoping there weren't any secret cameras watching him now. He hadn't thought to check tonight.

If there were cameras, then they had caught him crying.

Chapter Twenty-Six

Mal

FUCK DID HER STOMACH HURT.

The real Coney Island was nearly a thousand miles north of them. This bullshit carnival covered a few acres of parking lot, crowded with rickety rides and garbage food, all of it costing an obnoxious number of tickets, collected by shady carnies with too much metal shit in their faces and garish sleeves of tattoos. Mal hugged Ashely tighter whenever they were near one, even glanced at her husband a couple of times.

But Ray never glanced back.

And now her stomach was killing her.

She wanted to blame it all on that trashy food and maybe Ashley for encouraging (begging) her to eat it. Funnel cake *and* corn dogs. No wonder it felt like she had a bowling ball sitting in a basin of acid.

Except Mal knew that wasn't really where the ache was coming from.

"This is SO FUN, Mommy!" Ashley squeezed her hand again.

It should have made her feel better, but instead, it made Mal feel even worse.

"I'm so glad we're getting to spend this time together." She wondered if Ashley would believe her. Ray already knew she was a liar.

Ashley squeezed her mommy's hand even tighter.

Mal *should* be glad that they were getting to spend this time together. Mike could take care of the Rory Day case and all the other tiny nightmares that darkened her daily life. She could forget about her suspicions of Grimm for a week and tend to her family. Away from the toxic routines that had commandeered her life, she could finally reconnect with Ray and make everything like it used to be. Like she kept promising him that she would.

Instead, Mal walked the carnival feeling sick to her stomach for too many reasons. No, a giant licorice rope wasn't the smartest way to follow her earlier feedbag of funnel cake and corndogs (she'd had two). Nor was the churro. Ashley shared everything, meaning she had at least a bit of whatever Mal had if she didn't order whatever it was for herself. That was Ashley's main reason for encouraging Mommy to shovel all of that garbage down, despite Ray repeatedly warning her against it. So yes, Mal's terrible food choices were culprit number one.

But she was also sick of the way Ray kept staring straight ahead, as if allergic to the sight of her.

Nauseous from her detective's intuition insisting that something big was going down with Grimm, and she wasn't there to catch the man in his most heinous of acts or prevent him from carrying them out.

And downright bilious with the thought that he would

get away this time like last time, then be free to do it yet again.

"What ride do you want to go on next?" Ashley let go of her hand so she could skip ahead of her parents.

"I don't think I want to go on any rides right now," Mal admitted hand to her stomach.

"Not even the carousel?"

She shook her head and pressed on her tummy again. "Nothing that moves."

"Can I go on the carousel?"

"Of course, you can go on the carousel," Mal and Ray answered in tandem.

It sounded like music. She thought he might look at her.

He didn't.

"How many tickets is the carousel?" Ashley asked.

Mal handed her the entire supply. "Here you go, Ash. Our fun is now in your custody."

"What if I lose them?" Ashley looked down at all the tickets in her hand with suspicion.

"You won't," Mal said.

They walked to the carousel, then Ashley said goodbye and scampered off.

Finally alone, and Ray was still giving her the silent treatment.

"Are you going to be like this all day?" Mal finally asked.

He turned to her, his surprise seeming genuine. "Are you kidding me right now?"

She wasn't sure what to say.

So he took another turn. "You're barely here with us."

"It wasn't my intention to start an argument."

"This isn't an argument," Ray said. "But step one is

acknowledgment, and you can't even admit that you're not being present."

"That's because it isn't true. Or fair. I'm trying my hardest, and that's why we're here. But you couldn't be any colder to me right now."

"We're here because you got suspended from your job and were therefore finally dry of excuses. We're here because you *have* to spend time with your family. But the fact that it's an obligation is obvious by the way you're walking the carnival like a ghost."

"You don't think that's a bit dramatic? *I'm walking the carnival like a ghost.* Really?"

"You know what I mean, Mal. No matter your company or the scenery, you don't know how to disengage from your job and just be in the moment with your family."

"That's not true. Or fair."

"You say that a lot, Mal. But for a detective, you're sure comfortable bringing an embarrassing lack of evidence to the argument."

"Can't you just acknowledge that I'm trying?"

"Absolutely." Even colder than before. "The second I see it."

"That's not fair."

"Is it true?" Ray asked, seeming to look through her.

She didn't know he was this mad, hadn't realized things were this far gone.

"I'm sorry." She looked at him pleadingly. "Do you believe that?"

"Of course, I believe that you're sorry. But only in your way. Life keeps giving you chances, over and over, yet no matter what happens, I see you making the same mistake."

"And what mistake is that?" Mal asked.

"Not having fun with your daughter while you still can."

A sudden slap she hadn't expected. "Is that a threat? Are you planning on leaving and taking her with you?" She couldn't believe he had gone there.

Ray looked at her, his sorrow and disappointment both deepening but now garnished with surprise. "You really want to go there?"

Mal looked over at Ashley and saw her in front of the line, handing her tickets to a magenta-haired carnie. She looked back at Ray. "You're the one who *just* brought it up."

"No, Mal. I said, 'having fun with your daughter while you still can.' Because she's *growing up, but* I do appreciate you showing me exactly where *your* mind is at."

"I didn't mean that."

"I'm talking. It's my turn."

"Okay, Ray. I'm sorry." Another word, and she might vomit anyway.

"It's bad enough that you even circled the wagon of divorce, but I resent you implying that I would try and take Ashley away from you *the very first time you brought it up.* The things you've been doing and saying lately are not good for our marriage."

"I hear you—"

"I'm not done." He waited for her eyes and body language to comply. Once her body relaxed, he continued. "I've gotta ask you, Mal, and right now before Ashley comes back and starts skipping like a happy little girl between us, with no idea that Mommy might be thinking about moving on. I need you to be brutally honest with me right now: *Is this what you want?*"

"Of course not." It was hard not to cry and harder not

to vomit. "I love you and Ashley more than anything. I'm sorry for not really being here. I …"

"What's going on with you lately, Mal?"

"I've been working this case." She shook her head, not wanting to talk about it but knowing she'd given him no other choice. "Rory Day."

She stopped. She needed a moment to breathe. Didn't want to barf and couldn't afford to cry. Ashley's ride would be over soon.

"Are you okay?" Ray asked.

"I haven't been able to talk to you about what's going on because it's Grimm. I'm sure he's about to act again, but no one even believes me about the first time. Including you." The first tear, despite her efforts. "I'm terrified that I won't be able to stop him before he kills—"

Ray pulled her into a hug.

A few more tears, quiet and hot on her face.

He put his hand against the back of her head, then whispered, "This is the first time you've been emotionally honest with me in months. And exactly what I've been waiting for. I'm glad you're finally not trying to protect me from what you're going through. Nothing hurts more than you barging forward and shutting me out because you think you know best."

He pulled away, looked her in the eye, and finished. "We need to talk like this more often."

"I know." She nodded.

"I'm sorry. I swear I'm not trying to cut you off when we're having a moment, but you need a minute to gather yourself, and Ashley's ride just ended." He nodded toward the carousel. "So I'm going to cut her off at the pass and take her to get you some ginger ale."

She nodded, grateful.

"I'll be back." Then he dropped an unexpected bomb

before leaving. "I've been thinking a lot about what would be best for us. Couples therapy, Mal. Think about it."

He turned and started walking toward the carousel.

Mal went to a nearby bench and sat, thinking while waiting for her family's return.

The bone-crunching rattle of the rollercoaster coming from somewhere behind her sounded a lot like she felt. She never should have said anything. The embrace was nice, but a narcotic and nothing more. Certainly not worth its apparent tax. Couples therapy was the last thing she wanted. She'd rather go skinny dipping in snot.

She loved her husband more than anything in this world other than Ashley, including her job, despite what he thought. But Ray didn't know how to understand her. He had never stood over the corpse of an innocent life, snuffed out not too long ago, feeling the angry ticking of a clock that would never stop ticking, where every second lost was another the killer spent putting time and distance between him and his atrocity. He couldn't understand the burden of making sure killers were brought to justice. It was a lot on her shoulders, and too often, he added weight to the load.

Mal felt like her world was spinning out of control, and she needed everything to slow the hell down. Then she felt that spinning in her gut.

Mal leaped up from her seat and lurched three steps toward the nearest garbage can.

She gripped it by the edges and lost a gallon of liquid, gushing from her mouth like a mop bucket kicked to the floor.

She wiped her mouth and sat back on the bench.

A few people moved away from her. Fuck every one of them.

She could really go for that ginger ale.

And just as she thought it, Ray was standing in front of

her with Ashley standing beside him. He held out a cold can of Canada Dry.

"Ready?" Ray gave her an honest smile.

No, but she was grateful.

"Ready." She stood from the bench and turned to Ashley. "What do you want to do next?"

Chapter Twenty-Seven

Frank

Two DAYS and still no word from Freya.

Frank was tired of going out of his mind. He thought things could never get worse after Jenny, then truly believed it after what happened with Sarah. But it was like what he'd always heard about couples expecting their second child, wondering how they could ever love another baby as much as they had loved that first one. Before their hearts opened for more.

Pain was the same. He still had all the agony inside him from trauma with Jenny and Sarah, but now the ache of not knowing if he would lose Freya was killing him.

Frank had no idea if she recorded her father yet. Or if Dahl caught her trying. Perhaps Irene had committed to the course and was finally helping Freya.

Or *anything*.

He had the same small assembly of thoughts, stuck inside a tiny room with no way to release them.

Until he got a text on his burner from Irene. *Can we meet?*

His heart already racing: *Of course. When and where?*

Inside Scoop on Carson and Walnut?

I know it. Of course, he knew it. *When?*

I can be there in thirty minutes.

Then he would go now. *See you then. Anything I should know?*

Just want to talk next steps. Still scared.

You don't need to be, Frank reassured her. *See you soon.*

He had no idea if Freya told her about the cameras, but it was an excellent sign that she wanted to talk. Finally, something to move on.

He grabbed his hat and the fob and was behind the wheel of his Avalanche in less than a minute. The Inside Scoop wasn't the closest place to get ice cream at seven minutes away, but it was the best. It would hurt to go there, but he didn't dare suggest anything else. Whatever made Irene feel safest.

Whatever helped Frank get both her and Freya out of this.

He swung into the parking lot a little too fast.

He needed to calm himself.

So he killed the engine and listened to five minutes of Mozart before getting out and heading inside, hoping his old usual booth was available.

It was; the place was almost empty. Two families eating ice cream, and one of them looked like the outing was closer to coercion.

Frank ordered a single scoop of Mexican Vanilla and sat in a booth that kissed his memory, similar to the way the ice cream was melting on his tongue, or the marsala sat in his mouth every night.

He heard the tinkling bell and looked toward the door,

half-expecting to see Irene more than a quarter-hour early. But it was a mom and her young teenage daughter, making everything both better and worse.

Frank had probably been to the Inside Scoop a quarter of the times that Jenny and Sarah had gone together. They used to go there for girl time, when Dad was working late, or when Sarah wanted to have a talk with Jenny, or the few times it had been the other way around.

Jenny had wanted to order one of the Scoop's Espresso Nirvana drinks ever since she was six, so for the next eight years, he and Sarah had to tell Jenny no every time she asked. Too much sugar and too much caffeine.

"When can I have one?" Jenny always wanted to know.

Her parents agreed on fourteen and stuck to their guns until she finally stopped asking around her eighth birthday. It had been an arbitrary number, designed for their daughter to forget. But when they went to cash in her birthday certificate the Inside Scoop sent every year in the mail, two weeks after she turned fourteen, Jenny ordered an Espresso Nirvana without even asking.

As if he needed caramel drizzle, whipped cream, or toffee crumbs atop his agony, that was the exact drink the mom and daughter were ordering now.

He wondered if that girl really liked the drink or if it just made her feel grownup. Frank didn't think that Jenny really enjoyed her Espresso Nirvana all that much, at least not in the way she probably anticipated. He was so glad she got to try it before ... what happened. But she probably would have stopped ordering it once the novelty wore off.

It hurt like nothing else in the world to face the truth that he would never know who his baby girl would have grown up to be. He constantly wondered what Jenny would be like now if she were still alive.

Would she have made friends with Freya? Would she be fighting with Sarah about clothes or makeup, or music? Would she have a boyfriend, or like anyone? Or maybe she would have been more into girls. Would she still have thought unicorns were better than any other imaginary creature, or would dragons finally edge them out after a decade spent in second place?

Maybe he should order an Espresso Nirvana for himself. Especially now that his Mexican Vanilla was gone. He was still waiting, after all.

Frank needed something sweet to cut the frothing rage he felt from a man like Dahl simply existing. He couldn't understand how someone could bring a strong, clever girl like Freya into this world only to destroy her.

He was a predator Frank might have to chum. He wasn't the man who murdered Jenny, but he'd become his next best thing. Maybe Dahl would end up in jail, or maybe Frank would bury him alive a hundred miles away from the people he ruined.

And *maybe* that would make Frank whole.

Or at least help him to put some of his broken pieces together.

He could never find the right words to make Sarah understand, and that had always felt like a failure. She kept wanting him to quit, insisting that he did, unable to see why he couldn't stop searching for the killer. She thought that doing so was moving on, but he saw that surrender as the opposite.

But Frank had been wrong about his lack of spending time with her. That's what Sarah wanted more than anything, and he knew that. The problem was that at the time, he saw it as exactly that — a *want* instead of the *need* it was. Sarah was hurting just as much as he was, but they ached so differently that it became hard for them to suffer in tandem.

After Kirby came out of nowhere to ruin their already rocky marriage, she would have done anything to prove him wrong. She needed to know that Frank Grimm was still the man she married.

But the things that Sarah wanted to do could never bring him peace. And she could never see that they only made him hurt worse.

A memorial service with her broken body on display, waxy and patched with cosmetics to make-believe that her passing from this world hadn't left her looking like a block of cheese against a grater.

The constant visits to her grave — sure, he made those little excursions every now and then himself these days because sometimes that was the only way to hold himself together. But, back then, he wasn't ready.

Same for the constant talk about setting up a scholarship in their daughter's name. It all felt so futile. Exercises in self-flagellation.

None of it could ever bring Jenny back, no matter what, and every activity served as more salt on a freshly opened wound. There was only one way Frank would ever get two solid nights of sleep in a row again, without having to stay up three in a row just to earn it. And that was to find Jenny's killer and punish the man who took their little girl's life.

No matter how much she protested, Frank always secretly believed Sarah would have ultimately changed her mind. She didn't like seeing her husband as a hunter, but if he had actually managed to find the man who took their Jenny away, then put him in the ground where he belonged, surely she would have felt peace in knowing that monster was gone from the earth.

Or maybe that would have made Sarah see him as a different kind of monster.

Maybe she would have turned him in. Maybe he never would have had a chance at true redemption because he would have ended up in jail after thinking he'd found it.

He looked at his watch, second-guessing his decision to abstain from an Espresso Nirvana or another scoop of ice cream. Thirty minutes since his last text from Irene, exactly.

The bell tinkled about the door.

Frank looked over, expecting to see her.

But he saw the Demon of Heirloom instead.

Chapter Twenty-Eight

Frank

DAHL SAT in the booth across from him.

They stared for a long time, neither man speaking.

Finally, Frank glanced toward the menu and back. "I've heard the Espresso Nirvana is good." Then down at his empty cup. "And you can never go wrong with the Mexican Vanilla."

"I don't eat dairy."

"What does a wolf eat?" Frank leaned back, setting the stage for a reach into his pocket. "Whatever it can find?"

"I'd say a wolf eats Mexican Vanilla." Dahl pulled something out of his jacket pocket and dropped it on the table between them, keeping both of Frank's hands in sight.

Though he didn't need to pick up the note to know what it was.

"Is that a question?" Frank asked.

"Ask the right one, and things can change."

"What are you looking to change?"

"Maybe *change* is the wrong word," said Dahl, seeming to root himself in the seat. "Maybe the better way to say it is that the right question can lead to the proper elimination."

Another glance at the menu. "Sure you don't want something? Maybe we could share a milkshake."

Two grown men sitting in an ice cream parlor across from one another. Not quite glaring, but still staring *into* as much as *at* one another. One a monster for sure, though both might be. A pair of gunslingers standing equidistant from the batwing doors of the boomtown's rowdiest saloon.

Every breath felt like a terrible omen of revelations to come.

"You think this is a joke?" Dahl asked.

"Quite the opposite."

"Why aren't you leaving my family alone?" He snatched the note and waved it in front of Frank's face. "Care to explain why you gave your number to my wife?"

"We're neighbors. What if she needed to borrow sugar or something?"

"Oh yeah?" Dahl looked glad for that last answer. "What if she needs a jumpstart? Do you have a different number for that?" He shook the paper again, then dropped it on the table, leaned back in his seat, and clarified. "Because *that* isn't your real number."

"And how do you know what my real number is?" Frank didn't care or need to know; he just wanted the monster to keep talking.

"You think that's hard to find out?"

"Not at all." Frank shrugged as he slipped a hand into his pocket. "Thirty bucks or so oughta do it. I'm just wondering why you'd want to. Seems like a waste; that's like two months of Netflix." He paused to look thoughtful.

"Are the women in your house allowed to watch Netflix? Or just the training videos on following orders?"

"I can't decide if your obsession with my family is more sick or sad," Dahl said.

"Sad. For sure. What you're doing is sick."

"My wife was saying something about that." He nodded knowingly, piercing Frank with his gaze.

His hand fell from his pocket. Foiled again or just to be safe, it didn't matter. He needed to be careful. "What was she saying?"

"She says you think I've been abusing my daughter."

Frank said, "She told you wrong. I think you're abusing them both."

Dahl stopped nodding. "And what gives you that idea?"

No limit to the number of ways Frank could answer that. From beatings to verbal and psychological abuse to outright rape, this man was a monster in every way. Frank no longer had a doubt — not that he'd ever had much — about anything Freya had said.

He wished he'd activated the recording app on his phone ahead of time. But he would never have recorded Irene without her permission, and so he hadn't prepared. Such audio wouldn't be admissible in court, anyway.

He couldn't record now without his enemy noticing, and getting too direct with Dahl wouldn't get Frank what he wanted. Frank couldn't betray Freya's ratting her father out, so to answer Dahl's query, Frank leaned across the table, close enough to kiss the devil, then looked his enemy square in the eyes and told him the truth.

"Because I know a monster when I see one."

Frank hadn't planned to say what he just had, so he didn't know what to expect next, but still, the brute surprised him by laughing.

"I'm going to order an Espresso Nirvana while you finish your chuckles. Should I make it two?"

"Sure." The laughing stopped. "Why don't you do that?"

No one in line, so Frank went straight to the counter and ordered.

His back was to Dahl, so he couldn't be obvious.

He paid for his milkshakes, grateful that he had cash, then pocketed his wallet and stuffed the change in his pocket. It was the first time he'd ever been to Inside Scoop and not dropped it all in the tip jar, but he needed a moment to swipe his thumb across the glass in the pre-programmed pattern that activated his recorder. He couldn't use it in court, but he could use it to convince the sheriff's office of what was going on in the Dahl house.

"Drink it slow, or you'll get a head rush." Frank set the two Espresso Nirvanas on the table.

"Your concern for me is surprising." Dahl looked appreciatively at his drink.

"I hope the girl was smart enough to poison you."

"Let's see." Dahl took a sip. "Nope. Still alive. This really is delicious." He kept sipping. "You used to come here with Jenny, right?"

A pickup truck backing up in the driveway over his hand.

Someone swinging at a golf club but hitting Frank's top row of teeth instead.

The smoldering metal of a red-hot poker entering the flesh of an already infected wound.

Frank was taking the bait, and he knew it, but he couldn't stop himself. "How do you know I used to come here with Jenny?"

Dahl shrugged, now gulping. "Best ice cream in the neighborhood, right?"

"*How do you know I used to come here with Jenny?*" Frank repeated his question, this time through gritted teeth.

"An interview you gave right after you killed her, when you said how sad it always made you, thinking that the two of you would never go to Inside Scoop again."

Frank grabbed a handful of Dahl's hair, slammed his face onto the table, and knocked several teeth out of his mouth like pieces of a broken coffee mug.

But back on the other side of his imagination, he couldn't really do that, so instead, he stared back at the monster, picturing all of the ways he could ensure that no one ever found the body.

"Did you take her for ice cream before or afterward, Frank? Was the dessert to entice her or to make it all better once you were done?"

No response.

So Dahl continued. "Was she pretty, Frank?"

Still nothing.

"Do you know a monster when you see one because you're a monster, too?"

Frank might have to kill this man right here in public.

"Did you do it? Did you rape and kill your pretty little daughter?" Dahl kept leering at him. "Was … she good?"

Frank had barely been holding it in, but that's when he lost it.

This time for real, he grabbed a handful of Dahl's hair and slammed—

But Dahl wrestled out of Frank's grip and out of the booth.

Frank tackled him to the floor and started pounding his fists into the monster's face while Dahl kept laughing and laughing.

Then Frank got off of him, aghast, already knowing

what he had done. The mistake he had made … or walked right into.

Dahl stood, looking beaten and bloody, as he pulled out his phone. "You're so fucked, old man."

The parlor wasn't crowded, but everyone in the place was staring at the combatants. The enraged old man who had just attacked the much calmer man, now bloodied and calling the crime in to those who vowed to protect and serve.

Frank closed his eyes, knowing he'd let the monster win this round.

Dahl looked down at the screen, dialed something, then said, "I'd like to report a battery."

Chapter Twenty-Nine

Frank

FRANK WAS in the interview room. *Again.*

At least Mal hadn't been trolling the Inside Scoop parking lot. If she had been, then Dahl's little plan would have worked out even better for him.

A deputy did answer his call, and almost immediately, but Frank reclaimed a measure of control once back at the station. The Inside Scoop incident was an insult and beyond embarrassing, getting cuffed then escorted out of the parlor and into a cruiser waiting outside.

Frank didn't recognize the deputy, and the lack of familiarity was reciprocal. He was young, new to the department within the last year or so. He didn't appear to have any personal vendetta against former Detective Grimm or seem to even know who he was.

Frank didn't take it personally, understanding that the kid was just doing his job.

But he was grateful when Sgt. Johnson — a fellow

colleague in Frank's old life — intervened and told the young deputy not to book him.

"What am I supposed to do?" the younger deputy had asked.

And Johnson said, "Have Cortez interview him."

Frank liked that idea enough, so long as Mike didn't bring Mallory. He was a solid detective who did things by the book: decent instincts and a strong ethic. Not as effective as his partner, from everything Frank had seen, but Detective Cortez had the edge over Detective Black for the simple reason that he wasn't waging a war against former Detective Grimm.

He had been in the interview room for twenty minutes now and had spent the last half of them wondering if they were locating Mike or whether they were treating Frank as just another suspect awaiting interrogation, and the detective in charge wanted to make him sweat.

But then the door swung open. Not just to Mike, but to Captain Wilson.

The men entered, both looking agitated, then sat side-by-side across the table from him.

"What happened?" Mike asked.

Frank shrugged. "Assault and battery by the looks of it."

"We're going to need you to take this seriously, Frank," Wilson said.

"I've been taking it seriously for a while."

"What happened?" Mike asked again.

"I punched Patrick Dahl several times in his face. It was in public, and I threw the first and only punches. Anything he did to me was only self-defense. I'm sure the eyewitnesses will all agree. The place wasn't crowded, but what happened is obvious, and I was clearly the aggressor."

Wilson looked at him. "Why are you saying that?"

"Just telling it to you straight," Frank said. "Both because you'll have to make a judgment call about this one and because I'm hoping to illustrate how neatly this guy has set me up."

"He set you up, huh?" Mike sounded skeptical but not exactly disbelieving.

It was a start.

"Why would he be setting you up?" Wilson asked.

"Because he wants me out of the way."

Mike: "Why?"

"Because I know who he is and what he's doing."

Wilson: "And what's that?"

Frank replied in his most sober voice. "He's raping his daughter. He's also probably uploading videos of the assaults to the dark web somewhere and threatening to kill both the girl and her mother. They're in a dangerous, *deadly* situation, Captain. I'm trying to get them out of that situation. So in other words, I'm waving a big red flag in front of a frightened bull's face."

"And how do you know all of this?" Mike sounded curious more than accusatory, but Frank knew how to pitch his voice that way as well.

Not an easy answer. Sure, Freya had told him directly, but a natural follow-up question would be, *How did the two of you meet?*

He couldn't exactly say, *She was watching me break into houses.*

And Frank couldn't tell a story that Freya couldn't support if they got her alone.

"Once a detective, always a detective," he finally said.

"I'm afraid that's not gonna cut it." Mike shook his head.

Wilson was more direct. "We received an anonymous

tip that made a similar implication. You wouldn't happen to know anything about that, would you?"

Frank nodded. "Yeah, I heard about that."

"She was questioned."

"I heard that, too."

Wilson continued: "So you probably also heard that she said nothing was happening. That she didn't know why anyone would ever say such a thing."

"She's scared. You know how that goes." Then, "Is this an interrogation?"

"I'm actually not sure what this is yet," Mike admitted.

So Frank made a suggestion. "How about we make it a chance to put the bad guy away?"

"That is our business." Mike leaned back in his chair; it wasn't performative, he genuinely seemed to be figuring this out as he went along, same as Wilson. "You've gotta give us something to go on. You know how this works. Why don't we start with you telling us how you know all of this, maybe show us some evidence."

"I'm a concerned citizen. Telling you what I've observed so you can act before it's too late."

"But that's not the whole story, right?" Mike glanced at Wilson before turning back to Frank. "I don't think we'd be in here if that was the whole story. Why were you meeting Dahl at an ice cream parlor?"

"His wife texted and asked if I could meet her there. But he showed up instead."

Wilson was still just watching.

Mike said, "I'm sure you have that text exchange and could show it to us."

"Of course." Frank nodded.

"And this is on your regular phone?"

"A burner," Frank told Mike, with Wilson still hanging on every word.

"Why not give his wife your real number?"

It was asinine having to deliver answers everyone in the room already knew, but there was also no other way to round this corner of the board. "I gave her a phone and programmed my number into it. Her husband checks every call she makes."

"She told you that?" Mike asked.

"There's zero chance a man like Dahl gives his wife the freedom to use her phone as she pleases."

"*A man like that,*" Mike repeated. "You mean a man who would rape his own daughter?"

Frank nodded. "Among other things."

Wilson finally spoke. "It's important that we know how you're so sure of this, especially in light of the girl's denial during her interview."

"You know why she denied it, Captain." Frank expected better from him. "But regardless of what Freya said at school when she was scared out of her mind, I still know because she told me."

"We got an anonymous tip that you've been breaking into houses on your cul-de-sac. Is that true, Frank?" Wilson stared into his eyes, daring him to lie.

"Of course not." Frank managed to feel indignant, even though he had absolutely no right. "Why would I be breaking into my neighbors' houses?" Then he scoffed to prove the absurdity of such a ridiculous accusation. "I'm sure the 'anonymous' tip came from Dahl."

Frank was only the slightest bit worried about getting into trouble for breaking and entering, but his guts were in knots, thinking that the monster might slip out of this. He was troubled by the thought of tainted evidence. If the trial started with illegal activity, it would dead-end in court.

The room was silent, everyone waiting for Frank to

speak. He lasted a while, but they held the cards here, and he knew it, so he finally repeated his question.

"Why would I be breaking into my neighbors' houses?"

This time Mike started his answer before Frank hit the question mark. "Maybe you're looking for something — *anything* that will help you find out more about what happened to your daughter."

"As a former officer of the law, I would never want to ignore it. But if you think I'd break into places looking for information about what happened to Jenny, then wouldn't that just further eliminate me as a suspect in her murder? If I'm not a suspect there and suffered the loss that I did, wouldn't it then stand to reason that I'd have a vested interest in what might be happening to a girl who is now the same age that Jenny will always be, and lives right down the street?"

"I think that makes perfect sense, Frank," Wilson said. "That's why we're asking. If there's something here, then we need you to give us a reason—"

"Of course, there's something here. *You know there's something here.*"

"But nothing we can move on," Wilson said. Then he added, "*You know there's nothing we can move on.*"

Mike leaned across the table. "This isn't being recorded, Frank. It's just us three guys in here. Off the record, let's just take 'houses' off the table and say it's only the one—a two-story Victorian on 47 Heirloom. You think something bad is happening in there, detective gut, we get that. So, you wait until no one is home, then you break in and see something even worse than what you'd imagined. You keep nosing around the place because you want the girl to fink on her daddy. Either you can't or she won't, so you call in with an anonymous tip. Of course, she's not gonna say anything because she's afraid that Daddy'll kill her. So you go straight to the mom, but she finks on you instead, and Dahl shows up at the parlor. He wants you out of the picture, so he pushes your buttons. Gets you to deck him in the jaw and right in front of an audience. Impressive since he was pulling the strings of a man who absolutely should've known better or at least seen it coming. How much of that did I get right?"

"I'd say it sounds like a well-assembled theory."

"You mean in that none of it can be proven?" Mike clarified.

"I mean, I think you have enough to act on."

"You haven't given us anything." Wilson stood. "Sorry, Frank. But I can't help if you're not willing to cooperate. I don't think that you've done anything wrong here, and I'm sure you're onto something, but it's a dead-end for the department until you give us something tangible."

He looked at Frank, hoping that moment might come now.

It didn't, so Wilson finished. "I talked Dahl out of pressing charges and filing an order of protection against you. But he did say that if you go anywhere near him or his family again, he'll press charges and alert the press. I have zero reason to doubt he will. So unless you want Ty Kirby crawling right back up your ass and ruining your life more than he already has, I suggest you stay far away from this."

"So you're not going to do anything?" Frank asked, still sitting down and looking up at Wilson.

"What can we do?" Wilson shook his head, then looked back at his friend. "You're not naive about any of this. You know how it works. Are you breaking into houses?"

"No."

"Have you broken into Dahl's place?"

"No."

"Do you have a relationship with his daughter that you'd like to tell us about?"

"Absolutely not."

"Do you have any evidence to corroborate anything you're saying here?" That one sounded like Wilson's final question.

"I really wish I did."

"Then I'm sorry, Frank. There's nothing we can do."

"Does that mean I'm free to go?"

Wilson nodded.

Mike said, "Call us. Okay, man? We'll move on it the second we—"

"I promise I will." Frank gave him an emphatic nod, appreciating the genuine worry he could see on his face. Wilson's, too. "I'll give you a call if I can."

They offered him a car back to the Inside Scoop, but Frank declined and called himself a FASTr instead. He wanted the quiet ride to think. Maybe he should have said more, but he'd seen too many evil men slip through the legal cracks while innocents were convicted. It was a broken system he no longer believed in.

Frank couldn't afford to let the monster walk.

He'd keep looking for evidence but would not allow a terrible fate to befall Freya. So maybe this was it for him. Maybe he'd have to murder Dahl in lieu of Jenny's killer.

He'd disappear after that.

It wouldn't matter if he took the monster with him.

Chapter Thirty

Mal

MAL WAS GOING out of her mind.

Ashley was at school, Ray was on assignment, and she was stuck on suspension at home.

She did everything possible to get Grimm out of her head. She tried reading but couldn't keep her focus on the page. Fiction wasn't agreeing with her, and nonfiction made her want to research ways to make her adversary pay for his crimes, plus a tax for escaping punishment for as long as he had.

She tried watching Netflix, but all three of the shows she put on were more upsetting than entertaining. There was some true-crime bullshit that had holes wide enough for Mal to drive her Explorer through. The pure fiction was even worse. She finally tried some fantasy crap because it took too long before she scrolled to another show, and the trailer hooked her. Twenty minutes in, she wanted to throw things at the screen.

She *really* wanted to look through her footage of Heirloom Cove, send it up to her big screen, and spy on Frank while no one was home. But that was a promise to herself that she hadn't been willing to break. So far.

Music came next, but scrolling through options on Spotify only agitated her further. Everything either made her feel old or older, and that was idiotic because she wasn't even nearing her peak yet. Unless she had already washed out, thanks to Grimm.

The thoughts always circled back, no matter how hard she tried to escape them.

Mal was about to go outside for a walk in yet another attempt to detour her meandering, murderous thoughts, but she saw Mike pulling up to her curb as she approached the front door.

He wasn't just driving by while Mal was on suspension to bring her tacos. So this was either great or terrible. She greeted him at the door. "Did you come to hear how much I've been relaxing?"

"How many bottles does that take for you these days?"

She nodded for him to enter. "Are you suggesting that I open one? Because I can open one."

Mike shook his head. "You know I'm on—"

"Of course you are. So why are you here?"

"I needed to update you on something."

"Oh?" Mal was definitely interested. "You couldn't just text me?"

"I figured you'd want to hear this in person."

"So this is something you shouldn't officially be telling me."

"No." Mike shook his head. "I shouldn't be. But I thought you would want to know."

"You sure I shouldn't open a bottle?"

"There was an incident with Frank. At—"

"I knew it!"

"Calm down. It's not what you think." He walked past Mal and sat on her couch. Then he leaned forward while folding his hands between his knees. "He got in an altercation with his neighbor across the street. Punched him in the face, right in front of an ice cream parlor full of witnesses."

"Patrick Dahl, right? He thinks Grimm has been creeping around his daughter."

Mike nodded. "I've heard his side of the story."

"But? You're not seriously telling me you still believe Grimm?"

"Frank's story fits this other scenario just as well, Mal."

"And what story is that?"

"That Dahl set him up. Because—"

Mal scoffed.

"So. You're not even going to hear this?"

"I know what I know," she said.

"What's that supposed to mean?"

"I have cameras set up in front of the cul-de-sac. I saw Grimm go into 47 and stay inside for a good half hour. Now, why would he do that when Dahl has made it plenty clear on numerous occasions that he doesn't want the creeper anywhere around him or his family?"

"TO HELP THEM!"

Mike was on his feet a moment after Mal had finally sat.

"Whoa, wait up. Why are you so mad?" She asked from the couch.

"Why are you so impossible sometimes?" Mike threw his hands in the air and began to pace her living room. "I can't believe you put a camera on his street, Mal. You were asked to stay away, *ordered* to stay away. I'm your partner, and you're pushing me out. You're spying on Frank Grimm when you know you're not supposed to!"

"That's because—"

"He isn't hurting Dahl's daughter, Mal. And I believe that he thinks her father is. Wilson believes him too."

"Dahl reported that Grimm had been on his property on numerous occasions. He called in a specific encounter with Grimm when he was in the man's side yard for no apparent reason."

"I'm sure a reason was given," Mike said.

"Grimm said he was looking for a neighbor's dog."

"Maybe he was."

Mal was hoping he would say that. "The neighbor in question doesn't have a dog."

"And you know that for sure?"

"That isn't the point."

"Come on, Mal. Be a detective here. Take everything you know about this situation and turn it upside down. Couldn't Dahl have said all the same things to you if he was trying to frame Frank?"

"Why were they at the ice cream parlor?"

"Dahl's wife sent Frank a text, but he showed up to the meet."

"How'd she get his number?"

"Frank gave it to her, along with a burner."

"Alright, Mike. Same question: is it possible Grimm is playing us? He knows what the department is inclined to believe. Maybe that's what he's been doing for years and what he's still doing now."

"Yes, it's possible. But *nothing* points to Frank being the guy you think he is, other than your gut, which is what you always come back to."

"But you always trust my gut."

"Exactly. So what does it say that I'm not buying this now?"

That stopped her.

So Mike continued. "The question is, do you trust *my* gut, Mal?"

"You know I do."

"Except for this. Except for right now. Except for this one thing you can't for the life of you seem to see around."

"What makes you so sure?" Mal asked.

"You mean, besides the total lack of evidence? I was with Wilson when he talked to Dahl, and something isn't right with that guy. You can see it in his eyes. And I buy Frank's story that this guy was setting him up. So if that's true, then why doubt any other part of the story?"

It grated against her every instinct, but Mal had no choice but to follow him. "So, what now?"

"Are we on the same page here?" He looked at her as if not knowing what to expect.

"We are." She nodded. "Until Grimm gives me a reason not to be."

"*Until?* Or *unless?*"

"Unless. That's what I meant."

"There's a big difference between those words."

"I get it, Mike. Like you said, we're on the same page. So, *what now?*"

"I'm going to talk to the woman who conducted the original interview with Dahl's daughter."

"Okay," Mal said.

Mike walked toward the front door.

"I wish I could go with you." Mal stood and started walking to meet him.

He opened it and turned back to her. "Me too." Then he gave her a smile. "But some of us have to do twice the amount of work because others of us are on vacation."

"It's not a vacation."

"I bet you've been acting all ADD between trying to read and trying to find something on TV that can actually hold your attention, which is exactly what you do on every other vacation."

"Get out of here. The people need you to solve crimes and make Creek County a better place to live."

Mike stepped onto her porch and headed to his car.

"Make sure to tell me what happens after the interview!"

"Of course," he called back without turning around.

She closed the door, not knowing how to feel. If Mike was right, then she had to be so very, *very* wrong. Enough to make her a fool in front of the entire department. But the truth was worlds more important than her ego.

But she couldn't let it rest.

Mike had his gut, but Mal had something he didn't.

And the rules changed once Mike pulled up in front of her curb.

So she would be watching the footage again to see if there was any evidence that might prove him right or wrong.

She scrubbed through it, more conflicted than usual.

It was the same thing on a long repeat. The house was still, with the only curious note being Freya occasionally looking out what Mal assumed was her bedroom window.

So Mal was surprised and instantly interested when she saw something new.

She watched it three times in a row, wondering what it meant.

It was lights-out for Freya at exactly ten, without fail. She never looked at that camera past lights-out because there wasn't any point. Frank wasn't breaking into her place while she was asleep, especially if he wasn't even leaving his house. But this time, she scrubbed through the entire night.

And she saw a light go on in Freya's bedroom around

midnight. Dim, but there. It went dark fifteen minutes later.

Maybe Freya turning on a reading light or maybe looking up something on her phone or the computer.

Mal looked at more of the footage because, of course, she had to.

And no, that wasn't the only night.

Lights out at ten, then back on at midnight, just as precise.

There wasn't as much precision in the three other nights she saw, but they were all fifteen to twenty minutes.

Maybe Freya was secretly talking to a friend.

She could have been doing anything.

But a terrible, twisted thing in Mal's gut was now screaming that she might be wrong.

What if Freya's father was going into her bedroom at midnight to molest her?

Mal couldn't wait to hear more from Mike.

Because right now, she might be living a nightmare.

Chapter Thirty-One

Frank

FRANK HAD BEEN WATERING his lawn for nearly half an hour.

It didn't need that much water. Or any. The sprinklers were on a timer. But he needed to be outside and felt too exposed for a stroll. Even if he had the energy, a walk was too exhausting. Keeping the smile on his face while making the smallest of talk.

He'd gone for a short one already, borrowing Dolly from Rachel. But then she reminded him again why he'd decided to avoid going over with a light scolding about his not having been by for a few days, followed by an unbearably long and complicated narrative involving overpriced tulips at the grocery store, plus some story about a feud with some neighbor he didn't know and had never heard of who lived a few streets east of Heirloom.

Frank was only two houses down from Rachel's when he was accosted by an especially vitriolic Erin, not only giving him a full rundown on the whore fucker, but using a

243

string of increasingly alarming curses to articulate his latest escapades. Stan might appreciate her tirade as an art form, but it added acid to Frank's already sour stomach.

Maybe he'd tell Stan all about it when he came over for dinner.

It was probably time to go back inside. He'd been watering his lawn long enough to look weird.

He turned around to turn off the faucet, but something bristled at his neck and turned him around in time to see the monster slowing as he drove into the cul-de-sac, crawling by the time he was passing Frank.

The window lowered, and he found himself staring at Dahl's grinning mug, purple and puffy, splotchy and dark on his otherwise pale face.

He ended his smile with a wave, then rolled up his window.

Frank imagined him on the floor. Then he pictured himself stepping on the monster's throat while holding a bottle of whiskey until his mouth flew open, and he was gasping for air. Then he saw himself taking a long swallow and emptying the bottle into the monster's gaping mouth.

Then he'd drop the match.

Frank went inside and warmed his marsala in the microwave.

He needed to eat before Stan came over. Stan was "bringing dinner," which meant trash in a sack. Frank was looking forward to his company, but he didn't want to eat whatever garbage his cousin was bringing.

Besides, eating with Stan meant no conversation with Sarah. If he missed his side of that exchange, he would need extra hours to fall asleep.

He warmed the dish, this time with potatoes, and sat across the table from where Sarah would be if he hadn't destroyed both of their lives.

"Stan's coming over," he told her empty space. "Probably bring a half-gallon of ice cream and call it his dinner. I bet he'll eat it right out of the carton."

Sarah always said Stan ate like a pig.

"I wish you could be proud of me." He chewed. "For doing the right thing, even though it's hard and ugly." He drank. "And messy. I get it. But … I wish I could believe you were somewhere and that I have your blessing."

The lights flickered, and he wanted to leap out of his seat.

"Sarah?"

Then he felt like an idiot for expecting them to flicker again.

He drained his glass but didn't refill it.

Then he ate slowly until he finished.

He was done drying his dish and putting it away when he heard what sounded like someone pounding on his front door with a mallet.

He walked to the living room and opened it. "Why can't you ever use the doorbell?"

"Seems intrusive." Stan came inside.

"You think *that's* not? It sounds like you're trying to break your knuckles."

"Pain puts us in touch with who we are."

"I seriously wonder how you're my cousin."

"I wonder that same shit all the time. You hungry?" He held up two bags, walking backward toward the kitchen.

Frank shook his head as he followed. "You can't be serious."

"You said you've never had Sloppy's. So tonight's the night."

"There's a reason I've never had it. Can I just give you a polite, *no thank you*?"

"Not a chance, bitch. I do that chicken marsala shit

every other time I come here. You eat that crap so often your house smells like it right now. It's my turn. So Sloppy's it is." Stan started pulling burgers out of bags and setting them down next to mountains of fries.

"That's a lot of food."

"Fuck yeah, it is."

"You know I'll force one down to be polite, but—"

"You've never had Sloppy's, so I figured you'd want choices."

"You shouldn't have."

"You kidding me?" Stan looked from the buffet to his cousin. "Guess how much all of this cost me?"

"There is no possible answer that will make me feel better about what you're about to make me eat."

"Let's just say I paid with a twenty and could still fuck up a game of Space Invaders."

"Does that mean *play it?*" Frank asked. "Has anyone wanted to play Space Invaders in the last thirty years or so?"

"Retro is big."

"And is that an example of intelligent swearing?"

"What?"

"You're going to *F-up* a game of Space Invaders? That usage doesn't strike you as, I dunno, unnecessary?"

"It strikes me as *colorful.* It says to the listener that not only will I use my quarter to play it, but that quarter will be well spent rather than squandered, and the game will be sorry I played it. See: shorthand."

Frank shook his head in defeat and looked down at the table. "So, what am I looking at?"

"The fries are amazing, so you're definitely gonna wanna gobble 'em fast. They're hot and salty and hella delicious if you shovel 'em in your face in the next few minutes, but it's already been ten minutes from A to B, and if we wait too long, they'll start tasting like dry vag."

"Charming."

"*Descriptive*," Stan corrected him. Then he pointed to three different burgers in turn. "The True American, the Impossibly Delicious, and that last one is a limited offer; the You Can't Be Serious."

"It's a good question. You know why you can buy all of this food for less than twenty dollars, right?"

"Efficiencies in the marketplace. Which one do you want?"

"I really can't say none of them?"

"You can, but I will lord it over you forever. There's no retiring out of being cousins. Even if our friendship is mostly obligation, I still like you."

"I'm glad to hear it." He actually was.

Stan grabbed a fat handful of fries and shoved every one of them into his mouth. He wouldn't be talking for a while. But Frank dared him anyway.

"Which one of these will I hate least?"

"Tababibaeechoem." *Take a bite of each of them.*

"Absolutely not." Frank grabbed the You Can't be Serious. It was the closest, the most compelling, and likely to provide the most ammunition in his upcoming argument as to why Sloppy's was Satan's restaurant.

He unwrapped the burger and bit in without looking. He chewed and swallowed, expecting to vomit. "What the hell is in this thing?"

"I have no idea." Stan shrugged.

"Why is it so good?"

Stan laughed. "I know, right? It's totally vegan."

"You can't be serious."

"Exactly."

Frank sat in his seat and quickly finished the burger. Yes, he knew it was terrible. But it was also delicious.

Stan sat across from him. "You should really try the fries."

"This is more than enough." But then he grabbed a fry, and it was amazing.

"You should try the Sloppy's Sauce." Stan pointed. One of the dippers was already open and looked liked ranch, just starting to blush.

"No thanks." But then he dipped a fry into the sauce, and that was delicious, too. "I hate you."

"I know," Stan said.

Frank wasn't dumb enough to eat either of the other burgers, but he did have a few handfuls of fries. And like Stan's incessant swearing, the meal was an unexpected comfort. Frank filled him in on everything that had been happening, and without any hesitation in believing him like he'd seen from Wilson and Cortez.

There wasn't much Stan could do, including with Marco; so far, that had only led to a series of very dead ends. But he had Frank's back, and that was enough. They talked for two hours until he couldn't stop yawning. Then Stan gave him a hug that he meant and left him for the night.

Frank surprised himself by falling almost immediately asleep.

But then he woke to a ringing.

He was fumbling around, slapping his hand on the nightstand until it landed on his phone. Then he grabbed it and answered without bothering to look at the screen. "Hello?"

"He found the cameras!" Freya whispered.

"Where are you?"

"I'm in the bathroom!"

Frank heard a fist pounding on wood in the background.

Then, "WHO THE FUCK ARE YOU TALKING TO?"

"Call 9-1-1. *Now, Freya!*"

The call went dead.

He looked down at his phone and considered calling it in.

But it would take too long for them to get there. And Frank would have to make a move in the meantime.

No telling what he might have to do.

So he ran to the pantry, grabbed his gun from inside the canister of oatmeal, and raced out of his house, charging full speed to do what needed to be done.

Chapter Thirty-Two

Mal

"WHAT'S WRONG?" Ray grabbed Mal by the shoulders and tried to quiet her.

Only then did she realize that she had been crying.

"What happened?" she asked.

"You just started screaming in your sleep. Then you shot straight up in bed. I guess you had a nightmare. Do you remember?"

She did. And all at once.

But it wasn't anything she was about to say out loud.

"No." She shook her head.

Ashley dead and defiled.

"You sure?"

After a long pause, she said, "Just a lot of vagaries. Feelings more than anything specific."

"You can talk to me."

"I know. Thanks." She kissed him on the cheek. "I promise I'm fine, but I want to go and check on Ashley."

"Of course. Just try not to wake her."

"That's the last thing I want to do." Another kiss on the cheek.

Maybe things were getting better between them.

Ray was the rock she needed him to be; she just had to find a way to finally let him in like he deserved.

But right now, she needed to soothe herself from that nightmare. And the only way to do that was to peek in on her daughter and hear the sound of her breathing.

She quietly opened the door and poked her head into the room dimly lit by fairy lights that slowly transitioned from purple to pink and back again on a cycle all night long. There was something soothing about the colors fading into one another that made Mal want the lights in her room too.

Ashley's body was rising and falling in bed, tilted toward the door just enough for Mal to see the shirt that she shouldn't have been wearing to bed. It was her favorite one in the world — purple, with a unicorn barfing a rainbow — and aging too fast. She wanted to wear it during the day all the time, and also to bed. Mal told her she could pick one or the other. She chose daytime but would sometimes sneak it on after she was tucked in. Mal actually thought it was adorable and only pretended to be bothered.

Mal wondered if she should dare to creep inside.

Probably a bad idea, but she was doing less of those these days and really needed this one to still the disquiet inside her.

She inhaled her daughter's scent, kissed her on the forehead, and slipped out of the room.

Back to Ray, and now she was wide awake.

Maybe they could touch each other and—

But, no. Two steps from their room, she could hear him snoring.

She paused before taking another one.

Then she slowly turned around and started creeping toward the office.

Ray didn't know what time it was. Or how long she'd been gone. Even if he woke up again, it would only be to drift back asleep. Right now, his world was soup.

She flicked on the light, closed the door behind her, then turned on the live footage of Grimm's place.

She leaned forward, preparing to scrub it back to the last time she'd looked, but had barely moved the timeline — maybe five minutes' worth — when she saw him barreling out of the house.

She couldn't believe her luck.

Calling this in would be a mistake because how could she have possibly known about it?

Telling Ray would be an even bigger blunder.

She was in her pajamas, but what the hell. She could tie the belt on her longest coat in the closet by the front door.

She did. A minute later, she was in the car and racing toward Grimm's.

Chapter Thirty-Three

Frank

FRANK RACED INTO THE DAHLS' side yard, scanned the ground in front of the back door, then settled on a rock about the size of a Magic 8-Ball.

He moved the gun to his left hand and palmed the rock with his right. He held it overhead, wanting to smash the glass and let himself inside. But the monster might not know he was coming, and Frank didn't want to lose the element of surprise.

He checked the door, just in case, but of course, it was locked, and he'd run out of the house without grabbing his tools. Not that he'd take the time to pick a lock right now.

Freya screamed.

Only in his mind, but that was enough.

He smashed the glass, carefully opened the door from the other side, then entered the kitchen without bothering to quiet himself. Jack was out of the box already.

He barreled upstairs.

253

I'm in the bathroom!

He stopped in front of the bathroom. The door would almost for sure be locked, and checking would let the monster know that his fate had arrived.

Frank raised his leg and did something he'd done exactly three times before, holding his balance while driving the heel of his standing foot into the ground. He avoided the lock with his kick because hitting that would break bones instead of his target.

The wood splintered immediately. Like most modern doors, it was soft and hollow. Two kicks, and the thing exploded open.

The monster looked back as Frank raised his gun.

He loomed over Freya; the poor girl was in her underwear with her back against the bathroom wall. Blood gushed from her nose and gurgled from her sobbing mouth. Frantic panting made the battery of black and blue blotches dance on her body, looking especially mottled around her ribs.

Freya whimpered, *"Please …"* or something close to it.

Dahl straightened his shoulders, using his full height to make Frank feel the danger.

But there was no danger if you were willing to die.

"Please," Freya whimpered again.

The monster bellowed as he took a step forward. "YOU DID THIS!"

Frank shook his gun. "Another inch, and you're dead."

The monster believed him.

He fell backward instead.

Frank made the mistake of believing he was retreating one second too long.

The monster was suddenly behind Freya, yanking her into his arms to use his daughter as a hostage. He screamed again, not nearly as loud. "You did this!"

"What did I do?" Frank asked calmly.

The monster could mean anything, but Frank didn't care about his answer. It was best to keep the demon talking.

But the monster looked frantically around instead of answering as if expecting an escape hatch to appear out of nowhere.

Frank wasn't looking at the same man who had held his cool at the neighborhood barbecue or had orchestrated his own assault and battery at Inside Scoop. This version of Patrick Dahl was red-faced and insane. Panting, but differently than his daughter. His eyes were inhumanly wide and entirely crazed. Drool dangled from his drooping lip. He made the same accusation, this time in a snarl.

Frank gave him another decisive shake of his gun when the monster tried to inch forward.

He retreated, but again it was only a feint.

Instead of truly backing down, the monster used his surrendered step as a launching pad, first shoving Freya into Frank, then rushing past them and into the hall.

Freya fell into his arms.

Frank heard the door slam. "Where's your mother?"

"I don't know!"

He looked behind him, then back at her. "Did you call 9-1-1?"

"He busted in here and took it away before I could."

A second later, she was holding his phone.

"Tell them you were just physically and sexually attacked by your father. You managed to fight him off, but now you're locked in the bathroom, scared, mostly for your mother. Send officers immediately. Got that?"

She nodded, looking every bit as frightened as Frank wanted her to sound on the phone.

A gunshot tore through the silence.

Freya screamed.

"Run outside and wait for me there! Tell them all the other stuff and that an officer needs assistance."

Then Frank ran himself toward the monster's bedroom with his pistol drawn.

Chapter Thirty-Four

Mal

MAL WAS glad it was late and the roads were so empty.

No music, only the sound of her tires tearing at the ground, along with a heart that was working too hard and for too many reasons.

She ran a red light.

No big deal, nobody out.

If sirens started blazing behind her, she could roll down her window, put a cherry on her roof, and consider herself as having earned an escort she didn't want but was maybe, in the end, lucky enough to get.

Another red light, another no big deal.

But she couldn't run red lights *and* answer her phone. That was an accident waiting to happen.

Besides, there was only one person in the world who would be calling her right now.

So it kept ringing and ringing, luring Mal with better bait every time. Four rings, voicemail, then the cycle restarting with guilt coming in a wave, heavier whenever a new one rolled forward.

She should turn off the phone. That wouldn't solve the problem, but it would mute the issue for now. Silence the complication while she thought.

But Mal would have to be holding her phone, and surely it would ring in her hand. That would make her feel even guiltier.

Would Ray worry less if it went *straight* to voicemail?

No way out of this one.

And cross-traffic at the next red light eliminated her last excuse.

"I know, I know," she said instead of *hello*. "But I thought you were asleep."

"Where the hell are you?"

"I'm on my way to a crime scene."

"You're not working, Mal. Where exactly are you going?"

"I can't talk right now. The light turned green. I really need to go. I just knew you were worried because I wasn't answering."

The light changed and gave her permission to floor it.

"Where are you?" Ray asked.

"I just told you!"

"You didn't tell me anything. How about—"

"How about a little girl's life at stake — is that enough for you?"

"You're on suspension! Why didn't you just call Mike and ask him to send officers?"

"There wasn't time! I'm sorry, but we'll have to talk about this later."

"You can't just—"

She couldn't run the red light up ahead *and* talk on the phone.

Chapter Thirty-Five

Frank

THE BEDROOM DOOR BURST OPEN, and Irene practically fell out of the opening, blood spurting from her leg.

Frank ran over, caught her, and helped her to stand.

"Where is he?" he asked, wishing he'd just shot Dahl immediately instead of trying to get him to surrender. As much as he'd wanted to, a part of him had been reluctant to force Freya to see her father shot. She'd have enough trauma after tonight — assuming she lived through it.

"He went out the window." Frank made sure she was steady and then ran toward the stairs, calling out to her as he ran. "Freya is outside. I have to go. Sit tight. Put pressure on the wound. Call 9-1-1 and tell them everything about what he's been doing to both of you, but only after you let them know your lives are in danger!"

Frank was screaming at the end to make sure she heard him. He opened the front door, ran out onto the lawn, and bellowed. "Freya!" He couldn't care less who heard so long as she did. "FREYA! Yell back if you can hear me!"

He looked in the side yard, then peeked into the back.

Too many shadows. Too many decisions. Too many ways to die.

He ran back out to the front lawn, looked down the street, and saw it instantly. The monster dragging Freya toward Frank's house, one hand yanking her by the hair and the other pressed against her mouth.

Frank rushed after them, heart racing and already winded, but his adrenaline keeping him going. His gun was level with his body, but a clear shot felt impossible in the dark.

He lowered his weapon and ran faster.

Frank hadn't bothered to lock his front door before racing over, so now Dahl was inside with Freya. He wondered if the monster had any idea of what he'd just done, any clue that he had given Frank the best possible gift.

A few minutes ago, it had been the other way around. The monster was on his property. Patrick Dahl had been predator to Freya's prey. But now he was the game and Frank the hunter.

Two shots blew through the drywall about a foot from the door.

He edged his body past the threshold, entering only after he saw that the Dahl had made a misstep. Clearly new to this part of the horror show, he still held his daughter hostage, with his arm around her neck, now gripping the gun again.

But he also had one foot on the bottom stair, a hard enough shot without Freya bucking against him.

After wasting two bullets, he tightened his grip around Freya's neck, pressed the gun to her temple, and bellowed again. "You ruined everything!"

"You keep saying that," Frank said, perfectly calm. "Do you want to tell me what it is you think I ruined?"

"EVERYTHING!" He was a raw nerve of pure agony.

"Okay. I'm sorry for whatever it is I've ruined." He wasn't. "But I need you to think very carefully before you make a big mistake. Let's talk this out. Nobody has to die tonight."

"I don't want to talk to you."

"I'm the one who ruined everything. I imagine you probably want to talk to me more than anyone else right now."

Hard sobs, born in Freya's gut, the monster's gun still pressed to her head.

Still too far away, still too many shadows and uncertainty, still too many mistakes waiting to happen.

"I ruined your life … I get that. You're right," Frank said. "But I couldn't just stand by and watch this happen. You understand that … this was always a risk … that someone would upend the life you built for yourself. I'm just the one who finally did it."

"Don't come any closer!" Dahl was frantic.

And Frank froze in place. "Just put your gun down."

"You first."

"You know I can't do that, Patrick."

"Like hell, you can't."

"You let her go, and I promise I'll drop it … you can even shoot me if you want to, just as long as she stays safe. I know that somewhere inside, you love your daughter, don't you? We can stop this from getting any worse than it needs to be."

He nodded, sobbing. "What's the point? My life is over either way." The monster looked at Frank, daring him to answer.

Freya started choking, and he relaxed his hold.

"It doesn't have to be," Frank lied. "The police aren't here; it isn't too late."

"Of course it is!" For a moment, he seemed teased with defeat, but now his fury was back.

"It's not like it used to be," Frank kept on lying. "Psychiatrists understand this sort of thing better than they ever have. There's a reason you're like this. Maybe you won't even see prison. Maybe you'll wind up in a mental hospital where you can get the help you need. Where they won't judge you, but they'll listen to you and help you."

"Yeah, but I might just wind up in prison. And we both know I'll never survive." He was shaking his head wildly enough to worry Frank, make him afraid that he might lose control of his gun.

"The authorities know that guys like you rarely survive. That's why there are now separate wings in most prisons for—"

"That's not true — YOU'RE LYING!"

"It *is* true, Patrick. And I have friends who can make sure that's where you go. Friends who understand that you're just as much a victim here as anyone."

"I *am* a victim!"

"I know …" Frank nodded. "And I understand."

"What do you know? *How* do *you* understand?"

"You were right all along. Remember what you said to me at the ice cream parlor, Patrick? When you asked me if I know a monster when I see one … because I'm a monster, too? You're right. I am. You and I are different but the same. And if you let her go right now, I'll know how to help you … just—"

A symphony of sirens started yelling from somewhere far off but they were getting louder quickly.

"If you want the cops to see your side, then you have to

give them something. Letting Freya go is the easiest way to get what you want."

He let her go.

And she ran into Frank's arms.

"Go outside," he whispered to her, keeping his gun on Patrick. "Everything is going to be okay now."

"I know." A deep sob, then words that sounded like they required every ounce of her might. *"You're not a monster."*

Then she wiggled out of his arms and ran out the door. Frank slowly reached behind himself and pulled it shut, gun never leaving Patrick.

They were alone now, both of them quiet, staring down their barrels at each other.

Frank might die. But if Patrick fired, Frank wouldn't go alone.

Chapter Thirty-Six

Mal

ONLY ONE MORE RED light run before Mal was swinging hard onto Heirloom.

She could already see that the front door to 47 at the end of the street was wide open.

Her tires scuffed the curb as she killed the engine.

She ran toward the house, her ponytail flapping.

Into the house, gun drawn, calling out, announcing herself as a sheriff's deputy, ready to pull the trigger on anything that came within the orbit of hurting a little girl.

"Anyone in here?" Close to the top of her lungs.

"They're all outside." The voice was small, coming from somewhere behind her.

Mal spun around and saw Mrs. Dahl. *Irene.*

She lowered her gun. "Where are they?"

Still timid, the brittle words ready to break before they left her mouth. "They're outside."

Too many questions and no time to ask even one.

She nodded at Irene and raced out the door.

She looked around outside, saw nothing, then — *of course!* — she looked down the street at Frank's house.

Everything looked normal, but she knew it was anything but.

Mal raced toward the house.

She stopped at the sidewalk when she saw Freya squatting against a tree in front of the house next door, sobbing.

Mal holstered her weapon, so she could comfort Freya and show her a badge. "Where are they?"

Freya didn't say anything for a moment, unable to stop crying, trying to catch her breath.

Mal squatted beside her, hoping she wasn't wasting time, but feeling like calming the girl down was her first priority. Then assessing the situation so she'd know what she was dealing with before she went into Grimm's house.

Freya finally caught her breath and met Mal's eyes. "My father ... he t-tried to k-k-kill me, but Mr. Grimm stopped him. They both have guns, and I'm afraid—"

"It's okay. Go to your house and stay with your mom. Sheriff's office is on the way."

Sirens were blaring, help almost here.

Freya ran toward her house.

Mal wondered if she should wait for backup or go it alone. Every instinct said to wait, but she needed to see this through to the end. Besides, Frank might need help. And Mal had done nothing but fail the man for the past year.

She'd hate for his death to weigh on her conscience.

Mal raised her gun and approached the open doorway and the darkness inside Frank Grimm's home.

Chapter Thirty-Seven

Frank

THE MONSTER AIMED his gun at Frank's face, but he no longer looked like a man who wanted to shoot. Instead, he was lost and praying for salvation.

"How do you know they'll listen to me?" He looked around at nothing, his expression frail, and his movements frantic. "The cops, I mean."

"Because they want this all to go away."

The monster blinked; that was a mission he could identify with.

Frank kept on going. "This kind of thing gets reported, too many people make noise. You just need a story. Whatever happened to you all those years ago that turned you into this ... if you're willing to tell that story, then the right help will find you for sure. The mistake most people in your situation make is obscuring the truth of who they are. The past is too painful to talk honestly about." Frank shook his head to drive it home. "Even though doing so is the only way to get them out of it."

The sirens got louder. They didn't have long, a minute or two at most.

"Put down your gun, Patrick. Put it down so I can help you."

Dahl looked at him, wanting to believe. Then his expression broke, and he sneered, "You don't want to help me."

"Patrick." Frank looked at him seriously. *Earnestly.* "Right now, I'm the only one in the world who is even *capable* of caring about you. And that concern is only because of Freya. It's important that she lose as little of her father as possible."

But that wasn't true at all. Freya had never had a father. Only a predator in a parent's clothing.

Dahl finally nodded and lowered his gun.

Still, the screaming increased, the sirens now just blocks away.

"Kick the weapon away from you," Frank ordered.

Already beaten, the monster complied, shoulders slumped.

Frank walked through the living room, stopping in front of the gun but not picking it up. Then the predator looked down at his prey, now sitting defeated in a slump.

The monster looked up, saw his eyes, and realized what Frank had known for a while: Patrick Dahl would not be leaving this house alive, and Frank didn't care if the cops were swarming outside. If this was it for him, so be it.

Because he wouldn't want to live with the truth of what he was about to do.

That was the difference between him and a man like Patrick. Frank wasn't really a monster because a monster didn't live with the guilt. And no matter how much he wanted to end Dahl's life, Frank knew that doing so would curse him forever. He'd feel like a lesser man after pulling the trigger and would probably never want to pull another one again.

"Please … you said …" Dahl raised his hands, palms out in surrender.

"And what did *you* say? All those times your daughter begged you not to rape her?"

"No …" Shaking his head. "You can't do this …"

It was a shame that Frank had to hurry this along instead of savoring the moment. But the sirens were right outside, and this story had gone on for too long already.

"I can." He took another step toward the monster, but the former predator was a quivering mess. "And I'm going to." Another step. "I've seen this too many times … I know exactly how it's going to play out."

"But you said—"

"I lied." Another step until Frank was standing over him. "Just like you lied. Just like you've been making your wife and daughter lie for their entire lives."

Frank aimed the barrel right between his eyes.

Dahl cowered back, raising his hands as if they could ever shield his face from a bullet.

"I had to lie because there *is* no special prison for monsters like you." Frank shook his head. "And I'm not willing to take the chance that you'll ever get out and hurt anyone again."

"I swear that I won't!" He was crying.

And the sirens had stopped screaming.

"You're right," Frank agreed. "But you would have."

Even knowing he'd feel the torment of this moment for the rest of his life, he pulled the trigger twice—one bullet in the monster's face, the other in his chest.

Patrick fell back, already dying, his eyes widening with a final realization as the gunshot reverberated through the room with a deafening whine in Frank's ears.

He retrieved Dahl's gun from the floor and positioned it in his hand.

Suddenly, light behind him and a shadow falling over them.

A muffled shout, "Drop the weapon and put those hands where I can see them!"

The voice behind him wasn't a surprise. If someone was going to arrest him, of course, it should be Mallory Black.

The surprise was that Frank didn't feel like a monster at all.

Instead, he felt like someone who had stepped on a poisonous spider.

Dahl was dead because he needed to die.

Frank set his gun on the floor, raised his hands, then wiped the smile off his face as he slowly turned around.

Chapter Thirty-Eight

Mal

"DROP the weapon and put those hands where I can see them!"

Grimm put his gun on the floor, then he raised his hands and turned to face her.

"You wanna tell me what happened here, Grimm?" She looked behind him at the dead man. No chance Patrick Dahl was alive, no need to try and administer help.

"Patrick Dahl, the neighbor at 47 Heirloom that I told you posed a serious threat to his daughter, tried to rape her again tonight. Freya finally had enough and called me for help."

"Why you instead of the police?"

"I guess she trusts me more," he replied without emotion.

"Freya was at her house when she called you?"

Grimm nodded. "That's right."

"So why move the party here?"

"I'd say you have to ask Dahl, but ..." He glanced behind him, then back again. "Well, you know."

"What aren't you telling me, Grimm?"

"I'm not sure I understand the question, Detective Black."

She looked at him, trying to work out the missing pieces, or at least untangle this knot of omission. She didn't believe him, nor did she think he was outright lying. But Grimm did seem to be keeping an awful lot of things to himself.

But regardless of what happened, Mal felt certain of what she had failed to believe before now. Frank was innocent, at least of being the monster she had believed him to be.

"I need you to wait outside while I secure the scene." She finally lowered her weapon.

"Of course," he said without sounding surprised. "I'm glad you're here, Mallory."

A decisive nod, then he walked past her to wait outside as requested.

She followed him outside, then watched him walk over to a small tree in his front yard, just big enough to lean against without looking ridiculous. So he did, casting his gaze across the scene.

Cruisers and deputies were scattered around the cul-de-sac. A battalion of neighbors stood on their front lawns, some of them wondering and many already judging him.

The ambulance pulled to a stop in front of the two-story Victorian.

Freya led her mother out of the house, both of them in tears.

Mal thought Grimm might go over to check on them, but instead, he played the observer.

She checked in with one of the deputies, handed the

outside scene over to him, then went inside the house to investigate. There wasn't much for her to note — the entire affair appeared to have taken place in Grimm's entryway — and she couldn't stop picturing Mike's eventual gloating.

She finished inside, then went to explore the victim's house.

Freya's house.

Mal might find a few more answers there, but she was sure that much of what happened tonight would always remain a mystery. With the mother and daughter's help, she might get the evidence that Dahl was abusing them both, but that didn't come close to explaining the night's events.

More spectators spilled out onto their lawns, including a few Mal recognized from watching her footage. An older woman was standing a few lawns over holding Grimm's borrowed chihuahua, and the little rat dog was barking surprisingly loud.

She stopped in front of the tree and turned to Frank. "You wanna tell me what the hell happened here tonight?"

He turned from his observation and looked directly into her eyes. "Someone stopped a monster."

"I believe that. Can I also believe it was a clean shooting?"

He shrugged but didn't blink. "I think you've already proven that you're quite capable of believing whatever you want to believe."

It took a moment for Mal to answer. "I'm sorry about that."

A nod, then, "I know."

"So this was self-defense?"

"You saw the scene," Grimm said. "What do you think?"

"I see two shots by the door and another two in his chest. So it looks to me like Dahl missed and the better marksman won."

"Sounds logical." Grimm nodded. "Maybe the shooter was running toward the vic when it happened. That might explain the proximity."

"Okay. Then that leaves just one question …"

Grimm said nothing, waiting.

"Why only two shots?"

"I'm sorry?" Grimm said. "What's the question there?"

"I was out here with Freya for a few minutes before your shots, but I never heard the first two."

"Might want to get that checked out." Grimm tapped his right ear, offered Mal a professional smile, then turned to walk down the street.

Freya raced to greet him. They met in the middle of the street, and she jumped into his arms.

Maybe Grimm wasn't the killer that Mal had believed him to be, but was she letting a different kind of killer go free?

She had to let it rest. Let herself rest.

She raced home, her obsession finally over.

She had a deep need to see Ray, to apologize for everything and mean it. But she needed to see Ashley even more. To hold her daughter, to know she was safe, to see her breathing and perhaps even smiling like she sometimes did in her sleep.

The streets were empty, and the drive fast. Mal managed to make it all the way without crying.

But she lost it after climbing in bed with Ashley.

She held her under the covers—two bodies, big and

small, sharing their warmth. *I've seen so much of the worst,* she thought, *but I'll never let anything terrible happen to you.*

Ashley needed Mal to be more of a mommy, and from this moment forward, she would.

Ray needed her to be a better wife, and she could never let herself forget that again.

There were too many monsters in this world. It was Mal's job to catch some, but not all of them. And never again at the expense of her family.

Mal had never felt so sure of anything. And yet, she'd been wrong.

If she had gotten her way, Grimm would be in prison right now. Preferably for life. He had been doing everything he could to protect the girl, and yet she had been doing everything in her power to bring him down. Mal refused to see or hear reason, no matter how many times it was put right in front of her.

What did that say about her?

She knew and didn't like it. Fortunately, there was a better question.

What would it say about her if she didn't do anything to change, now that she knew?

Mal could do better, and she would.

Grimm had probably killed Dahl in cold blood, but there wasn't a person on the force who would want to prove it, and she'd be a pariah for trying.

Why would she want to?

In the end, a monster was stopped. And besides, this wasn't her case. Mal was off the clock, on suspension, and ready to fully enjoy her family for the days she had left.

The door opened.

She looked over and saw Ray's silhouette in the threshold.

"Are you okay?" His voice was gentle.

She nodded in the dark.

"You're crying," he told her.

"They're good tears."

Ray walked over and crouched by the bed.

Then he pulled Mal into his arms.

"I'm so sorry," she said with her head to his chest.

"I know."

Epilogue

SIX MONTHS LATER ...

FRANK CRADLED the marsala in his left arm while he knocked on the door with his right hand.

It swung open to a beaming Irene, at least a thousand watts brighter than she'd been six months ago, shivering with a trauma blanket on her shoulders in the middle of the night.

Freya's transformation happened even faster. There were still a lot of tears, but less all the time and her wider smile had barely any acne around it. She had gained ten to twenty pounds — hard for Frank to tell with her baggy clothes — and they looked good on her. Healthy. Same for her hair; not only was it fuller, there seemed to be more of it.

They opened the door, and he entered.

"Let me guess?" Freya grinned at him. "Is it … chicken marsala?"

"Why would I bring that?" Frank made a face at them both. "I always bring marsala." He presented his covered dish with both hands. "This is octopus."

Freya shook her head. "Is not."

"Is. Still alive, too. We're gonna cut it together."

"Now I know he's lying," Irene said.

"How dare you." Frank smiled. "It's a baby octopus. We're going to cut the little thing into bite-sized wriggling pieces, suction cups and all."

"You're a terrible liar." Freya shook her head again, then added a codicil she should have kept to herself, even though she couldn't, and Frank saw it coming. "I can't believe you got away with murder."

"Freya!" Irene exclaimed.

"I've asked you to please not say that, even in private," Frank said.

"How many times has he asked you to please not say that?" Irene asked her, talking over Frank.

They all laughed, but nothing else was said. Nothing else needed to be.

Life was different for them all.

He'd not told them he'd killed Patrick in cold blood. They thought Patrick tried to shoot him. It was better for them to believe that, for both their peace of mind and to keep their stories straight.

Murder was his burden. No need to share it with two people who'd already had their fill of misery.

He would never really eat octopus, but he was a lot more adventurous than marsala these days. Sarah understood. They still talked, but Frank felt less guilty than he used to. Finding a way to properly channel his energies changed everything.

He ate with the Dahls twice a week, once at his place and once at theirs, but he always did the cooking because he had the most time. At least that's the way he wanted it to seem.

Stan knew better because Frank told him everything. They had breakfast every morning where they plotted and planned, and Stan helped him out with his secret project.

It felt especially great to finally be using Jenny's insurance payout for something constructive.

"It is marsala!" Irene said as she took the dish away from Frank and immediately removed the lid.

"What did you expect?" Freya asked. "He burns everything else."

"I do not burn everything else." He'd burned a few things.

"Can I show you something before dinner?" Freya asked.

"Whatever it is, I already love it." Something he would have said to Jenny before he lost her. Hearing himself saying it out loud now was a reassuring strain of hurt.

They sat around the table, and Freya set what looked like a journal atop it.

"You sure you don't want to show me after we eat?" Irene asked. "The food is going to get cold."

"His marsala tastes the same either way. Right, Mr. Grimm?"

"Frank. How many times do I have to tell you?"

"All of them," Freya said. "I will call you Mr. Grimm forever, especially now that I know how much it annoys you."

"This is what I get for slaying your dragon?"

"I thought we weren't supposed to talk about that?" Freya smiled and slapped her hand on the journal. "But *this* is what you get for killing—"

"FREYA!"

"Freya …" Frank sighed.

She opened the book and showed him her drawings. Pictures of their time together, taken with her pencil. A nice set this time, the best on the market without being obnoxious. Frank would have been happy to buy her all she wanted, but the monster was well-insured — not because he cared about leaving anything behind for his wife and daughter; the insurance was another avenue for investment.

"That's when we went to the Inside Scoop." Freya pointed at the page, then pointed again to the new one as he turned it. "And that's when we went to the park. See the ducks?"

Frank looked from the drawings to Freya. "Are you trying to insinuate that I'm having trouble with my eyesight?"

"She does that to me, too," Irene said. "All the time."

He kept turning the pages. Drawings surrendered to genuine photographs. There weren't many, but they hadn't known one another long, especially as the kind of friends — or *family*, he kept having to remind himself — who took pictures together.

"Do you get it?" Freya asked.

He closed the book and looked at her. "These are so I don't have to live vicariously through other people's photos, right?"

"Exactly." Freya nodded. "When life breaks up your family, you might have to make a new one."

Irene said, "Thank you for helping make ours."

"It's the best part of my life now." One of the two, for sure.

He couldn't help but smile.

"See!" Freya jabbed a finger at him. "I told you: he's always smiling now. Ask him."

"Ask me what?"

"Freya thinks you have a girlfriend," Irene said.

"No." He shook his head and answered honestly. "I

don't have a girlfriend. I've just been getting out a lot more these days. Out of this cul-de-sac."

"I think he has a girlfriend." Freya grabbed the journal and finished her thought. "I'll draw a picture of what I think she looks like and get it back to you."

"I'm scared to see what you think my girlfriend would look like."

Freya agreed. "I'm brave to even think about it."

"We really should eat," Irene reminded them. "Before the food gets any colder."

They ate and laughed, still teasing him about his secret girlfriend as they polished off the marsala.

Then they each had a small bowl of Mexican Vanilla from the Inside Scoop.

And said *goodnight*. Until next time. In just a couple of days.

Frank walked back to his house, went inside, then turned off his light.

But he didn't go to sleep.

Because Frank was only pretending.

Now he was onto the other best part of his life.

He donned his jacket and hat, grabbed his keys, then went out to the car.

He drove fifteen minutes to the warehouse Stan had both found and rented for him.

He went inside, then turned on the lights and his bank of surveillance screens.

Getting out of the cul-de-sac was long overdue. Frank had widened his search and was now monitoring a dozen different monsters.

He had his eyes on one man in particular.

An open sore of a man named Malick Briar.

Next time, he would stop the monster sooner.

If Malick was the man Frank believed him to be, then he was yet another monster to slay.

Maybe he was the man who took Jenny from him. Maybe not.

But he was almost certainly the man who murdered Rory Day.

The second Frank had proof, Malick Briar would die.

The End...

Frank throws himself into a new investigation, hoping to finally find his daughter's killer. But when he uncovers high-level corruption, he realizes he can't trust his old colleagues.

Will Frank's rusty skills be enough to stop the killer before another girl dies?

Read Hidden Honor today!

A Quick Favor

Thanks for reading *Hidden Justice*.

If you enjoyed this book, please consider writing a review of it on your favorite bookselling site so other readers can enjoy it too. Just a couple of sentences would mean a lot to me.

Thank you!

Nolon & Dave

About the Authors

Nolon King writes fast-paced psychological thrillers set in the glitzy world of entertainment's power players with a bold, insightful voice. He's not afraid to explore the darker side of human nature through stories featuring families torn apart by secrets and lies.

Nolon loves to write about big questions and moral quandaries. How far would you go to cover up an honest mistake? Would you destroy your career to protect your family? How much of your soul would you sell to get the life of your dreams? Would you cheat on your husband to keep your children safe? Would you give in to a stalker's demands to save your marriage?

David W. Wright is the co-author of edge-of-your-seat thrillers including the best-selling post-apocalyptic series *Yesterday's Gone*, the paranoid sci-fi *WhiteSpace* series, and the vigilante series, *No Justice*, as well as standalone thrillers *12*, and *Crash* which was recently optioned for a movie.

David is an accomplished, though intermittent, cartoonist who lives in [LOCATION REDACTED] with his wife and son [NAMES REDACTED.]

He is not at all paranoid.

He is "the grumpy one" on *The Story Studio Podcast* with fellow Sterling and Stone founders, Sean Platt and Johnny B. Truant.

You can email him at <u>david@sterlingandstone.net</u>

We swear, he almost never bites. Unless you feed him after midnight.

Also By Nolon King

Hidden Justice

Hidden Justice

Hidden Honor

Hidden Shame

Hidden Virtue

No Justice

No Justice

No Escape

No Hope

No Return

No Stopping

No Fear

Once Upon A Crime

Once Upon A Crime

Twice Upon A Lie

Three Times a Murder

Dead For Good

Dead For Good

Left For Dead

Dead Of Night

Wake The Dead

Dead For Life

Stand Alone Novels

Pretty Killer

12

Blown

Miserable Lies

The Target

Secrets We Keep

Close To Home

Heat To Obsession

A Simple Kill

Tell Me No Lies

Red Carpet Black

Fade To Black

Victim

Also By David W. Wright

Hidden Justice

Hidden Justice

Hidden Honor

Hidden Shame

Hidden Virtue

No Justice

No Justice

No Escape

No Hope

No Return

No Stopping

No Fear

Karma Police

Jumper

Karma Police

The Collectors

Deviant

The Fall

Homecoming

Yesterday's Gone

October's Gone

Yesterday's Gone Season One

Yesterday's Gone Season Two

Yesterday's Gone Season Three

Yesterday's Gone Season Four

Yesterday's Gone Season Five

Yesterday's Gone Season Six

Tomorrow's Gone

Tomorrow's Gone Season One

Tomorrow's Gone Season Two

Tomorrow's Gone Season Three

Available Darkness

Darkness Itself

Available Darkness Book One

Available Darkness Book Two

Available Darkness Book Three

WhiteSpace

WhiteSpace Season One

WhiteSpace Season Two

WhiteSpace Season Three

Stand Alone Novels

12

Crash

Emily's List

Threshold